Finally AFTer
ALL These years!
(And yes, my editor made all
the Spelling corrections). I
Love you Mom,

DIARMA

Michael Staley

Publication assistance provided by *GSP-Assist*, a service of
Great Spirit Publishing

Great Spirit Publishing

Springfield, Missouri
www.greatspiritpublishing.yolasite.com

ISBN 13-978-1500939090
10-1500939099

Published in USA.

WHAT THE READERS SAY ABOUT
DIARMA:

"Provocative, insightful, magnificent." ~ *Thomas Seidel*

"A rare and magnificent union of substance and style."
~ *Elisabeth Alexandria Smith*

"A piercing perceptive psychological thriller
unlike any other I have read." ~ *Eve Marie Bose*

"Michael Staley has very simply tapped a new dimension in
literary experience. Read it." ~ *Debi Nobrega*

"If you liked John Fowles' *The Magus*, you are going to
love Staley's *Diarma*." ~ *Kimberlee Mongillo*

"The fact that this work was originally penned some forty plus
years ago lends credence to the concept of 'Timeless.'"
~ *Allen Rowe*

"Builds to a climax that is an absolute mindblower."
~ *Michael Brown*

"A must read for anyone in a position of power and
influence over others. Period." ~ *Daniel Vitanza*

"Incredibly visual. What a movie this would make!"
~ *Helga Brandenburg*

"*Diarma* – Wow, what a book…it's quite magnificent."
~ *Barbara Quin*

The entire spirit of this book is dedicated to the concept set forth in the following words:

"It is time we admitted that all men are not created equal though all should be born with equal human rights, and until the many can be educated out of the false assumption that biological superiority is a state of existence as opposed to what it really is - a state of responsibility - we shall never come to a more just or happier world."

~ John Fowles

ACKNOWLEDGMENTS

To Dr. Richard Maurice Bucke (1837-1902), whose classic work, Cosmic Consciousness, first published in 1901, and now available in paperback through the Citadel Press, documents in enlightened detail the fourteen instances of Cosmic Consciousness that have occurred over the past two thousand years of man's recorded history. I heartily recommend the work to all who are interested in furthering their insight into themselves and the Universe.

To Little, Brown and Co., Inc., for permission to quote from John Fowles' The Aristos and *The French Lieutenant's Woman*.

To Rider and Co., London, England, for allowing me to quote a parable that appears in Roy Dixon Smith's *New Light on Survival* appearing on page 139 of this work.

To Sanford Meisner, acting coach extraordinaire, whose ability to direct oneself to oneself should well be the envy of many a psychoanalyst.

AND FINALLY, to Anthea Alexis and Bradford Boobis, without whose being this work very simply would not have been possible.

M.S.

PROLOGUE

I AWAKENED to the sound of my own screams as my head banged against the stone floor. Strong hands pinned me in place, then lifted me a moment before I was unceremoniously flung back to the bed. Their possessor released me and walked to the far corner of the circular dwelling. He folded his arms to his chest as if to say, "We're stuck with each other, friend. Make the best of it."

I managed to raise myself to a sitting position and inspected my dwelling of the moment. It did not compare in the slightest to my prior accommodations. There was only one window high up and it was barred. Everything was gray, the gray of sectioned granite. The bed I was lying on was a cushioned wooden plank suspended by two large linked chains pinioned to the wall. I looked to the immensely thick steel girded door with its cast iron ring grip and fully realized my whereabouts. I was in a dungeon, a medieval dungeon. I wondered momentarily if I was still in this world at all and then my jailor confirmed it for me:

"You have one hour to prepare your defense."

Or had he? The man opened the door and left, locking it behind him. I half walked, half stumbled to the door and pulled back the slot guard that covered the small rectangular opening, forced my head through it, wondering the whole time "Defense against what?!" Without breaking stride, the man turned his head, having apparently plucked the query from my mind, and declared, "The Specimen exists, doesn't he? Isn't that enough?"

He continued on a few steps. As he reached the ladder which was obviously his point of exit, he halted, did an about face and with eyes that bored clear through me, added, "The Specimen is charged with two specific counts of Insufficient Humanity." Then he did something that chilled me to the bone. He smiled at me in a most benevolent manner and then bowed his head ever so slightly before disappearing up the ladder and through a trap door.

I knew I had returned to the void but hardly the one I had so methodically tried to escape only weeks before. I knew that void. It had depressed me, drained me of all impetus and ultimately catalyzed me into a suicide attempt, but it had never terrorized me, not in the manner my present predicament did. I groped out for reality, any reality, but only felt sandwiched between horror and criminal perversity. I felt incapable of making the choice between them. Was the "experience" still on? Or had it not been an experience at all? Had it really happened just as it appeared to have happened? Or had some device, some sophisticated forms of special effects been employed?

The image of her plummeting body sent everything else on its way. No one, NO ONE, would go to those lengths to prove a point, a point that obviously still very much eluded me... no one sane, that is. Had I fallen into the hands of lunatics, or was it my own lunatic fringe I was ensconced in? What had she said to me? "*One man's logic is another man's lunacy and vice versa...*" or was I dead? Had I passed over to the other side and my just desserts?

My eyes quickly scanned the room, resting on what they sought. I walked to the small basin and stared into the opaque mirror above it. Yes, I recognize the face but is that the ultimate proof?

I heard the door unlatch. I was certain no more than a half hour had gone by and so assumed they, whoever the hell "they" were, had decided my defense was so flimsy as to be non-existent, thusly not requiring the full hour preparation time. I couldn't have cared less. I had already decided to keep absolute silence for the duration of the "trial." It simply didn't matter anymore. For all intents and purposes, I was dead.

In actuality, though, I hardly knew it at the time, the exact opposite was true. In my totally confused and self-serving state, I could not be expected to perceive that "for all intents and purposes" the moment that follows death is precisely the same as precedes birth. Bearing this in mind, they had me exactly where they wanted me, for prior to metamorphosis there must first be catharsis.

But perhaps I should start at the beginning, if there truly is such a thing…

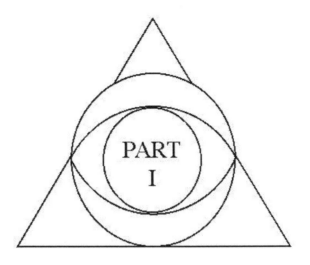

PART
I

THE SPECIMEN

"A specimen of research that is to be examined with
the help of a microscope has first to be carefully
prepared, cleaned, freed of extraneous matter, and
kept firmly under the lens."

~ Nyanponika Thera

NEW YORK CITY, THREE WEEKS EARLIER

It seemed to be in perpetual frantic motion, limbs clinging, releasing, grasping again; darting simian eyes that shot mania everywhere at once. It was inextricably trapped, unnaturally confined, deprived – the antecedent to depraved.

Suddenly, the small creature's eyes flicked to mine and in that split second my involvement shifted from the vicarious to total empathy; in that fraction of an instant, I became that terrified, lost, caged primate... and so, as the others came and went, my eyes alone remained transfixed on the living/dying spectacle.

From the corner of my mind's eye I watched my finger lightly tap my temple to indicate the bond now established between us - that I, too, was incarcerated by my own mind, my own being. For the first time in my life, I fully, organically understood the essence of futility.

Without taking my eyes from it, I slowly walked the perimeter of the domed enclosure searching for a door, an exit. There was none to be found. It dawned upon me then, almost as a revelation, there was, of course, only one way out.

I waved a farewell to the scampering spider monkey and, as I began to leave Central Park Zoo, some unseen force lifted my head and sent me a question in the form of a feeling: Was there really some omnipotence observing me from the same perspective as I had been scrutinizing the monkey? Or if it did, indeed, exist, did it even care?

There was one thing I did know, however. With unmistakable clarity, it had come to me. My little monkey friend had mentored me well. I no longer wished to be a prisoner of Time, Space, and especially Form.

As I looked to the sky, the rumbling roar of distant thunder punctuated my thought. The sun was disappearing, and so was I.

****

****

As I stepped into the night I noted that it seemed appropriate there were no stars or moon to illuminate my dimmed existence; all black and blue, a cobalt cosmos slashed with silvery slivers diminished me.

I was struck by the thought of what an incongruous sight I must make: suited and tied, carrying an attaché, strolling leisurely, even nonchalantly, straight towards the ocean, down the deserted beach. Well, almost deserted. Wasn't that the figure of a man seated in the sand some distance to my left? No, merely a piece of sculptured driftwood, a cursory inspection concluded.

Aside from a gull here, a sandpiper there, my privacy was complete as was my being ludicrous. I knew what I was – a twentieth (or any-ieth) century misanthrope, but only in the highly personalized sense of the word - repelled by my own humanity.

I found my spot a mere five yards from a slap-happy sea. I removed my jacket, loosencd my tie, and inhaled deeply. The air was thick, humid, and oppressive. I seated myself Indian fashion, unlatched and opened my case and commenced to extract my life from it. The first evidence of my being that I chose to obliterate came in the form of a marriage license. At one very brief passing point in time it had represented the ultimate union to me; at another, somewhat more prolonged one, the ultimate deception. As it was the latter that scarred my mind, I only glanced at it peremptorily before shredding and casting it windward.

Next came a diploma, actually three diplomas; all, to my mind, scripted testimonials to social hypocrisy, even amorality, and they definitely did not warrant a final nod before finding their strewn fate in the now nominal sea breeze.

The third ceremonial sacrifice took the form of a military discharge – "Honorable" – but of course I opted to reduce this documented insanity to ashes.

Next, a large manila folder containing photographs of my paintings, indeed, my first love, which was to be supplanted by a second "love" of a more practical nature as I grew into what was expected of me. Admittedly, were I a deeper soul, I never would have allowed that to happen.

I looked at them all briefly, pausing at the last one completed over ten years ago - a self-portrait that seemed to investigate me as I did it. I must have flourished a prescient brush that day as somewhat vacuous eyes stared through me as if to say, "What took you so long?"

At first reluctantly, then deliberately, I tore them in half one by one, and then into quarters, eighths, and finally sixteenths before sending them gracefully on their way.

I stretched in place and glanced quickly around before extracting the second to last item. Cremation or manual destruction? My fingers answered for me as they methodically tore the birth certificate into tiny pieces no larger than confetti.

Bravo Christos! All that is left of you is your body and, coincidentally enough, all that is left to remove from your briefcase is the revolver. End of the road.

My stare demonically focused on the spinning cylinder; I finally broke the chamber, and then, true to my vow, removed four of the five bullets.

No. I was not about to make a game of it. It was not being done in the spirit of a final concession to whatever life was left in me; rather, I was choosing this prolonged manner of self-extermination for quite a different reason, and I did not care, or know, if it was a valid one. It was indeed a personal one, so intensely personal that I will not divulge it... yet I rob you of nothing.

Be my guest, dip into the well and mercilessly penetrate the layers of your own existence, and then retrieve a particularly excruciating and totally indefensible contradiction to your being; your raison d'être. It's lurking within you somewhere. Painfully extract it and insert it here, for…

It was to be my penance, my personal justice. Remittance long past due finally paid in full.

I turned my head skyward just as God's veins sliced the night sky, spun the chamber once and placed the barrel to my right temple.

The thunderous roar almost inadvertently caused me to pull the trigger. Another branch of lightning illumed the black. I lowered the weapon as I felt my nerve going. Something felt off to me, had intruded upon me. Up until this moment everything had felt absolutely correct in the pursuit of my demise but now something had gone askew and I needed further impetus to restore my resolve.

Of course, it was out there waiting for me. The sea. I had always loved and been fascinated by her on the one hand, awed and frightened by her on the other. And so I would challenge her one final time. Perhaps she would take me.

I stripped completely. I checked my watch and noted that even man's time had chosen to run out on me this particular night as the dying battery barely ignited the time and date: August 13, 12:06 AM. I automatically placed it in my outside suit coat pocket before realizing the mootness of gesture. Then, as if on cue, the moon suddenly emerged from behind a palate of inky fluff beaming a pathway that bathed my body in a ghostly glow, quite appropriately, I thought, as I succumbed to her thrashing embrace.

III

And fickle, too. She proved to have no use for me and so spewed me back. I lay face down in the wet sand for several moments as the water lapped at my feet before turning on my back and staring at the free form charcoal cloud that was slowly re-obscuring the platinum moon.

"At the instant the moon disappears from sight is the moment I'll do it."

I struggled to my feet and half-walked, half-stumbled to my belongings. I did not bother to dress. Without taking leave of the moon, sat in the sand, spun the cylinder once and placed the gun to my head... and waited. A warm breeze caressed my body just as the most untimely of thoughts invaded my brains.

Why now, of all times, does that full moon conjure up a proffered host at Holy Communion? The window closed and, as I had promised myself, I pulled the trigger. Nothing but a deafening CLICK and the too quick accompaniment of a barely audible sigh for which I immediately felt guilty. This time, a seagull perched on a wave, and when it took flight, without spinning the chamber, once again I depressed the trigger... CLICK.

I felt the strangest sensation in my lower abdomen while at the same time I felt my hand trying to pull the gun away from my head. The vibrations (for lack of a better word) increased and began moving upwards into my chest, settling in my head. I felt as though I were leaving my body. Suddenly, I realized that once I lowered the gun that now felt as though it were making its own escape through my sweat-soaked hand, would I be able to raise it again?

I felt paralyzed in that position. I felt the "vibrations" abating, thusly returning to a normal state of consciousness. The sense of accompanying euphoria all but disappeared; that I had failed some sort of cosmic test and was now being given the go-ahead to terminate my puny life. With all my remaining mental fortitude I tried to squeeze the trigger. I could not. I needed something, a further extension of the macabre ritual I was enacting; yet another catalytic agent of the dark forces enveloping my brain. I opened my mind to all motivational stimuli and came up empty. I finally settled upon the first manmade sound I heard and waited ten minutes of incalculable time for the roar of an automobile engine igniting in the distance. Or had I imagined it? Concocted it? Come on, Christos, only one, possibly two more pulls of the trigger…

Suddenly, I started to weep. Not for the reasons you suspect. Something much simpler. I had miscounted and had just discovered my mathematical error – had pulled the trigger three times, not four.

And so, with an inner strength that had I possessed all along would have surely averted tonight, I returned to the gauntlet. I looked to the sea and decided on the seventh wave to pound the shore. I knew this would be the one and quite unexpectedly my fear shifted to resolve. In that instant I knew I had passed my "test." Here comes the seventh wave now… CLICK. The fourth click.

I was no longer in possession of my mind. It did not know from "games." It only knew one final thing was left to be done. It seemed to what was left of my mind that someone else's hand now held the gun; someone else's finger was squeezing, squeezing, sque… CLICK! The loudest click of all. Five.

When the initial shock finally dissipated allowing my faculties to return, thus grasping the absolute inconceivability of the moment, I responded quite naturally for a man of my particular bent. Still holding the gun to my head, lunacy pulled the trigger several times in rapid succession (five times to be precise and then a sixth for good measure).

Poised on the precipice of catatonia, I forced my hand to lower the weapon, broke the chamber, and stared at its vacancy in pure astonishment. A mirror image? Memory eventually came to my rescue and I searched the sand methodically, then wildly, ultimately fruitlessly for the discarded four bullets. I slowly rose to my full height and began searching for a sign of human life. I ran my hands slowly, even sensually down my body as if to confirm its existence. And finally, I raised my head to the blue/black and from the innermost cavity of my gut came a chastisement that pierced the Universe…

"YOU SON OF A BITCH!"

In my traumatized mind I could not be expected to see, let alone hear, the irony in that blasphemy. Rather, my perception of the moment took a far more physical course as I collapsed in the sand, wept, and slept until dawn.

A mosquito awakened me abruptly as a half-mast sun poured forth another goddamn day. I lay in place until it had revealed all of itself, then rose, dressed, and headed directly for my car, my mind a tortured vortex of the previous night's events.

I stopped so suddenly that I momentarily lost balance, backed up slightly, and read the "message" that had been engraved in the sand a few feet from where I had spent the night. I burst into near hysterical laughter as the irony of it consumed me. My mind flooded with image after image of some do-gooder in flowing white, racing through my belongings while I had indulged my would be watery demise, hurriedly gathering up the bullets, emptying the chamber, and then scurrying off before I washed ashore, but only to return in the dead of night to bestow upon me this cryptic one word, one concept ray of hope neatly executed in script for me to discover upon awakening: PASSAGES, it proclaimed.

By this time the energy drain from the raucous-cum-hollow laughter had brought me to my knees (obviously where I was meant to be) and so I forced myself upright to view the strange elliptical circumference that surrounded my resurrection. It resembled a large egg from which something, had taken a bite from the underside... PASSAGES... What the hell did that mean? I started to laugh once again, albeit forced and hollow in tenor. Suddenly, I peered in all directions, settled on the ocean herself, assumed my most MacBethian posture, and addressed her in my most stentorian voice:

"Passages of what, my uninvited benefactor? Time? Passages to what? God? There is no God, my momentary messiah. Passages to what? To whom? Wait a minute, wait a minute, you do-gooding son-of-a-bitch... I've got it!" I slapped my brow in mock revelation. "Passages to myself! Right? Well, you are the sly one, my unsolicited savior. Hey! Come on, tell me. Am I right? Is that the abstract pearl you're leaving me with? And just what is this odd oblong surrounding it? What's its symbolism, oh wise and revered one? Why, you stupid, well-meaning bastard, whoever you are, if you're going to leave me with a Great Message, for Christ-sake, make it crystal clear, not some goddamn... give me an answer, goddamn-it-to-hell! Not another fucking problem to contemplate!"

I had managed to work myself into quite a rage and had to calm myself while walking to my car.

Looking back on it now, I have to admit that, even though I had indeed chosen that particular tack, had quite instinctively responded to the message in the sand in just that manner, somewhere, in a far less chartered territory of my brain, I abashedly admit, if only for a flash of a moment, I did indeed entertain a somewhat more mystical solution to the sequence of events. I did not dwell on it however, for doing just that would be an open admission of the existence of that which I had come to vehemently deny.

The drive back to my Manhattan apartment will take some two hours, but rather than take you on that excursion, I will take you on another:

What species of animal is this that would contrive and implement such a manner of self-demise?

I do not know. I will tell you this much, which is the part that I do know. I did not attempt to take my life out of desperation, momentary or otherwise. Quite the contrary. It had not been conceived in a surge of depression or a peak of emotion – quite the opposite. Rather, the act was nurtured by and predicated upon a lifetime of experiences that unrelentingly, uncompromisingly told me I was nothing more than "a fish out of water," a being partially, then totally estranged from the world as it is, and so quite naturally, equally alienated from its human inhabitants.

At times I had even entertained the thought that I was of another species altogether. In my early years, I had indeed tried to be like the others, but children possess ultra-sensitive barometers and responded to my "I want to be like you" overtures by backing even further away. Hell, they knew.

As I grew older, I came to appreciate, even cherish my individuality and gravitated towards spending even more time alone. I do not mean to imply that I was a social recluse, even though admittedly of a non-social temperament. I was not. My professional life, but more importantly certain natural biological advantages, precluded this. For instance, as I entered my late twenties I became quite attractive to women, especially a certain type of woman a few years older than myself. Strong women. Although I did not find the satisfaction I sought on a total level (even and especially with my wife), these women did supply a temporary respite sexually and instructionally, the latter solely on a worldly level however, for they did not feed that part of me that did not belong to this world – my essence that cried out unceasingly for support, recognition, confirmation. And so, at times I was even forced to doubt my sanity.

Ultimately, all this culminated in what I call congenital spiritual restlessness. It came to pass that nothing stimulated me; nothing satisfied me. Only the idea of something, not the reality of it could momentarily fulfill me, for when actually experienced, and I had the means to experience most anything, or anyplace, this world offers, after the initial novelty wore off, the restlessness, the boredom, would overwhelm me.

Lately, as though governed by some perverse law of diminishing returns, the dissatisfaction would come in ever increasing proximity to the event until finely nothing could void the feelings of alienation.

It was as though I never really belonged here.

It was as though I was never meant to be here.

It was as though I had experienced it all and finally nothing had meaning for me.

Ah, yes, the great cliché, *"Peace comes from within."* From within a shell?

I could tell you more, much more, but what would be the point, for I know now, not then, that I am far less an individual than a syndrome – a byproduct of a society, the natural excrement of a system that has aligned itself to the wrong God – money, power, status – a society on the verge of bankruptcy.

And so, as time accumulated at the lowest possible interest rate, I became precariously but solidly ensconced in The Fringe – straddling two worlds; stranded between two separate realities, unable to cope or function in either, ergo, last night born of circumstance, experience, instinct, intelligence, and lack of communication. I was truly marooned in this existential void that gapped the world of Illusion and the world of Truth. I lived in Limbo, for that is precisely what is meant by that religious designation, though the ignorance of "holy" men conspires to define it through abstract definitions that are far more geared to further confusion than understanding. I was its reluctant inhabitant, governed by the forces that prevail there: Inertia, Frustration, Confusion, Ignorance, and Guilt. For a long time, I remained engaged in a brutal test of brinksmanship, stagnant, until last night when I freed myself of one of the forces, but only one: Inertia.

I spent the remainder of the day and half the night seated in a large tufted black leather chair, staring at the wall. Twice, I broke "trance" to go into the bathroom and stare at my reflection in the mirror.

My options were simple if threefold: return to the lifestyle I had become familiar with, had lived for several years now; had taken me by the hand to that stretch of beach. Or, slashed wrists in a warm bath, or perform a metamorphosis of sorts. Break out of myself, but how, doing what?

The following morning I took my first positive step: I called my firm and announced my retirement, much to the shock and dismay of my two partners. It wasn't exactly going to send shock waves through the architectural community, but it was going to jolt a few of New York city's finest contractors, for I was the most imaginative and productive member of Christos, Wallach and Black, in my day, which was no longer.

The rest of the day, as well as Saturday, was spent calling and occasionally personally contacting various and sundry travel agencies, even though a similar experience of a month previous had proven fruitless as they had indicated, quite convincingly, that "The idyllic atmosphere you seek, Mr. Christos, it is simply no longer available on season or off. If you would be willing to concede one or two of your demands, etc., etc."

It had been a most disheartening experience, pointing out that not only my world was fast disintegrating, but the planet at large as well.

My luck did not change for the response to my current effort was identical to the extent of being computer programmed. There just did not appear to be a haven of the sort I insisted upon in the locale I was equally adamant about on the whole of the planet. They had either become too popular, too polluted, or were too extreme weather-wise to my taste; or they were "island paradises" but somewhere in the South Pacific, not the Mediterranean/Aegean areas and had virtually no life or conveniences on them at all. Several agents had suggested the outer-Caribbean as being the area most compatible to my demands, within realistic limits, of course. I was not interested. My roots were in Europe, more specifically Mediterranean, and I instinctively, genetically, felt drawn to her.

I finally tired of "We'll give you a call if anything comes to mind," and decided to research potential areas on my own, which is why I am just now entering Rizzoli's on Fifth Avenue.

"May I be of assistance, sir?"

"Thank you. Has anyone published a book on the theme of Islands of the World?"

"Let me check the catalogue for you, but I have a feeling, though heaven knows why, that no such work has been compiled. Specific island territories, yes, but as for all encompassing study, I doubt it. In the meantime, why don't you browse through the travel section? Just exactly what did you have in mind, sir?"

I told her and she set me off in the proper direction. I had just entered the sector marked "Travel" when I caught sight of something that caused me to stop dead in my tracks. I reached over and took the magazine from the rack. I suppressed a smile. It was a publication entitled, "PASSAGES." It sold for $5 a copy and by its psychedelic cover was obviously of the Avant Garde class of periodical that had become so popular of late. I began to thumb through it and very quickly ascertained that its message was too self-consciously dedicated to the means and ways of self-realization. I felt I owed it to the magazine itself to read an article, any article, but could not get past those images that once again dashed thru my mind, only this time my seashore savior had a copy of PASSAGES tucked neatly under his/her arm and was consulting it from time to time as to what steps to take in order to prevent the death of a lost soul in the sand. It was no use, so I returned it to its place somewhat disappointed in having the mystery solved once and for all.

Shaking her head back and forth, she approached me.

"Apparently, no such book has been compiled, sir. Did you find anything suitable if any of the other books?"

"I haven't really looked yet."

"Please, take your time." She gestured to an immense oak table.

I had still not been able to match the pictures in the books to the ones in my mind by the time I left some hour and forty minutes later. The photographers assigned to compile them had been of very little help – seemingly on the payroll of the local tourist board – for rather than shooting high and wide angle perspectives allowing a full view of their subjects, they seemed obsessed with soaking up local color or expressing their aesthetic sense thru a porcelain relic here, an intimate close-up of an indigenous exotic plant there.

It was just this experience that decide if it for me. After all, just because a few travel agents had been unable to locate – and fewer photographers had been unable to capture – my utopia, was not to say that it did not exist. I would simply concentrate my energies on getting across the Atlantic, hardly a problematic contingency, and once there commence explorations of my own.

Sunday, I rested, took a quiet drive in the country, and mapped out my plans for the following week. I would withdraw my savings and sell my car, as well as other assets such as my cabin at Lake Minnewaska, stocks, bonds, and profit sharing annuities. With the monies realized I would be well set for from three to four years, but only for that length of time, for I was going to hold nothing back, monetarily or momentarily. Rather, I was glad to live out that time as if a physician had gazed meekly over his glasses and gently announced, "I'm terribly sorry, Mr. Christos, but you only have three, possibly four, or as little as one year left to live."

I dined out that night because I felt better than I had felt in a long time. Life seemed to be stirring in me once again. Of course, I did have to, several times that eve, silence the little voice that uncompromisingly repeated the cliché, "Come on, Christos. You really believe you can run away from Alexander Christos?!" I found the best antidote to this loquacious intruder was yet another glass of wine, and so, by the time I returned home around midnight, I was mildly drunk.

I had ordered up my life for the next few years and that was exactly how I was going to live. It was my last non-providential lingering thought before drifting off.

"Mr. Christos? Mr. Alexander Christos?"

I rubbed the sleep from my eyes, propped myself up on one elbow and with my free hand groped for my cigarettes.

"Hello," said a telephone voice I only barely recognized as my own.

"Oh, I am sorry. I didn't mean to wake you, Mr. Christos. This is Leigh Hall, of Voyages Unlimited. You came to see us about six weeks ago. Do you recall?"

"Yes, Leigh, I recall the meeting quite well. We could not do business."

"Yes, that's right. Are you still interested in finding such a place?"

"Of course. Do you think you've come up with one that meets my requirements?"

"That's what I'd like to discuss with you. Could you come by the office at six this evening?"

"Fine."

"Good. The office will be closed for the day but I have some work to catch up on and there's someone I'd like you to meet who will be able to better describe the place I have in mind. She is not available until this evening. Do you still have my card?"

"Yes, somewhere... in my wallet, I believe. Give me the address again in case I've misplaced it."

"Twelve East Sixty-Fourth Street, Suite 1011," Leigh said. "At six, then. Just knock and I'll let you in."

"See you then, Leigh," I said. "By the way, what is the name of the place you have in mind?"

"Diarma. It's a very unique island. I'll tell you all about it when I see you."

"Would you mind spelling it for me?"

"D-I-A-R-M-A. As I said, you'll… Mr. Christos… Mr. Christos, are you still there?"

But I was not still there. I was in quite a different place altogether and in the process of traveling there had hung up. Actually, I had dropped the receiver and quite by chance it had landed in the cradle. My fingers had inadvertently opened, thus sending the receiver on its plunge because I am half Greek and classically fluent in the same. Diarma just happens to be the Greek word for "Passage."

VIII

I arrived at the glass and steel offices of Voyages Unlimited at six sharp. I tried the door and found it locked. I knocked several times until I discovered the tiny pearl bell and depressed it. I was peering through the opaque glass when a feminine flash of cocoa brown appeared in silhouette a moment before the door opened.

It was not the young and quite beautiful Leigh Hall, but rather a handsome woman, late fifties, I gauged, who extended a long-fingered, affluently-adorned ivory hand as she flashed a smile so contagious that I was disarmed at once.

She stood appraising me for a long moment and the corners of her mouth as well as these of her eyes shamelessly indicated that she was more than pleased with her visual perspective. At the precise moment I was beginning to feel uncomfortable, she effused yet more warmth, took me by the arm and led me to a small outer office at the far end of a marble corridor. We entered and I was somewhat overwhelmed by the precision, order, and cleanness of lines that was her domain: all points, planes, and circles. She motioned me to sit and offered coffee, tea, or a drink.

I declined and she immediately walked to magenta drapes and drew them back, revealing a panoramic vista of Manhattan's upper eastside. She poised herself in the cushioned window box and continued her inspection of me on the one hand while barely containing her joy on the other.

"Mr. Christos, you are a very lucky man. If you believe in luck, that is."

I smiled and replied, "Please call me Christos, just Christos, Mrs....?"

"Forgive me. Rand. Millicent Rand, and it's Miss, or Ms., if you prefer, I don't."

She held up her hand as if to ward off any forthcoming flattery and then granted me her most demure smile as she added, "Just call me Millicent. But should you contract my name to Millie, consider our relationship terminated."

"I wouldn't think of it, Millicent. Is Miss Hall going to be here?"

"She is lovely and I'm sorry to disappoint you but she had a last minute booking for one of our retainer clients and had to dash off to set the specifics."

"Oh, I'm far from disappointed. Please give her my regards."

And then Millicent Rand did something I found to be quite extraordinary. She allowed her eyes a mock bow of Victorian coyness, which a woman of her age could not have normally accomplished sans affectation.

"Tell me, Mr. ... excuse me, Christos, may we now assume we have established our collective affluence in dispensing the social amenities?"

I laughed, "Yes."

"Good. Let's get down to business. Tell me, have you heard of the island of Diarma?"

"Only inasmuch as Miss Hall mentioned it to me this morning," I half-truthed.

"Well, not many have. Come over here and I'll show it to you."

She walked to the west wall, whose entirety consisted of tiny multicolored bulbs, that when ignited became a world atlas. She singled out Southwestern Europe with her hand.

"It is located here, in the shoe of the Mediterranean, and as you can readily see is virtually an island unto itself. Its closest neighbor is the Granadian province of Spain to the north. It is bordered on the south by Morocco, once again over a hundred miles distance. To the west there is no land for two hundred miles plus, until Tangier, and to the east, also roughly two hundred miles, Algiers. One might say that Diarma is the imperfect radius of the diameter I have just shown you. As you can see for yourself, absolutely no land whatsoever exists between the radius and circumference."

She turned to look at me then, for approval I would imagine, but I had barely heard anything she said. Rather, my gaze was transfixed on the shape of the island itself, which was precisely the exact proportions that had been engraved in the sand surrounding my "message."

"Are you all right, Christos?

"What? Oh yes, fine… excellent… so far, so good. Please go on."

"Now, Leigh tells me that you are looking for a place that is quiet and beautiful, lightly inhabited and unpolluted, yet not totally devoid of activity or basic creature comforts, per se, correct?"

"Exactly."

"Very well. At this point I think it best just to plunge into the unique qualities of the island. I assure you your basic requirements are more than fulfilled here. To begin with, Diarma is not open to the public. It is a privately owned corporation with fifty-one percent of the shares held by its overseer. The other forty-nine percent is divided into plots of land owned or to be owned by the permanent residency."

I shifted my glance to a beige pigeon who had just found a temporary respite on the outer window ledge.

"What we're really talking about here, then, is tantamount to a private club, and if that is the case…"

"Don't be so hasty. At least give me the courtesy of hearing me out. I have indicated to you that Diarma is unique in its concept. If after I have told you as much as I am at liberty to tell you at this stage, you still feel it is not right for you, there will be time enough to register your rejection. Until that juncture, however, I insist you remain open to me."

From charmer to taskmaster was a very easy transition for Millicent Rand. Somewhat chagrined, I nodded affirmatively.

"When the island was originally purchased and conceptualized, some four years ago, guest privileges were extended by the owner on a highly selective basis for the express purpose of interesting exceptional individuals in specialized fields of endeavor to visit the island and, if it became acceptable to both host and guest, donate their specialty to the island in exchange for which they received a share in the island and permanent residency, as well as all living necessities.

"The list of initial guests ran the gamut of two basic subjects professors to scientists; skilled blue collar workers for the construction of essential living facilities to a librarian; from a dentist and surgeon to a musicologist; from an expert theological staff to an astronomer from a renowned ecologist to an equally accredited parapsychologist; from a top international lawyer to a quite famous animal behaviorist.

"In short, the island was being staffed as a societal entity unto itself with one basic exception: As the aims of Diarma are like those of no other society, past or present, that we know of, the basis of selectivity as to residency was uniquely conceived to say the least."

She paused for a moment. Was that the barest trace of a smile forming at the corners of her mouth, or was she simply pursing her lips?

"I initially placed six of the people some two to four years ago. They now maintain permanent residence on Diarma, and each and every one of them has found a peace and sense of fulfillment in this lifetime they never dared dream of, let alone hoped for."

Again she paused, this time for effect, before continuing:

"Now, at the time of its initial growth, funds were limited and had to be dispersed on a priority need basis; therefore, one of the professions not sought at the time was that of an architect. It was decided that the present medieval structures should stand until such a time as would be realistic to implement changes that would complement the conceptuality of the island's goals, which are visionary to say the least. I can unqualifiedly state that within its four-year existence, Diarma has already established its foundation, thrusting it light years ahead of its time. And so, the architecture must correspond. When Miss Hall showed me your registration card revealing your profession, as well as your preferences – and you are quite an exceptional architect from what I have been able to find out – I could only assume the hand of providence had shown itself once again, for four days ago this arrived."

She handed me the communique:

> *Dearest Millicent,*
>
> *The time has come to commence structural changes as relates to the physical facilities here on Diarma. Would you please begin at once to find us a uniquely qualified architect? The arrangements for compensation and remuneration remain identical to those initially set forth: a share in the island and permanent residency, or a share in the island and permanent guest privileges.*
>
> *Thank you so very much. Look forward to seeing you in December.*
>
> *Warmest Regards,*
> *Alethea*

I placed it on her desk.

"You know, Millicent, I'm not really interested in an employment opportunity, enticing as it may sound. On the contrary, what I had in mind was an extended holiday."

"I understand that, Christos, but let me explain something to you. If, upon acceptance of your application to visit Diarma, you decided to actually go there, you go as their guest for a three-week period. All your expenses are paid, including round trip travel, and, if at the end of that period you wish to leave and not return, you are committed to nothing else.

"If, on the other hand, the island wins you over and you decide you would like to be considered for either residency category, this will be discussed and either mutually agreed upon or not. In either event, the demands on your time will be minimal, at most consisting of two dinners at the overseer's home."

"What we're talking about then is a three-week expense paid vacation."

"Precisely. Should things work out, all you could possibly lose would be three weeks out of your life. And I promise you that, quite contrary to a deficit, those three weeks would be a wonderful experience for you. The island itself is devastatingly beautiful and its aura, magnificent."

I continued to stare at the letter as I spoke.

"I noticed there was no mention of money, per se, as to employment."

She looked at me for a moment as if gauging whether or not to let me in on a secret. "That is because there is no money on Diarma. One might say that the currency of Diarma is Connection."

Before I could speak she held up her hand and added,

"That is all I am at liberty to tell you about the internal workings of Diarma at this time. Actually, it is more than I should tell you. Should you decide to apply, and your application accepted, I will be instructed to forward a pamphlet to you that far more explicitly outlines the aims as well as general features of the island. However, one must physically experience Diarma to absorb the full benefit of its ambiance, and for that reason, its overseer operates on the premise that it is far better to have a potential resident discover things for himself once on the island. Diarma... is its own best representative.

"So, what do you think? Would you like to fill out an application?"

I rose and walked to the window and gazed out into the filthy summer sky. I addressed my response to a cone of belching black smoke.

"From what you've just told me, the island sounds... perfect. Perhaps that's why it's a bit hard for me to accept. In any event, I'd like a couple of questions answered before I commit myself one way or the other."

"Such as?"

"You keep referring to an overseer. Does the overseer have a name? And why have I never heard of this place before? You indicated that it has been in existence for four years now, and until this minute, I've never heard of it. Why is that?"

"The overseer does, obviously have a name; however, it would mean nothing to you, and he died quite recently. His wife, who is eminently qualified, is carrying on his work and is, in fact, the island's present overseer."

"Her name, then?"

And her tone changed to one of coldness as she replied, "I'm afraid that's quite impossible until your application has been accepted. You know her first name anyway. It was on the letter you read."

I turned to look at her, investigating her eyes for some evidence of deception, even hoax. I could find nothing but a trace of annoyance and adjusted to it.

"Forgive me, Millicent, but you've indicated that a society exists whose aims appear to be postulated on openness and enlightenment, is that correct?"

"Openness most definitely. Enlightenment is a term that, unfortunately, has been bastardized down through the ages and is now subject to as many interpretations as the individuals who have claimed to have attained it."

"That was an impressive statement but it does not alter the issue which simply is that I find the fact that the overseer of an advanced living state refusing to divulge something as basic as her name to be paradoxical at best."

"Then you are either not as bright as I was led to believe or extraordinarily naive for your years."

She made no attempt to repress her sigh as she rose and took a place by me at the window.

"As I lean towards the latter, Christos, I am going to take you into my strictest confidence. I only hope you are a man to be trusted."

She quickly went on as if to save me the discomfort of an ineffectual reply.

"I told you that the Diarma overseer died quite recently, but what I neglected to tell you was the manner in which he died. He was assassinated."

Her eyes went askance into nothingness before continuing.

"This would have been revealed to you once on the island. I am only divulging it now because I sense very strongly that you, more than most, would find meaning and fulfillment on Diarma. I felt that the moment I saw you. You may call it intuition but you may not call it 'women's intuition.' He was assassinated for the same reason all great visionaries are killed, and by the same element – that group of power-hoarding individuals who recognize a real threat to their way of life, their 'power,' their worldly riches, and most important, their reason for being. I told you that he conceived and successfully implemented a new and far better way of living life on Diarma, and he has done so exclusive of an economy that requires money. Need I further extrapolate on the magnitude and impact of such a success on modern day society? So they killed him, in Zurich, while crossing a street on the way to a forum in which he was going to publicly reveal for the first time the enormous strides made on Diarma. No, you did not read about it, nor did you hear about it. His death went unnoticed as far as the public was concerned. A back page hit and run, period. I have the article. Would you like to read it?"

No, I nodded, and then asked, "A conspiracy?"

"Most definitely, but not in the sense you think. He, like Christ, and more recently, Gandhi and King, was the conspirator, for he conspired against the system, and the system, any system's most fundamental law is self-preservation. They simply exercised that 'right,' and so, for the time being, Alethea feels a certain degree of secrecy... perhaps discretion is a better word... should enshroud the island. It is for this reason only the barest of information is given in an initial interview such as this. Once your application is forwarded and reviewed, she will have a much better sense of you; ergo, the pamphlet I mentioned. Ironically enough, it is with his death that the present opening for an architect becomes realistic, for it is with the insurance monies finally realized that the construction of the new facilities may now begin.

"I have told you much more than I am allowed, Christos. Please honor this confidence and query me no further. Do you with to apply or not?"

"Yes."

"Good. I need some statistical data and also, there is a short questionnaire. It will only take a few minutes."

I followed her back to her desk, lit a cigarette, and waited to be examined.

"Full name?"

"Alexander Christos – no middle name."

"Date, place, and time of birth?"

"January 9, 1975, Montreal. I think it was around seven in the morning, but I'm not sure. Is it important?"

"No, it's just something they like to know, if possible. Let's see, that makes you thirty-nine. Citizenship?"

"American."

"Ancestral origin?"

"Greek and Spanish, equal parts."

She actually dropped her pen and did not attempt to conceal her surprise.

"What's so strange about that?"

"Nothing. Nothing at all. It's simply coincidental, pertaining to the Legend of Alboran… Oh, dear me, there I go again, divulging information I really shouldn't be giving out at this stage."

I decided to press my advantage and so smiled my sweetest smile and asked, "Pray tell, Millicent, what is Alboran?"

"Simply an historical facet of Diarma that would have been revealed to you through the pamphlet."

"Could you be a little more specific?"

"Christos, you're incorrigible! Very well. Diarma was originally the Island of Alboran. Up to four years ago, actually. Its legend is quite unique, even infamous in Basque folklore."

"Would you, perchance, have a copy of that legend?"

"Just exactly what section of Spain did you mother come from,

Christos?"

"The Basque country, Millicent."

"My God, that's incredible, you'll realize just how incredible once you've read the legend. I'll look for one before you leave, all right?"

"Fine."

"Let's get on with it, shall we? Marital status?"

"Divorced."

"Children?"

"None."

"Parents living?"

"Both deceased."

"Brothers, sisters?"

"One sister but I haven't seen her in years."

"Present employer?"

"None."

"Really! How fortunate for Diarma. You'll be looking for work, then?"

"No, I retired."

"Then how fortunate for you... Now, the questionnaire is confidential, so after completing it, place it in this envelope and seal it. Use my desk. I'll be down the hall."

PLEASE ANSWER ALL THE QUESTIONS AS BRIEFLY
OR AS EXPANSIVELY AS YOU DEEM APPROPRIATE.

1. *Are you presently affiliated with any organized religion?* No.
    If answer is "no" or "yes," do you believe in God? No, not in the usual context of what God is and does. If I believe in anything at all, it is some sort of noninvolved, non-caring force that simply just is.

2. *What is the state of your physical health?* Unfortunately, excellent.

3. *Have you ever killed anything?* Yes.
    If answer is "yes," what did you kill and at what ages did you kill it? A bird at age twelve and several mosquitoes, flies, spiders, and cockroaches, at all ages.

4. *Do you believe that "money is the root of all evil"?* No, but man's

love of it may very well be.

5. *What is your definition of evil?* Anything that keeps you from being your true self.

6. *Are you heterosexual?* Yes, it is my greatest curse. *If answer is "yes," what qualities are you drawn to in the opposite sex?* The same qualities I am drawn to in a member of my own sex: strength, gentleness, intelligence, sensitivity, physical beauty, and non-inquisitiveness.

7. *Are you familiar with the work of Bradford Boobis?* No.
If answer is "yes," what are your feelings about it?

8. *Do you believe the Human Race to be a basically good and sane species?* I strongly suspect not. All I can really believe is that the whole of humanity itself is nothing more or less than a course in the curriculum of the Universe, which we, as well as I, have obviously failed.

9. *Have you ever read* The Magus *by John Fowles?* No.
If answer is "yes," what do you think he was trying to point out through the work on a deeper level?
If answer is "no," are you familiar with its overall concept? No.

10. *Have you ever read the work of Dr. Richard Maurice Bucke - Cosmic Consciousness? If "yes," what are your feelings about it?* At the risk of having you believe I am near illiterate, no.

11. *How do you physically envision God, or whatever you have personally labeled It? (If answer to Q 2 was "No," simply write "N/A").* As a pair of enormous eyes with the lids shut.

12. *Have you ever read the teachings of Gautama the Buddha? If so, what are your feelings about them?* I can finally give you a "Yes." Enough to recognize that his teachings are both pessimistic and nihilistic. The creed and methodology he proselytes appears to me to be totally self-serving. I must also confess that anyone who was revered, or claimed to be The Fully Enlightened One, which, by dictionary definition breaks down thus: He came to the answers about all things in the Universe - should be looked upon with a somewhat jaundiced eye. According to my understanding of Buddhism, the entire process of evolution (after evolution produced Him, of course – He's the exception) is nothing more or less than doomed species masturbation… On second thought, maybe he's right. In all fairness, it is entirely conceivable that my Western mind is unequipped to grasp the subtle distinctions within the Lamist doctrine.

13. *Is there any single individual, past or present, which you look up to with great respect, even awe?* Jesus Christ, but He is an impossible dream.

14. *Do you consider yourself to be a courageous person?* Only if I answer this question honestly.

Thank you for allowing us to take such liberties.

D
I
A
R
M
A

* * * * *

As if on cue, she walked into the office and, for a moment, I wondered if she had been spying on me, but when she smiled that smile I could not bring myself to the accusation. She gathered up the questionnaire, placed it in the envelope, and sealed it.

"What did you think of the questions?"

"Precocious and relevant."

"Touché. Please try to understand that there must be some form of initial screening process for reasons other than, as well as, those I have indicated. What you have just completed is not a test, but rather a carefully thought out method through which Diarma can glimpse an initial insight into the applicant's character, disposition, intelligence, and thought processes. If, for some reason your application is turned down, the questionnaire will be returned to you and I assure you no copies will have been made.

"And, please, don't take the rejection personally.

It will simply mean that all things considered, Diarma would not be a mutually beneficial experience. If, on the other hand, you are accepted, it will be as if walking into your own home or that of your dearest friend. Of course, along with the questionnaire, I will enclose my impressions, which I will tell you now will be most favorable, but their weight is only an influencing factor, not the influencing one."

"I'm only surprised they didn't ask me if there was a history of lunacy in my family."

"Don't be. If you were insane, you most likely wouldn't know it, so what would be the point? Are you?"

"I don't think so."

"See what I mean?"

She checked her watch and guided me to the door.

"I have one more interview to conduct this evening so you'll have to excuse me."

It jarred me badly. Somehow I hadn't even considered the possibility of there being "competition." I actually felt a pang of jealousy – of possessiveness. She seemed to sense this and said almost in the manner of placating a child,

"Take my card with my private number. Call me if you have the need. We should have an answer in a week to ten days, possibly sooner. If you are accepted, they will wire and instruct me to send on the pamphlet to you. If upon reading it you decide you would like to visit Diarma, it will only be a matter of days before travel arrangements are set. I do so hope it works out. I know that you would fall madly, inextricably in love with Diarma. I personally maintain guest privileges, you know. I visit twice a year for a month and every time I come back reborn."

She extended her hand and I eyed her somewhat flirtatiously as I said, "Millicent, if you are representative of what the island accomplishes, then I would be worse than a fool not to accept... I almost forgot the legend. Did you find a copy of the Legend of Alboran?"

"Wait here for just one moment. I ran off a copy of it while you were filling out the questionnaire."

She walked hurriedly back to her office and returned moments later with a sheaf of papers in her hand.

"Because of the rare coincidence that occurs here, I copied the Legend directly from the pamphlet. When you've read it, kindly destroy it, as there are one or two references to Diarma in it."

"Of course. By the way, I assume you know the Greek meaning of the word Diarma?"

"Indeed, I do," she said, with an almost mystical twinkle in her eyes.

It was as I entered the street to flag a cab that I realized her card was still in my hand, along with the photocopies of the Legend. I started to put it into my pocket when I decided to give it a glance and what I saw stopped me so abruptly that I almost succeeded in flagging a truck with my entire body. The card was of simple tasteful design and its script announced:

Dr. Millicent Rand
Psychiatrist
212-555-4757

My astonishment gave way to laughter – Diarma was taking no chances.

The hour of arrival at my apartment coincided perfectly with the disappearance of the day. From my tiny terrace I gazed over the Hudson River and watched a tangerine sun sandwich itself between a monstrous building complex and New Jersey's euphemistic version of a mountain. I disappeared inside for a moment to mix a fast compari and soda, reappeared on the terrace where I set it down on the small tile table where it remained untouched. I flicked the switch that sent a single beam of amber light spot-lighting the lone chaise lounge and then I lunged into the prize:

THE LEGEND OF ALBORAN

Diarma's (Alboran's) history is unique, if not more so than its obvious natural advantages. The earliest record of societal habitation is believed to have been established by the highly technologically advanced Minoan Civilization as early as 1700 BC. Alboran was used as an area of religious(as opposed to spiritual) retreat inclusive of barbaric rites wherein human as well as animal sacrifices were offered to the gods by way of a three-thousand-foot plunge down the interior of the volcano that was situated dead center in the middle of the island. The volcano spewed forth its dissatisfaction during one of these ceremonies.

In the year 1450 BC, and for the next thousand years, the island yielded little or no recorded history other than legendary allusion and the more concrete evidence that it remained a "sometime area of retreat for the reigning monarchs of the times." It is generally held that the volcano, though not active during this period, was the main deterrent to any form of permanent settlement.

In 1272 AD, Alboran became a Spanish possession. Some forty years later, it was bequeathed to the Duke of Alba for "services rendered of an extraordinary nature" during the Great Crusades. The Duke visited the island frequently with certain selected guests and is quoted in his colorful memoirs as referring to it as his "island paradise." It was he who bestowed the name on the volcano that stands to this day: La Boca de Dios – God's Mouth. Once again, no permanent settlement was either encouraged or actuated for, while Isle Boca de Dios never actually regurgitated, it was indeed prone to a not infrequent belch.

The Duke and Duchess bore a son, Francesco, and with his entry into this world, the Legend of Alboran was also born.

Francesco was a most exceptional specimen of humanity, strong, handsome, intelligent, and kind. As the years passed and Francesco matured into young manhood, a relationship with a distant cousin, Philipe de Valencia that had been nurtured from childhood also ripened. By the time they were twenty years old they were inseparable. They were more like brothers than cousins, both possessing almost identical character traits and intelligence. While Philipe was the more aggressive, Francesco was more compassionate. It is said they became so close they would think the same thought at the same moment. Their relationship epitomized the healthiest of love between two members of the same sex... until Allysia. They came to be the "gods" of their times... until Allysia.

In 1350 AD, when they were both thirty and still single, Allysia, a Greek Princess, came into their lives and changed them, as well as the course of Alboran's history, forever. The three of them met while Philipe was on holiday on the Greek Island of Paros, and at the outset it appeared the union had been conceived in

Heaven. She was their female counterpart in every sense of the word - the perfect ménage-a-trois sans-sexual-involvement. They became inseparable companions on an incredibly equal level. For a time they seemed content, even overjoyed to share each other's minds and emotions, but then, of the latter category, one of them became rampant - passion and lust; and, it happened to all three of them at the same time.

Allysia fell madly in love with both Francesco and Philipe, and vice-versa. The relationship between the two men, spanning more than a quarter of a century, disintegrated at an astonishing rate. Ultimately, because there was no other manner in which to determine who was to be graced with her favors, a joust was ordered, as was the custom of their times. Francesco and Philipe were to engage in mortal combat – winner takes Allysia and the loser's land holdings.

The dons of the respective families, though greatly saddened by the turn of events, rose to the duteous occasion and ordered the contest held on the neutral Island of Alboran. The outcome of the joust was to set the course for the ensuing five hundred years of Alboran's history.

Wholly aside from the historical implications, the joust, in and of itself, was strictly one of a kind for it was to produce one winner and one loser, who, oddly enough, were the same person: Francesco. He became both victor and defeated for he refused to inflict the final thrust of the sword into the fallen Philipe; instead, he buried it to the hilt into the dirt next to his unconscious opponent and walked to the far side of the arena knowing full well the consequences of his act. Legend has it that as Francesco stood over Philipe, his short sword poised for the death thrust, a golden glow emanated from his presence moments before he buried the weapon into the ground.

He had committed a crime of a social nature, shaming both families, and his punishment was not only the loss of Allysia and his land holdings, but banishment to Alboran for life.

Princess Allysia, of independent spirit, had other ideas, however, and chose to remain w1th Francesco. In the ensuing years they had a child and she was said to have been a most beautiful one possessing not only great physical beauty but extraordinary intelligence and sensitivity as well.

Francesco and Allysia decided that the combination of genes had been so fortunate that in future generations they would maintain the bloodline and only that bloodline.

It came to be an obsession with them. It proved to be a great error, nevertheless, when their daughter, Nikolin, came of age, Allysia went to the Basque country of Spain, where Francesco's true roots were, to find her the "perfect mate" - Rudolpho, for it had been determined that female offspring would be betrothed to Basque males; male offspring to Greek females.

The second generation only appeared to support their theory of purification. Twins, a boy and a girl, were born to Nikolin and Rudolpho, and, once again, they seemed to have inherited only the best genetic traits of both sides.   However, by the time the twins reached adolescence, a quirk began to surface, and against the advice of both parents and grandparents, they became obsessed with purifying the line even further. When they were seventeen, they incestuously produced their own child - Anarose, and Anarose was reputed to have been the most ravenously beautiful, exceptionally talented, and inordinately spiritually attuned child imaginable.

As Anarose grew to young womanhood, her spirit became so independent that any and all attempts to manipulate her into carrying on the purification rites were ignored and even shunned by her. Possession of virtue became obsession with virtue. At first, this course of action was predicated on the intuitive knowledge that to further inbreed, or even procreate at all, would bring about disastrous results.

By the time she was twenty-five, another explanation

had revealed itself to her: that her particular life span was a totally superfluous experience; that it never should have come to be; that she was nothing more or less than an illogical extension of her parents (as well as their parents) demonically focused sense of immortality; that for some bizarre and completely invalid reason she had chosen to incarnate through them and had erred vastly. Additionally, she felt that this genetic quirk had revealed to her that she had very simply been purified right out of this world... and so, her second obsession supplanted her first – death, or more correctly, extinction.

Anarose realized this in 1602, pursuant to the Island's only recorded violence up to the present day, save the joust itself.

A few days later, the day of her burial services, as if God Himself were bellowing His anger, the volcano erupted and wiped out the island, virtually splitting it in two. The half-housing La Boca de Dios remained fixed; the other half drifting far down Africa's west coast pursuant to the strong head winds and tidal waves that ensued.

Legend has it that the nocturnal winds that prevail nightly on Diarma are a direct result of that eruption. For obvious reasons the island was uninhabited for the next two hundred years. In 1758 AD, the island was leased from the reigning Duke of Alba, who with great foresight, refused to part with it on a permanent basis, by a Frenchman, Marquis de Sade, none other than the infamous one - who had come upon the island quite by accident and was overwhelmed by its beauty which now included the lush foliage that remains today - the result of the lava entering the soil.

Donotien De Sade was one of the wealthiest men in Europe and spent well over the equivalent of three quarters of a million dollars restoring and constructing a full community. His plan was to have the island as a commercial but private resort for the titled and nobility of Europe. It was to be wide open with gambling and prostitution, as well as facilities that complimented his legendary penchant for perversity; a paradise of lust and sadism for the more liberal man and woman of his day.

The final construction of the physical facilities was completed in 1762. As if on cue, La Boca de Dias began to belch its disapproval. Although legendarily adventurous, the Marquis was not one to tempt Fate itself, and so departed the island, never to return. The grumblings had been tantamount to a false alarm; to this day, the volcano has never uttered so much as a groan.*

The Duke of Alba regained possession of Alboran in 1778 upon lease expiration... with an entire community added free of charge. However, he never visited it nor did either of the two successive Dukes of Alba.

The island remained uninhabited until its present overseer took possession almost two hundred years later pursuant to the sale of the island by the Spanish government for the sum of two-point-five million dollars. The sale was outright.

No lease terms exist.

*In 1925, a team of geologists declared the volcano dormant, though not decisively extinct.

* * * * *

Four days later, I called her, far more to substantiate her reality than on the pretext of wanting to know if anything had developed. A voice recording enthusiastically greeted me, informed me of her present unavailability, and at the tone of the beep, instructed me to leave a name and number so that she might return my call.

Within twenty minutes the rest of her was talking to me wherein the conversation consisted mainly of small talk, and I strongly suspected that she fathomed my real intentions. She had no news as of yet.

I exhausted the remainder of the week in the diligent though vain role of detective. The latest edition of the Rand McNally Atlas showed no island of Diarma in the area she had pinpointed. It did show a singular island of minute proportions called Alboran, and I suddenly recalled I had a friend in the diplomatic corps who had spent considerable time in and around the Mediterranean.

I reached him later that night – no, he had never heard of Diarma; Alboran, yes, but he had never visited it - merely an atoll in the Spanish Mediterranean, he had been told, a small resort community.

I contacted the overseas conglomerate that provided telephone service to the area and was told they serviced no island called Diarma or Alboran for that matter, which only confirmed that the island was without telephone communication, which I had half expected anyway.

My last ditch attempt in the line of sleuthing was to have sent a cable to Alethea in care of Diarma/Alboran, with instructions that it be returned to me if undeliverable; however, at the last minute, I decided this might not only be a breach of hospitality but security as well.

In all truth, I was merely filling in time until the pamphlet arrived, for by this time I had definitely decided to accept the offer which I never doubted for a moment would be forthcoming, competitors or not. Through whatever medium, Diarma had come to me, not the other way around, and so, it was only logical that I was meant for it and vice versa. Besides, I couldn't wait for the plot to thicken.

"Christos? Millicent Rand. I hope I didn't disturb you."

"Not at all… as a matter of fact, I was just going through my clothes, selecting appropriate items for…"

"I don't know quite how to say this… I was so certain you would be right for Diarma… They've turned down your application, Christos. I'm terribly sorry."

Several moments elapsed before I heard my voice say, "Did they give any indication why?"

"No, they never do in these cases. I simply received a wire this morning, instructing me to continue looking for a qualified architect."

"I see."

But I didn't see. My mind was a swirling mass of confusion fast becoming overwhelmed with anger.

"Christos, are you still there?"

"Yes. Well, I guess that's that."

"I'm afraid so. I'm truly terribly sorry. It just didn't work out… I was so certain you were The Seventh Man. Good-bye Christos."

"Wait! Millicent… Millicent?"

The line was dead. What the hell did she mean, "The Seventh Man"? Who the hell was "The Seventh Man"? The seventh resident?

No, that can't be it. She had indicated there were several residents presently on the island. Some esoteric Diarma designation for applicants, I decided, for lack of anything better to conjure.

And then the anger turned inward for I realized in that moment that the basis for the rejection was most likely derived from the flippancy of tone readily apparent in some of my answers to the questionnaire.

Ten minutes later I had dug out her card and dialed her number in an attempt to salvage the situation, but rather than herself, or the voice recording, I was greeted in a very mechanical manner by yet another recording: "The number you have reached is out of service… if you wish further assistance, please remain on the line…"

There was no "further assistance."

A simple disconnect, and when the anger finally subsided, I felt panic wedge its way into me. I suppose one positive thing did come out of it, however; any lingering idea that I had been the victim of a hoax or complex manipulation vanished, as had the island.

What did not vanish was a ferociously escalating desire to be there.

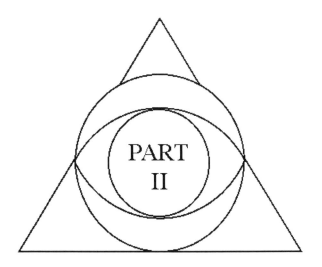

PART
II

CATHARSIS

"Many a man deludes himself into believing he possesses power of one kind or another. There is only one real power – the power that brings about understanding – and he can indeed possess it."
~ Diarma

My plane landed in Madrid the following night. In the morning I rented a car and headed for Granada, my destination Motril, a port town situated some hundred and ten miles northeast of Alboran. I had planned on making a leisurely trip of it encompassing two days but my mounting excitement literally drove me through the night and I arrived in Motril a little after three in the afternoon the following day.

I ate a fast lunch and went immediately to the harbor to charter a boat, but there were no takers. Some even laughed at me. At first I thought it was my pigeon Spanish, but then I realized that their laughter was hollow - that the most common reaction to my request was one of astonishment tinged with fear. Was it the volcano that frightened them? They were, after all, an unsophisticated people undoubtedly given to superstition. Apparently, my command of their tongue was just not good enough to get across the question.

Out of desperation, I doubled my charter fare and was finally approached over dinner by an expatriate American who introduced himself as Rambeau, to whom I took an immediate dislike.

"Yes," he said, he would take me to Alboran, but for double my doubled fare as high tide would not take effect for four nights and the trip would be perilous. He would take me tonight, shortly after midnight, so that he could return to Motril by seven the next morning, thus not missing a precious day of fishing: the lobster were running, he explained.

None too happy with the departure hour, as it would place me on Diarma a little after three AM - hardly an hour to welcome a guest let alone an intruder - I accepted the man's terms at once. The fact that I was indeed to become an intruder concerned me only minimally for I simply repeated to myself once again, "Diarma has come to me," and would just have to take a wait-and-see stance until the moment of truth.

*****

It was that most seductive of Mediterranean nights, grandiosely displaying the stuff romantics' fantasies overflow with, that poets vainly attempt to imprison even as their very souls scream out to leave well enough alone. Quarter-mooned, brilliantly starred, every plane, each image, cosmically distinct; entities of beauty unto themselves that when combined and rendered a whole, contrived a perfect visual seascape.

Rambeau approached me at the rail, uncorked a bottle of wine and offered a glass. Reluctantly I accepted. I wished this man to keep his distance, not to intrude on the serenity that was, but not wanting to appear rude, I drank it in two gulps and excused myself on the pretense of getting some rest.

As it turned out, it was no pretense. The hours of flight combined with those on the road had taken their toll, for as I lay down on the cot, I drifted off almost at once.

I awoke to the man's none-too-delicate touch. It was three forty-five. My head ached slightly – wine always had that effect on me. I was informed that Alboran was just coming into view, and the man's expression and tone queried, "Why would anyone want to go to that Godforsaken pile of rocks? Sure, it's beautiful, if you're an iguana," he actually said.

I rubbed the sleep from my eyes and made out the outline of La Boca de Dios. I had some difficulty distinguishing the island's general form and dimensions until we were almost upon it. We were making our approach from the northeast into the cliff exposed section that guarded the massive sprawling base of the volcano. I assumed this course was the only feasible means of entry. As we came yet closer there was no sign the rough seas were subsiding and I began to worry about the tide.

As we continued inland, the jutted cliffs and rock-laden coastline took on awesome body. In the dead of night they resembled an ominous stone militia guarding the entrance to their castle. I looked down just then and fully realized just how low the tide was and began to wonder how the hell we were going to affect docking.

That is precisely when I heard the engine come to a full stop. We were still a good mile offshore. Rambeau put in a salty appearance and informed me that this was the end of the line due to tide conditions. I thought the man had a perverse sense of humor to say the least. What did he expect me to do, swim the last mile with two pieces of luggage?

No, he replied, he would sell me an army surplus raft he just happened to have along. It had been patched a few times but was certainly seaworthy. By this time, I was convinced the man was serious, but I could not bring myself to believe the suggestion in the face of the frothed rage that were my stepping stones to Nirvana.

I asked Rambeau to circle the island and allow me to debark on the beach side which he had indicated existed on the opposite side.

"You ever hear of reefs, mate? At low tide, yet?" came his reply in a tone that suggested I was only slightly more advanced than an imbecile. "One little swell and you and your raft would be cut to ribbons. The tide's rising on this side. It'll be a might bumpy but you'll make it. Now, what's it to be? You want the raft or not? You don't look like no Johnny Weissmuller to me, pal."

*****

Soaked, bruised, and bleeding, I beached in a tiny cove shortly before dawn. It had taken almost two hours to traverse the lone mile. Completely exhausted, I reversed the raft and passed out on it.

XII

With the help of the sun (my watch had not survived the embarkation), I gauged it to be mid-morning when I awoke. I felt somewhat chilled and at first thought it was due to my wet clothing, but then I realized that the air temperature was quite cool, much cooler than I had expected for a Mediterranean isle in August. Perhaps the result of the previous night's winds, I surmised.

As I stood and oriented myself, I became acutely aware of the bodily damage I had incurred a few hours earlier. There didn't appear to be an inch of me that wasn't sore.

It was then, as I looked down at my feet, that I noted two things that were highly unusual. The first was of the category of natural phenomena - black sand, something I had only read about before; the second was a phenomenon of quite a more human nature - someone, during the night, had come upon me, cleaned and bandaged the worst of my lacerations, and then retreated back into the night. I decided it was an act of an oddly hospitable nature.

As I looked to the ocean I had to shield my eyes from the water reflected glare. Somehow I had expected greater feelings to have been elicited from my romantic viewpoint. I turned towards the sheer rock cliff which blocked from view all other vantage points. I certainly could not get worked up about that either; quite the opposite, for I suddenly realized that, aside from trying to swim all the way around to the other side of the island, which I had no intention of doing, the only way out of my present predicament was virtually straight up, and, I had always had a fear of heights - which I suppose explains a lot.

The one piece of real estate that was visually accessible to me was the upper portion of La Boca de Dios looming high in the sky, but that particular morning, even it held an ominous quality. I entertained the thought that perhaps at any second it would indicate its disgust at the intruder's invasion.

I managed to snap myself out of my depression while combining essential needs into one suitcase that could be belt-slung over my back - a most necessary concession to my imminent mountain goat metamorphosis.

At first at a decrepit pace I began my ascent and then I elatedly discovered that the angle was far less perilous than I had initially perceived. Strong foot and hand holds appeared magically every step of the way, almost as if they had indeed been placed there just for me. I paused for a breather and ogled another sight I had never seen – a rich and fertile fir tree, at least twenty-five feet from stem to stern, growing at a forty-five degree angle straight out of a cluster of rocks. My spirits as well as my body were rising steadily and then the former went berserk as I finally crested the cliff face. My senses, primarily visual, were treated to a bombardment of beauty that defied any prior description and suddenly I realized Rambeau's inability to appreciate anyone's wanting to visit this place. Through natural circumstance, and Diarma's clever contrivance, no one other than guests had been privy to this viewpoint as they were forced to approach from the northeast due to tide conditions; my present perspective was solidly guarded by what was indeed a stone militia.

Much in the manner of a cinematographer capturing an epic spectacle, my eyes slowly panned the horizon, devouring each and every aspect in the process.

It was as if Someone had commanded Something to combine all the most magnificent terrestrial exotica and symmetrically place them in one locale, but rather than the mere calculation of a sculptured paradise being the scheme of things here, the invocation of feelings had been the criterion.

I imagined the omnipotence had expressed itself thus:

"OVER HERE, GIVE ME THE FEELING OF FRESHNNESS, INVIGORATION!"

And I gazed through binocular eyes to the inland border of the crescent beach into the spruce, firs, and pines extending over the entire southwestern portion of the island and creeping northerly up the slope of La Boca de Dios.

"THAT'S NOT QUITE IT!" It admonished. "SOMETHING IS MISSING. GIVE ME THE FEELING OF COOLNESS!"

And I discovered the waterfall cleansing the narrow sparkling brook just as a doe darted into an L-shaped meadow.

"NOW, GIVE ME THE FEELING OF EXPANSIVE CLEANLINESS AND CALM!"

I shifted my gaze a few degrees to glistening white sand that fed into aqua glass that was only occasionally disturbed by the barest ripple.

"EXCELLENT. A TOUCH OF PARADOX WOULD DO NICELY HERE. GIVE ME THE FEELING OF UNLEASHED POWER, EVEN RAGE!"

I turned around and saw and heard the thrashing whitecaps against the ragged granite, as well as the towering blindingly white lighthouse whose very foundation was an enormous hexagonal rock hovering a few yards into the sea herself.

"ALL RIGHT, NOW I WANT SERENITY AND TRANQUILLITY. RIGHT OVER THERE WOULD BE PERFECT!"

I looked down the slope directly in front of me into a valley of green meadows and heather glens decorated with wild flowers of only the brightest of colors, the focal point of which was a shimmering pond that flaunted geese and swan as an occasional fish broke the surface in seeming celebration.

"NOW, THE COUP D' GRACE – SOMETHING MAJESTIC, PROUD, INVINCIBLE... A MOUNTAIN... NO, TOO PLACID – A STRONGER SYMBOL OF POWER AND NOBILITY IS REQUIRED HERE... A VOLCANO. PLACE A VERY LARGE VOLCANO DEAD CENTER IN THE MIDDLE OF IT ALL.

FANTASTIC! IT'S PERFECT. ALL THAT REMAINS ARE A FEW MINOR CONCESSIONS TO THE SPECIES WHO SHALL PRIMARILY INHABIT IT.

"FIRST, AN AREA FOR A FEELING OF COMMUNITY…"

I stared down into the small charming village that wound itself halfway around the base of La Boca de Dios.

"LASTLY, A FEELING OF CONNECTION TO THE PAST AND THE FUTURE."

As I scanned the slopes of the volcano, I saw where man's hand had taken up where "God's" left off: from the antiquated stone structures to the huge bubble dome that pinnacled the very crest of the volcano.

I trekked onward and was able to see that security had also been provided for, for descending the lower slopes were terraced levels housing trees, plants, bushes, and crops yielding vegetation and fruit in abundant varieties.

I had read about the unusual phenomena created by lava flow but until this instant had never experienced such incredible dimensions of natural beauty, and so, quite naturally, I resumed my hamletward trek with a surge of energy I could not recall experiencing since early childhood.

XIII

"What in God's name happened to you? You look half-drowned. Are you all right? Please, come with me. We weren't expecting you just yet. Come along now, I'll take you to the infirmary and then notify the overseer at once."

I had just entered the outskirts of town. The professorial looking gentlemen led the way and within the hour I had been properly iodined, rebandaged, and tetanus-inoculated. My guide then led me out of the village and up a narrow cobbled path for about a quarter of a mile until we reached a castle-like structure complete with turreted towers that bore the legend Pensión.

I was turned over to an elderly gentleman who appeared from behind a gold scrolled registration booth who in turn led me up a winding stone staircase to a higher floor suite of large rooms that were rather Spartan in decor and immaculately maintained. The parlor consisted of basic creature comforts, a huge marble fireplace fronted by gargoyle andirons and an immense box window that provided a sensational view of "Cleanliness and Calm." I checked the clock and asked the kindly elder to knock on my door in two hours and then walked through the small foyer that obliquely led to the bedroom. I went immediately to the French doors that guarded a small balcony and as I stepped out on it realized my great fortune. I had been assigned a corner room and my present point of view extended out and over the sheer cliff coastline that had been my point of entry. I looked down and gauged the distance to the sea to be over a thousand feet.

I turned my head to the sound of deep throated mooning and saw perched on the parlor ledge two ruby-eyed doves bobbing their heads back and forth, appraising their new neighbor.

When they took flight, I did also and two doors later discovered the bathroom, stripped, and leisurely soaked myself in the over-sized tub.

After somewhat presumptuously unpacking, I laid down on the room's only concession to luxury – a canopied Louis the Fifteenth, and waited.

As I fell asleep, I had no idea whatsoever when the note had been slipped under my door:

> *Christos,*
>> *You are expected at seven PM sharp. The gentleman in charge of the Pensión will supply you with directions.*
>>> *A.*

The cat was obviously out of the bag. I had half-expected this as I was certain that either my initial host or my mysterious Florence Nightingale had given her a very specific description of me. Actually, I felt relieved, much in the manner as when as a child I had finally been caught in a lie.

Next, I turned my attention to the tone and text of the communiqué. Was that coldness, even anger that under lied her message? Or, was I misinterpreting mere economy for terseness? As I had not met her, I had no way of knowing. I gave way to the latter innuendo, not by power of reasoning but rather sheer optimism - another long dormant feeling that had been reawakened by Diarma... besides, the last thing I wanted to do was exhibit an unsure or nervous attitude at our initial meeting – quite the opposite was the rule of thumb. In any event, as it was now five-thirty, I had some ninety minutes to find out.

I dressed and stepped back out on the balcony and smiled. My fine feathered friends had returned and at that particular moment it was quite obvious that the she was more than a little disgruntled with the he, for she was busily chastising him with pecks, gnaws, and grunts.

Now you may well think me a sexist for automatically assuming that the she was the aggressor. Not so at all. It is simply that one cannot deny a certain universality of masculine/feminine experience, as you shall bear witness to in a moment…

XIV

A magenta forest became chartreuse… deep purple plains half mooned it… mountains of flame and blood mixed with pale, almost vanilla peaks, rose gracefully to the very tip of the cosmic window. Was that beige rimmed turquoise a lake? It was a second ago… now it was a river becoming an ocean. Suddenly, the mountains, forest, plains, lake-river-ocean became one as the sun's rays shifted ever so slightly with its descent potpurring the images, and then, in a fraction of an indiscernible instant, my Africa-in-the-sky dissipated into elongated, indistinguishable brush strokes of pastel hues crowning the sea, mutating into the royal blue that is the Mediterranean night.

I tore my eyes away from the spectacle and saw her seated at a large white wicker glass-topped table with matching chairs, and although her back was to me, I sensed that she sensed me.

I approached her slowly and the sound of my footsteps on the grass seemed inordinately loud to me. I was suddenly filled with the feeling of discomfiture, even alienation. There was something unreal, surreal, of almost forced theatricality about the situation in which I found myself. It was as if I were walking into an incredibly beautiful painting – a masterpiece – with everything in its proper place but me.

Pausing to glance around, it then struck me with full force: It wasn't me – it was she, seated there at that table in that perfectly poised position, her total attention focused on the vestiges of the colorama, and beyond, far beyond. It was as if she had been positioned there intentionally by the artist as the focal point of acres and acres of green rolling lawn; the radius of miles and miles of sky. Then came the first indication that this was real life happening now, this instant, for the canvass suddenly came alive, but only slightly and for the briefest of moments as her silver hair splayed softly in the breeze, then, still life once more.

I was directly behind her now. She had still not moved nor in any manner acknowledged my presence. I was at a complete loss for words. Even a simple "Hello" seemed neither natural nor appropriate in that moment; worse, I didn't know what to do either. Her ambience was overwhelming. My body finally made the decision for me and I found myself walking past her to the opposite chair where I very simply froze.

She granted me a communication. Her right hand, which had been cupped to her forehead, moved outwards slightly. This miniscule sign of acknowledgement indicated I was to sit and that I was not to think about, much less dispute, that oh so economically commanding gesture.

She maintained her gaze of a budding star through magenta lensed glasses and then deigned to view me through that same perspective. Her somewhat angular, exquisitely sculptured face remained totally expressionless, and then she very simply astonished me beyond words as she removed her glasses and I stared into enormous gray-green eyes flecked with gold that shone the whole of feminine experience. A timid voice in my head told me to say something, anything, but a stronger intuition quelled it. Her expression - perhaps optical penetration would be more apt - did not alter the tiniest of degrees as she broke the silence with,

"Tell me, do you believe 'Beauty is in the Eye of the Beholder'?"

She immediately returned to her star.

Once again, I was badly thrown off balance. The last thing I expected to come out of her mouth was a queried cliché. I started to feel at ease.

"Yes," I replied.

"Then, besides being a most presumptuous, extraordinarily selfish, dangerously impulsive young man, you are also a fool."

She shifted her gaze to the Aurora Borealis before proceeding with her attack.

"If, for any reason, I did not find that spectacle beautiful, would that make it not beautiful? Beauty is what beauty is. By the same token, it is not beautiful because I find it so. That applies to people as well as sunsets, from where the expression originated. I can only hope and pray that you are not a dangerously irresponsible individual as well when you leave Diarma tonight in less than two hours at nine o'clock, to be exact, never to return. By that I simply mean you are to tell no one what you saw or that you were even here, for if you do, you will bear the brunt of the responsibility for jeopardizing the life's work of over a hundred people, to say nothing of the most evolutionary concept available to man since Jesus Christ. Do I make myself perfectly clear?"

She re-donned her glasses, rose, and headed for the topiary edge of the crest. All that was to be said had been said. The meeting was very simply over and, as there had been such conviction in her tone, such damnable truth in her choice of words, I did not doubt her for a second.

I sat immobile in the chair and gazed upon her slender, erect body, searching desperately for some appropriate rebuttal. I looked to my heart for an apology but nothing seemed adequate for, in that moment I was indeed dumbstruck with the full force of my "selfish," presumptuous, "impulsive" act.

I was conscious neither of rising or walking away. I must have gone a good twenty feet before she stopped me dead with, "Of course, that's only one possibility."

She was halfway to me now, her entire being welcoming, and when she reached me, she extended her hand, smiled, and said, "My husband believed that one of the major approaches to the expansion of the human mind towards its ultimate goal of objectivity, was to continually confront it with situations, experiences, that forced the active consideration of all the possibilities inherent in the understanding and valid evaluation of those situations we are prone to involving ourselves in. It's all right; you are not expected to grasp the concept instantly. A course which we give here called "Penetration" is taught for the express purpose of strengthening this mental capacity. In time, the diligent student, after great discipline, as well as many and varied experiences, can come to see all the possibilities. They actually flash visually before him, in his mind, in ordered sequence, thus allowing the totally perceived truthful response and reaction."

The best I could muster up in "totally perceived truthful response and reaction" was a very perplexed look.

"As I said, you can't be expected to grasp the concept instantly, but should things work out between us, in September you would be enrolled in this course, as well as others, and I promise you that in time you would come to learn to consider all the possibilities before making a decision, arriving at a conclusion, or in your particular professional capacity, placing a pencil to a drawing."

She took my arm in a familiar manner suggesting we had been friends for years, and steered me back to the table. Suddenly, I felt as though I were being mentally seduced and began to get angry.

"I really don't know what the hell you're talking about. First, you treat me as if I was a leper, and then in the next instant we're bosom pals. To my feeble mind, that's game-playing, Lady, pure and simple."

"I will tell you this only one time, Christos, so please believe that it is coming from a most sincere place in me. The one thing I never indulge in is 'games.' My words to you as you were leaving were 'Of course, that's only one possibility,' which implies what to you?"

"That there's another possibility, of course, but of what?"

She waved off my question with one of her own.

"Did you believe my indignant reception?"

"You know I did."

"Did you believe you were being fairly and justly treated?"

"Yes, if a bit harshly."

"I did not ask for an emotional response, only an intellectual one. Yes, the truth, more times than not, is harsh, especially when you have gotten away from it. Until you become familiar with it all of the time, until you live in it, then, by comparison, everything else is harsh."

"Well, excuse me. Just give me a minute and I'll step out of my humanity. I've been trying to shed it for years anyway – and we'll get on with it."

She scrutinized me for a moment then and suddenly burst out laughing.

"I wonder why it is that our species feels such a strong need to cling to negative emotional responses, as if to relinquish them would be to 'step out of one's humanity,' as you put it."

"They do seem to be a large part and parcel of our existence. Emotions, that is."

"Of course. But the object is not to prolong the negative ones or void the positive ones. Rather, it is to purify them, all of them, so that love becomes unselfish love; joy, pure joy, and anger, oh yes, anger, unmitigated, non-cynical anger, the kind of anger that is justly and forcefully directed to the only recipient it truly finds justification in – injustice. Now, I ask you again, did you believe you were being fairly and justly treated?"

"Yes, if a bit harshly."

She ignored it with a look that went askance.

"Am I to assume you meant what you originally said to me in your initial greeting? Or, this some sort of multiple choice?"

"I always mean what I say, Christos."

"Look, Alethea – may I call you Alethea?" She nodded her assent. "I've always considered myself a pretty bright guy, but you've really lost me. Just exactly what did you mean, then, when you said 'That's one possibility'?"

"That there is another possibility. There always is. For instance, you were intended, even manipulated, into being here. The rejection was simply a way of testing your ingenuity and tenacity."

"You're joking, of course?"

"Am I? You're here, aren't you? So I say to you that that is an equally plausible second possibility."

"You mean to say that all this, beginning with the message in the sand, was all a manipulation to get me to Diarma?"

"I know of no message in the sand." She looked me dead in the eye.

"If what you are saying is true, suppose I had failed your test and had not pursued Diarma?"

"You still do not understand, Christos. Why do you insist on closing yourself off to only two possibilities? I didn't say the second one was true, nor did I say the first possibility was true, but let us for a moment suppose that the second possibility is the valid one. So, in answer to your question, 'What if I failed the test?' as I did not have to consider that problem, I obviously cannot give you an answer. In short, we are not dilettantes here on Diarma. We only force the active consideration of a real problem or situation at hand. In other words, Christos, you're here, and for the time being, isn't that enough?"

"Yes, I'm here, but for how long?"

She smiled and replied, "That is strictly up to you. I have offered you two possibilities, and for our purposes here and now, let us suppose they are the only ones. Unless, of course, you wish to inject one of your own. As I see it, you have a very simple choice to make."

I thought seriously of injecting one of my own but something stopped me. I felt as though I would be cheating in a complex game and it seemed premature, even inappropriate, as I had no idea as to what either the stakes or the ground rules were, so I simply said,

"I elect the second. I would very much like to stay."

"Well, that's a relief, I am certainly glad to know you didn't come all this way just for us to find out you were stupid.

"By the way, those two traits, ingenuity and tenacity, are held in extremely high regard here, for were they lacking, there is virtually nothing we could do to instill them… do you begin to see the value of what I just put you through? Of course, I could have sat you down and chastised you thus: Christos, there are two possibilities here. I'm either one, so angered by your presumption in coming here uninvited, or two, I'm delighted you made it. But had I done that, you would not have experienced the possibilities... Yes, yes, I know you are a little suspicious of me, but reservations aside, can you begin to appreciate the value of that kind of experience of living fully in the moment for better or for worse?"

"I will concede you that."

"Concede? This is not a contest, Christos, be assured of that. I thought I made that clear a little earlier."

Her look was so intense it sent a chill through me. She milked the moment exquisitely before plunging on.

"What we work for here is better, but in order to ultimately sustain that being, one must become familiar with the other side so as to know how to avoid its pitfalls. Now, you'll have to excuse me for a few minutes. I've prepared a light supper for us. We can eat out here if you like..."

Whilst we had dined "under and with the stars," as she put it, she stressed to me that even though classes were not in session for me, that if I felt so inclined, I should utilize at least a portion of my time on Diarma to work on myself. She suggested that I practice Penetration on a very simple level, utilizing Zen principles to intently investigate something, an object, fully, from one point of view, and then after exhausting it, force myself to turn my mind a hundred and eighty degrees and look at it with the same degree of intensity, then if this proved successful, to try to stretch my mind even further and see it from yet another point of view. In short, to cover as many points on the circle of inspection as was possible for me to do. She also suggested I use people as "objects" when exercising myself in this manner. She seemed to place additional stress on this latter facet.

She had then plunged into the inquisition of my life in a most simple and natural manner. We were poised between watercress soup and arugula salad when she said, "Tell me about yourself."

And tell her I did.

The beauty of the surroundings and the candor of her aura combined to liberate me and I found myself unable to stem the flow of things I had been both unwilling and unable to express in years. My revelations took us through the next hour and the entire main course of fresh abalone and garden vegetables, during which time she had merely nodded in confirmation, listened intently, and interrupted just twice to have me clarify a thought that appeared murky in substance to her. She seemed to possess a built-in barometer that could adroitly divine those places in me that got in my own way, yet she had been surprisingly gentle in pointing them out to me.

When I had literally run out of things to say, I awaited her comments or questions, but none were forthcoming. Rather that other-worldly look entered her eyes as she gazed past me to the sea.

Over lemon balm tea and fresh fruit compote, she discussed her late husband. She told me the truth about the circumstances surrounding his death and I responded with the proper degree of outrage and shock. Millicent Rand would have been proud of me.

*****

She checked the moon as if it were a suspended timepiece and said rather abruptly, "It's time to call it a night. I have to leave for New York tomorrow and will be gone for two or three days. Enjoy yourself, Christos. Your time is strictly your own; however, bear in mind what you are professionally here for and be prepared to offer me an architectural prospectus at our final meeting, which will take place the night before you leave."

She stood, reached into her pocket, extracted a small hardcover booklet, and handed it to me.

"This book of thoughts was authored by my late husband," she said. "When you return to your room you will find the pamphlet Millicent told you about as well as some other reading material.

All the quotations in the pamphlet that are signed Diarma come from this booklet. Don't attempt to read it in one sitting - it was not intended for that. Glance at it from time to time and contemplate the thoughts. I think you will find it interesting. Do you have any questions for me before we say good night?"

"Just one. When Millicent called me to tell me I had been turned down, the last thing she said to me was 'I was so certain you were the seventh man.' What did she mean by that?"

"When Gautama was queried as to how he answered questions from his disciples, he responded thus: 'There are some questions I will answer; there are some questions I cannot answer; there are some questions I choose not to answer.'"

"How very oblique of you."

"Anything else?"

"Yes, as a matter of fact. What happens when a bad apple surfaces in your barrel?"

"It's covered in the pamphlet but I'll tell you the bottom line: banishment from the island for life."

"My, my. Comparisons to the Buddha in one breath and to the Old Testament in the next. You're beginning to scare me, Alethea."

She smiled then, almost sweetly, had it been possible for her to do so. She said, "You have nothing to fear from Diarma, Christos. It is one thing to play God and quite another to think you really are. Those are all the questions I will answer for you tonight."

I glanced at the blank cover of the small booklet as she walked me to the Mallocean-walled approach way. Much to my surprise, she kissed me lightly on the cheek before disappearing through an ivy-covered archway. Staring after her, with slightly trembling hands, I opened the booklet to a random page and read the first quote I encountered:

"If you wish to accomplish a great deal of true substance in this life, you must remain as anonymous a personality as is humanly possible; however, if your goals are stylistic ones, the exact opposite holds true."

I closed it and then re-opened it to the title page. It read, *THE DIARMA MIND*, and where the author's name should have appeared there was nothing.

****

XV

****

"Man conceived 'utopias.' They exist to be worked towards, not to be attained. To the one in the cave millions of years ago, the quality of life that prevails today, flawed as it most certainly is, exceeds his wildest aspirations... and yet, we have him to thank for it."
~ The Diarma Mind

When I returned to my room I found the literature awaiting me on my bedside table. I laid the pamphlet aside for a moment to see what other goodies had been laid out for me. There was a paperback copy of a work called *Cosmic Consciousness* by Dr. Richard Maurice Bucke; *The Diary of Milarepa*, a translation by Evans-Wentz; *The Tibetan Book of the Dead - Bardo Thol*, translated by Evans-Wentz; a nine-by-twelve book of reproduced paintings of Bradford Boobis entitled *Boobis*; and, finally, a small book by John Fowles entitled *The Aristos*

In short, every work I had indicated I was unfamiliar with on the questionnaire, and a couple more thrown in for good measure. Attached to the pamphlet was a short note: "Christos, it would serve you best to read the books in the order placed - from top to bottom." And then, in the event that I had mussed the order, the works were kindly listed for me. I removed the note from the cover and viewed the design.

TOPOGRAPHY AND STATISTICAL DATA

The island of Diarma (formerly called Alboran) is sixteen kilometers long and at its widest point spans twelve-point-five KM. Its soil is some of the richest on this planet and its crops yield fruit and vegetables of virtually every variety. Flora of an exotic nature is highly indigenous to the island.

Diarma (pronounced die-are-muh) boasts one peak, an extinct volcano, into the crest of which was built the living and working quarters of its overseer.* The entire southwestern coast is blanketed by sugar-fine beaches that feed into the Mediterranean Ocean whose temperature maintains a constant sixty-four to sixty-eight degrees Fahrenheit. The reefs in this crescent area do not allow for docking facilities, therefore, access to the island is gained through a northeasterly approach which offers the paradoxically dramatic cliff-laden and perilously rocky coastline. Docking and debarkation are affected only during high tide by dinghy or row boat.

----

*The word "estate" is purposely not used as it connotes class as a part of nation: rank, state, or condition of life.

The community of Diarma itself, that is to say, the service facilities, lie in half circle at the base of the volcano. Residences are interspersed on varying levels of the volcano's ascent affording magnificent views. Beach homes, for those with permanent guest privileges, dot the southwestern coastline but are set back far enough so as not to be an environmental eyesore.

The middle ground between the village and the interior beach border descends in terraced levels and is exclusively for plant and crop life, as well as the minimal livestock we maintain. The air temperature is consistently between sixty-five and eighty-two degrees Fahrenheit, light humidity. Calm and peaceful during the day, summer eves are renowned for the lashing winds that prevail only during sunless hours.*

----

*Undoubtedly accounts for pollution-free atmosphere – a sort of natural air conditioning.

The first thing its new owner did was change the name of Alboran to Diarma - Greek for "Passage." The second thing he did was import a team of geologists to survey and assess the volcano's mouth. It was discovered that time had bridged a solid rock ledge that spanned the entire interior circumference of the peak some twenty feet beneath the actual crest. He had it filled with iron ore and concrete, not to prevent an eruption, for it would not, but rather to form the foundation for his home, flush with the volcano's peak. This magnificent structure stands alone against the medieval architecture that dominates the remainder of the island's buildings as a symbol of Twenty First Century Plus. Surrounded by rolling lawns, topiary, trees, and exotic flowers, it offers a view of life that words cannot even begin to capture, as does all of Diarma.

Since its inception, Diarma has been working toward its sole objective: the implementation of an evolved society on a small but realistic scale; a societal portent of the future; a living, working example to the rest of the world that a separate reality can (and must) be established and lived; a reality far more valid than its prevailing counterpart: the world of illusion and deception - the planet as a whole.

The measures of evolutionary institution are best reflected in its educational curriculum. It is important to note that the method of instruction utilized by the Diarma Institute of Learning has completely made "classroom technique" obsolete, and in so doing, has implemented a new methodology that not only intellectually saturates the diligent student, but emotionally and spiritually as well.

Among the courses offered are:

Penetration: The practice of the consideration of all possibilities.

Communication: This course emphasizes the perception of universal emotional response as a language unto itself.

Epistemology: The study of the root of human knowledge.

Universal Consciousness: A scientific as well as philosophical study of man's relationship to the Cosmos, combining the techniques of modern science and Great Artifacts with the universally correct dictums of the great spiritualists.

(The evolutionary teachings of Christ, Buddhist Meditational Techniques, Socrates (logic), the paintings of Bradford Boobis, Para psychological Phenomena, etc., etc.)

History Of and Communication with Lessor Evolved Species: Diarma has great love and respect for all forms of life and feels that the need for Connection between members of its own species must also include all other species in order to organically realize true connection to the Universe.

ECONOMY

Diarma is a self-sustaining society whose currency is, once again, Connection.* To be more specific, we all serve each other's needs, both in the mundane and evolutionary sense. For example: the resident in charge of the basic clothing goods store receives his meals free from the grocer, or at the community eating facilities; the sewage plant operator gets his academic instruction free in exchange for his services, and so on and so on.

A community fund is maintained for exigencies as well as minor necessities of a social growth order that require initial cash investment. The fund is sustained through the minimal export of plants, ceramics, and fish. These activities are engaged in solely by the senior citizenry that has been invited to live out their days on Diarma in exchange for these services. They hail, for the most part, from neighboring Spain. Residents may draw up to $5,000 a year for travel or other contingencies that require their presence on the "mainland."

\---------------------------------------

*Money is the language of a reality we basically deny."

~ Diarma Mind

GOVERNMENT

There is none in the sense that anyone is aware he is being governed. To label it, it is an evolved form of Democracy sans Capitalistic influence – a sort of Democratic Socialistic Theocracy, or, as we have labeled it, Universalism. The only laws that exist are those that are implicitly known by every rational human being. As, in its four year existence, there has been no infractions of same, the obvious punishment – initial probation, then banishment, depending on the seriousness of the offense, or frequency of same - has never been exercised.

PRIMARY ASPIRATIONS

Individuality is held in the highest possible regard on Diarma. Our entire collective force is geared towards the realization of one's individual potential, for it is implicitly understood that the only real value the distinction of individuality has ever or will ever have is in its ultimate contribution to the whole.*

----
*The Diarma Mind

It is also felt that the price of the loss of the sense of individuality is the fully potentialized process itself; that this is indeed the most desirable of objectives.* It goes without saying that Compassion and Understanding are the natural guidelines within which we aid one's realization of one's individuality (the scrupulous applicant screening process), for we have no desire to potentialize a Hitlerian personality. It should be noted that Compassion has many faces.

Diarma feels that this is the only valid instructional process for Twenty First Century man through which enlightenment, in the truest sense of the word, can be achieved; that it cannot be realized by solely following, no matter how diligently, the passages left by another, be it a Christ or a Buddha, not in today's world; although as a guide or stepping stones, their messages are invaluable, their enlightenment came from precisely that which we advocate on Diarma: the realization of their individual potentials.

"Man is his own Universe and the Universe is a realm of Infinite Possibilities, of which you are one."*

----
*The Diarma Mind

RESIDENCY CATEGORIES

There are three basic residency categories at this stage of our development. All hold equal privileges and stature:

Permanent Resident - basic services, non-evolutionary.

Permanent Resident - evolutionary functions.

Temporary Residents - Liaison and evolutionary functions.

This latter category has been extended to those who were instrumental in formulating and acquiring the island's needs, initially and on a continuing basis, yet still remain attached, professionally or otherwise, to the world at large.

They are entitled to visit the island four months out of every year and are assigned one of the beach cottages. While here, they are treated with full permanent status privileges.

MISCELLANEOUS FEATURES OF INTEREST

An up-to-date small clinic staffed with a physician and surgeon, dentist, and two nurses, is operational twenty-four hours a day. It is rarely visited. No psychiatric therapy is provided as the residents are extremely healthy in mind as well as body.

An extensive library provides a most serene atmosphere situated on the upper-west slope of the volcano. It is both an enclosed and open air structure and is open twenty-four hours a day.

An open air theater is located in the small community. It is utilized when a professor of one of the subjects feels that the most communicative method of instruction would be through the human embodiment of the text.

There are two eating establishments on Diarma. They are both open air and are situated at either end of the half-mooned community, thus affording alternate visual splendor. They both serve for the two daily meals six days a week. There is a "sector for solitude" provided for those who do not wish to be disturbed while eating; thus, the untimely intrusion of one's thoughts (something held in very high regard on Diarma) is avoided.

A FINAL WORD

As our guest, you enter the island as if coming into your own home or that of your dearest friend. All the island has to offer is yours for the taking. You will need no money. You are our guest in every sense of the word. We do, however, ask that you do not introduce certain things that are not made available here:

All tobacco products. All alcoholic beverages. (A carafe of wine is available with the evening meal.) All forms of drugs, be they of the smoke-variety, hallucinogenic, hardcore, or pills such as "uppers," "downers," or any form of tranquilizer, etc., etc. Of course, firearms or weapons of any type whatsoever are forbidden.

At the end of your stay you may apply for permanent guest privileges in exchange for your professional services, which, if approved, will entitle you to full Category III status. If you are being considered for category I or II status, this will be discussed prior to your departure and, if approved, you may affect residency anytime within a six month period post your departure. In either or neither event, we extend our warmest invitation to you to come to Diarma and we guarantee that, even with this relatively brief exposure period, your life will change for the better.

D
I
A
R
M
A

*****

"In the final analysis, there is no such thing as a 'good' or 'bad' experience. It is experience itself that is the sole catalyst to growth."
                                                              ~ *The Diarma Mind*

Come, we offer you the experience of a lifetime.
Several lifetimes.

"We are all in flight from the real reality.
That is the basic definition of Homo Sapiens."
~ John Fowles The Aristos

The glow from the warmth of a single beam of sunshine gently announced it was time for me to begin my second day in "paradise." I arose, walked to the balcony, and stared out over the seemingly infinite shimmering expanse. I heard the light rap on the bedroom door and turned to see a young girl, tray in hand, bearing juice, coffee, and croissants. Wordlessly, she walked to and through the French doors and placed the tray on the small table. She smiled as she bid me "Good Day" and "Good-bye" in the same breath, turned and left as unobtrusively as she had come.

While leisurely consuming my breakfast I looked straight down to the sea and delighted in an emerald green seaweed pattern of almost perfect geometric design that had embossed itself in the turquoise, visible to the eye only from an appreciable height.

I was wondering where my squabbling friends had gotten off to when they apparently plucked the thought from my head as they gracefully revealed themselves soaring through the air engaged in playful acrobatics – obviously, a good night's sleep had done wonders for their respective dispositions.

I walked briefly indoors to get a cigarette, realized I had none, and so, suffering slightly, dressed and made ready for my immediate future whose itinerary initially demanded indulging the virtues of a long quiet walk on the beach.

An hour and a half later, I decided to exchange the seashore for the forest. I am just about to discover what will become one of my two favorite spots: the base of a huge blue spruce adjacent to the waterfall, whose exposed root ends form a perfect seat that extends lazily into a most musically inclined brook.

Now, Christos, remove your shoes and socks, nestle into your "seat," and cool your feet while allowing your sense of smell to be assaulted by blooming laurel. Inspect the waterfall closely and discover that it is indeed manmade – a work of art and definitely one of his greater achievements. With this thought, begin to realize the incredible resources that have gone into this idyllic setting… the rustle of leaves, the flight of motion as a small fawn dashes in front of you, pausing long enough to respond to your surprise as opposed to your glee, and darts off.

From this vantage point, the entire scheme of the island reveals itself to you. Look straight ahead and you have a perfect V of the two-toned blue that is the union of ocean and sky.

Look to your left now and see terraced levels that appear to have been maintained by a master Japanese gardener that bear apple, peach, orange, lemon, and fig trees in full blossom against the backdrop of the multi-hued west slope of La Boca de Dios.

Turn a hundred and eighty degrees and peek through golden-ray-illumed underbrush over the earthen red tile rooftops of the smaller edifices in the tiny hamlet, and, as a bonus, follow the flight of a regal pair of cinnamon pink-and-black striped Hoopoes to a picture postcard shot of the almost make-believe harbor.

Lean all the way back now and relax any tension that is left in your body. Look straight up into the perfect symmetry and organizational splendor that is your immediate roof, to say nothing of the virtual prism of light shafts just now displayed by the sun's subtle shift.

Come back to a sitting position now and peek around the base of the trunk into the last of the four definitive directions. Feast your eyes on the portion of the volcano that is a partially sun illustrated triangle of valley framed by the perfect irregularity of jutting cliffs.

The melodious clang of the steeple bell announcing the noonday meal tells you it is time to rise and begin your walk back to the village. It is then that you notice that you hardly deserved the passing grade you have just given yourself in your first Penetration class, for there are two squirrels, no more than six feet from you that have been visiting you for how long?

*****

Each and every further step of acquaintance only supported the care, maintenance, and exquisite beauty of the island. Not once did I evidence the terresticide that man is so irresponsibly prone to.

And so, with only one thought on my mind, I gave myself over once again to my sense of smell and literally followed my nose through sea salt, ozone, wild flowers, and pollen carried on the...

I jerked my head towards the blurred-at-the-edges images and strained my eyes to bring them into focus. A strange, almost silkscreen effect seemed to encase them. It was then that I heard and felt the high pitched ultra-sonic sound that seemed to permeate my very being. I had just entered a small wood and the flash of color and movement that caught my eye was a good two hundred yards away. Just as it would come into focus long enough for me to perceive it, then it would again begin to distort, first at the periphery, then inwards. I watched, fascinated, and discovered that with each sequence the scene would stay focused a little longer before disappearing once again. The vibrations continued to roll through my body, increasing until they reached a zenith before leveling off.

I'm just making out the vision now... it is the interior of a second story bedroom but the wall that normally would have hidden the room's interior has been removed... or perhaps doesn't exist. The room appears very dated. A figure... a man... naked. He is lying on his stomach on the narrow bed... going out of focus now... but the colors are so vivid, so beautiful... reconstructing itself now… ah, yes, the man again, and next to him a large velvet chair with clothes piled upon it… is the man's body gyrating? Or is that just the picture going out of focus once again… yes, that must be it for it has blurred now… perhaps if I get closer… but I cannot… I am riveted to where I stand… here it comes again… the man is in movement… suddenly his body collapses and he sinks down into the bed… no, not the bed… a woman… he has been making love to a woman… the man is getting up now… disintegrating now…

I was just feeling the voyeur when it reappeared… the man is completely dressed now… his clothing appears antiquated… elegant seventeenth or eighteenth century dress. The woman, nude from the waist up, is seated in front of a mirrored bureau, running a brush through her dark locks… the man looking over his shoulder at his reflection, positioning a black top hat on his head, reaching for gloves now and putting them on… fading now… the vibrations decreasing also… coming back into focus again… with one hand, he is offering her a large bouquet of flowers while with the other, placing shiny coins next to her on the small vanity. She turns to look at him with her heavily made up yet quite astoundingly attractive face… she seems to have no expression, and just as I am getting the feeling that it is me that she is really looking at, everything dissolved.

But the now low-toned vibration remained with me, tapering off until it completely dissipated some ten minutes later, the amount of time it took me to reorient myself to reality.

And so, from what my original thought had been while trekking towards my noonday meal – which of the alternate eating establishments to grace with my presence – I now had quite a different food for thought, and for the ensuing hour, masticated them both quite thoroughly.

Having always been fascinated by parapsychological phenomena, I had read of the famous Versailles Incident of 1901. In my mind, there existed a parallel somewhere. In that year, two academically-oriented English spinsters had apparently walked into another dimension through a time warp of sorts, and though their account was at first received with a high degree of skepticism from both psychical and non-psychical sources, some forty years later, it was considered to be one of the most unique experiences of retro-cognition ever recorded for documentation, as the two ladies claimed to have strolled through Marie Antoinette's private garden, complete with the infamous lady herself seated quietly under a tree engaged in the painting of a picture.

Was class in session for Alexander Christos? Was this part of the "intellectual, emotional and inspirational saturation" the pamphlet had described as "obsolescing classroom technique"? If so, I had to admit its effectiveness, but to what end?

I had, of course, chosen the "sector for solitude" as I had consumed my meal at the seaside dining area, but as I removed myself from same, I began to wonder just how much solitude I was to indeed be afforded on my island paradise.

I spent the remainder of the day just wandering about, familiarizing myself with the terrain and facilities. Just before six o'clock, I returned to the spot where I had seen the apparition. I found the exact locale, and not much to my surprise, no evidence of the morning's phenomena could be uncovered. As a matter of fact, there was rather incontrovertible evidence to substantiate the opposite, for the wooded area wherein had hung suspended the second story room, was spiked with its most clustered inhabitants yet tree after tree stood no more than ten to twelve feet apart, and so manipulation of the event began to take a backseat to its authenticity.

A little after six, I dined in the cliff view eating facility. Over a cold platter of shrimp, lobster, crab, and a baked potato, complimented by a carafe of wine, I watched the sun disappear into the sea, as well as the incident into the recesses of my mind.

As I arose from the table I felt a wave of tiredness come over me and so decided to retire early.

After my bath, I lay down on the bed and reached for the last book on the list. It wasn't that I was being necessarily arbitrarily rebellious in so reversing the reading order; it was just that the other works felt to be too heavy for me to immerse myself in at the present moment.

Fifty pages later, I understood just why it had been placed on the reading list. Many of the thoughts expressed in The Aristos, not all, seemed pertinent to my state of mind. I was suddenly feeling restless, so I walked out onto the balcony and stared down at the furiously white capped ocean. Awed by the hypnotic rhythm of the thrashing waves, I almost lost my balance to legendary winds that had begun their nocturnal duties. Without warning, I am suddenly overwhelmed by the feeling of wanting to be on that rock I am gazing down upon, and so I give way to it.

XVII

*"Thus far in our evolution, the essential role of the
female of the species (ultimate) is that of the
catalyst; anything that brings about change without
being directly affected itself."*
~ *The Diarma Mind*

Mind and body assembled there a few minutes later. Much to my amazement, I found myself in a spot completely unscathed by the whirling winds. The cliff-face was my guardian and the huge rock I was about to assault was perched into the sea a few feet from where I stood. I removed my sandals and waded to its most gentle incline, then hoisted myself aboard. I discovered a narrow ledge on its seaward side a few feet below where I stood, that when stretched out upon formed a perfect bed, complete with a pillow of lichen. I gazed into the brilliantly adorned sky and concentrated on not concentrating at all; on just becoming one with my surroundings.

I would have succeeded were it not for the abrupt sound of an object breaking the stillness of the calm pool that literally rested beneath me. This particular inlet was not at all agitated by the tumultuous waves that had made their presence clearly felt everywhere else around me.

Startled and shaken, I raised myself to a sitting position and began to investigate the rippling concentric circles. I had just decided that my intruder had been a large species of fish when I saw her swimming beneath the surface, naked, towards a tiny cove a few feet to my right. It was then that I realized that she must have been directly above me on the rock when she dove.

She may well have submerged a woman, but she emerged a goddess. I wondered if she could see me and decided she could but had simply not noticed me. At that instant her milk white body was backlit by the white gold moon imbuing her with an almost supernatural quality. She tilted her head to one side and began drying her hair. I was investigating her profile while at the same time wondering how she had so totally protected herself from the sun, when suddenly she turned her head slightly and our eyes met. I recognized the face immediately, even without the makeup. It was indeed a face of astounding beauty though subtly tinged with wantonness; a face not of classic beauty, but rather of classic feminine experience that somehow conveyed vulnerability and defiance in the same expression. Her eyes completed the paradox – they managed to split a full response in the same moment. The first half revealed surprise, even shock; the second said, "Go ahead, be my guest, feast your eyes." Then, she instantly turned her back and donned a one piece Indian affair that flowed to her feet. She gathered up a single flower, sniffed it briefly, and began to walk off.

In my enthusiasm to get to her, I lost my balance and fell most unceremoniously into the sea. As it turned out, it was the wisest thing I could have done, for my scream of surprise turned her around and her own laughter halted her. Smiling, she shook her head lightly back and forth as I emerged from the surf in the character of some inept nautical monster of the night.

When I got to within a few shivering feet of her, I smiled my most male smile and because I could think of nothing else to say, said, "Do you come here often?"

To which she supplied a somewhat more reserved corresponding female expression and replied, "Every night, but now I will have to find a new place. You have stolen my favorite spot from me." She placed the dark flower once again to her lips.

At that moment, the beam from the lighthouse passed over us and I realized she had violet eyes. She was the most incomparably beautiful creature I had ever seen. Violet eyes, as if that face and body had not been enough. Somehow, I managed to compose myself.

"Perhaps we could arrive at a compromise. Either you wear a bathing suit or next time I won't look."

Those eyes obliqued to some place between coldness and sadness as she said, "There won't be a next time," and immediately resumed her stride.

It was the last thing I had expected to hear. It threw me badly. Such incredible femininity, even coyness, in one moment, and then that. I shouted after her, "Wait a minute. At least tell me your name!"

Without breaking step or turning around, she called back to me, "Names are unimportant. If you must label me, invent one of your own. Good-bye."

"Good night," came my perplexed rejoinder.

I watched her disappear around the base of a cliff. I did not attempt to follow her; instead, I returned to "our rock" and after an hour or so of reliving (as well as tinkering with) the encounter, returned to the Pensión.

****

XVIII

****

"Man's curiosity is insatiable and
it is its own justification."
~ Jacques Cousteau

With my three companions, jasmine in full bloom, the sensation of sea spray, and the loner of all bird species, an incredibly bold Blue Rock Thrush, I waited for her the following night but she did not appear. Not in the flesh, that is. Through other dimensions she had never really left me throughout the day. With only the previous night's brief contact, it was as if she were walking around in my mind. It was a totally new experience for me and so I delved into it by indulging in a sort of variation on the island theme: Penetration… on a fantasy level.

I held "conversations" with her through my morning walk. I investigated her through the noon day meal, scrutinizing her gestures, evaluating her peculiar manner of speech, discerning her mystique, which is, of course, a paradox in and of itself. My only rest from her came during my seaside nap when she mercifully chose not to enter my unconscious. But, of course, when I awoke and discovered my overly reddened state, it was she who ever so gently applied the tanning cream.

I was becoming obsessed by her to an adolescent, unhealthy degree, and so over dinner I attempted to get to the root of the obsession. What I came to made me turn away from myself in disgust.

Was I "in love" with her? Not hardly.

Was I seeking her as a friend? No.

Am I simply attracted to her on a male/female basis? Yes.

Isn't that enough? At least for openers? No.

Why not? Because I sense something about her, something supra-vulnerable.

Then perhaps considering your track record with the opposite sex you should leave it alone. Wouldn't that be the responsible thing to do? I suppose so.

It's settled then.

No.

You don't want to do the responsible thing? I guess not.

The attraction must be very strong then. Label it, Christos. Go ahead. Label it. All right. Fifty percent lust. Fifty percent curiosity. Are you satisfied now? Besides, perhaps she's simply part of a scenario.

We're all part of a scenario, Christos.

I arrived at "our rock" a little after eight. At about ten I finally decided that she was not coming and descended the rock to return to my room.

I almost squashed it before seeing it. I reached down and gently scooped up the delicate flower. I had never seen a black rose before and was not certain I was seeing one now for I happened to know that horticulturists had been trying unsuccessfully for centuries to cultivate one. It was definitely black and its scent was magnificent. It smelled of her, naturally.

It had been a precisely executed gesture on her part, exactingly tantalizing, not devoid of the shroud of mystique that engulfed her, yet just enough of the reality of her to uplift my sunken spirits. I was suddenly not tired at all. I felt I must do something, anything to keep her alive in my mind for I did not trust that the stuff dreams are made of would keep her with me through the night, and so I decided to search for her, braving the cliffward edge of the island from where I had watched her disappear last night. It was pretense, of course, for I knew I would not uncover her, but like the proverbial bloodhound on the scent…

Through partially submerged caves whose fields of depth appeared endless, to and thru a sunken pine forest that eventually led me to a cul-d-sac that demanded a darkened offensive of a craggy precipice, I stalked my imaginary prey until I called the game on account of exhaustion some two hours later.

*****

Bone-tired, I hastily undressed and got into bed. I began to drift quickly and was consciously aware of being pulled into the twilight void that separates awake and asleep states.

I bolted upright in place, took a mini-moment to orient myself, and strained my ears to the sound. My body was covered with cold sweat and seemed paralyzed with fear. I was just about to discount it as a non-real state when the unmistakable shriek of terror pierced the night once again, but this time fell off into a weeping, wailing sound that finally ended as unexpectedly as it had begun, almost prematurely.

I was on my feet now. On the terrace now. Again! But louder and no tapering off, just a final strident chord of death. It had been the loudest and most terrifying shriek of all. It had been of the dimension of sound that did not allow for speculation as to its point of origin. It had distorted the night from nowhere and everywhere at once. The only thing I could be certain of was that it was a woman's scream, a young woman.

My eyes continued to scan the vacuum as the winds buffeted against my body, but my mind was in another place altogether for what had awakened me had jarred me from that moment that precedes dead sleep had been something else. Not the scream, not the wailing, but a word, one word. A name, my name, and it had come to me in a dimension I had never before experienced. It had been as if she had been standing next to the bed, had spoken directly in to my right ear when she had said my name, when she had implored, "Christos." Then nothing. Then immediately after nothing, the scream.

And even though it had sounded as if she were in the room, I had instinctively known she was not. I had most definitely recognized the voice… both from within the room and without.

Still shuddering with fear, I returned to my bed to lie awake "considering the possibilities."

XIX

"Because something exists one should not place an
immediate value judgment on it:
good or bad, right or wrong.
Truly, it only makes it there.
That is the purest meaning of existence."
~ The Diarma Mind

My first thought when awakening from all of an hour's sleep had been to force a confrontation with Alethea to find out if class was indeed in session for Alexander Christos.

However, upon clearing the cobwebs, I realized she was not due back from New York until the following day, and so would just have to wait. The one thing I couldn't come to terms with was the fact that Alethea had explicitly stated that during the three week stay I would be strictly on my own. No exercises or classes of any nature would be imposed upon me, and, although she had struck me as being manipulative, quite possibly highly so, I would have bet my bottom dollar she was not a liar. So for the time being, I was forced to accept the bizarre as opposed to the contrived. And because I am who I am, I actually preferred it that way anyway.

There was one area of the island my explorations had not yet taken me – the southwestern upper slope of the volcano – and this morning seemed as good a time as any for its conquest.

By mid-morning I had traversed my way to within a hundred feet of the crest (and Alethea's front yard for that matter). I was marveling at the purity of air and total lack of humidity as I rounded a bend and saw it:

It looked to be a rock buttercup somehow extending itself out from the slope seemingly poised into the sky itself. The width of its circumference was bridged by an oak bench someone had obviously built to specification.

I scrambled downwards until I came to a point almost directly above it and studied it more carefully. It really did resemble a large buttercup. Its half-foot high lip went with amazing regularity full circle except for a tiny portion that connected with its natural bridge, also no more than a foot wide and on an upward angle of thirty degrees from where it connected to the slope. I came closer, hugging the hillside using bushes and small trees as handholds. I began to speculate on how this tiny volcanic atoll had come to be for I realized that its composition was the bleached rock of petrified lava.

I stared down at it from my high angle perspective and imagined myself high in the sky above it. From this viewpoint it took on the character of a tiny barren planet complete with mountain ridges, flat plains, dotted cities, and where the rock pockets had collected rain water, identified two lakes and a snaking river. I looked once again at its narrow approach way. It was no more than six feet from slope to buttercup, but hardly an ordinary six feet. Three large steps or two gigantic ones, I decided. After all, I thought, someone not only crosses it, but also managed to get the bench across. Never mind that there is no railing to hold on to. Never mind that if you lose your footing you drop three thousand feet plus.

I got right to the very beginning of the bridge way, leaned my back against the hillside, and calmed my breathing. I focused my eyes on an imaginary point on the horizon as far in the distance as I could envision, straightened up my body, and without wavering my glance, took the three necessary steps, with the last one, reaching for the back of the bench.

It had been well worth the price of admission. At first, I just sat on the bench, my feet dangling over the edge of the lip. The sensation of total isolation was of a nature that thrilled me. It was as if I was literally perched in the sky, I could, if I wished, look straight down and view the valley, the beach, and the ocean, but upon experimentation, found that the greatest feelings were elicited by looking straight ahead. I then lay flat on my back and felt the tiredness of two sleepless nights enter my body. For a moment I was frightened to sleep there. What if I tossed and turned in my sleep? But then logic rescued me – in almost forty years, even as a small child, I had never fallen out of bed.

I was thinking of her as I fell asleep and was indeed dreaming of her when I awoke to her. She was standing behind the bench, holding onto it, in the three square feet or so of buttercup that was available to her. I had no idea just how long she had been standing there observing me, but I noted the smile on her lips indicated she was pleased by what she saw.

It was the first time I had seen her in daylight, which had the sole effect of enhancing her beauty. She seemed to belong to the exact spot where she stood. The colors of her skin, eyes, hair, and clothing blended perfectly with the natural motif of the tiny glen that was her hillside backdrop - heather her - heather it.

She undid and removed the soft shaded purple mantilla, allowing her ebony hair to plunge just below her shoulders, and draped it over the back of the bench. She came round and sat down beside me. She sighed and looked very perplexed as she addressed her remarks to a scampering blue lizard.

"What am I to do with you? I have forfeited my other favorite spot to you and now you usurp this one as well."

My impulse was to reach out and put my arm around her as if consoling a child, but at the last moment I sensed it was not the prudent thing to do as it was certain to be misinterpreted, and so, with that same arm suspended rather awkwardly in midair, a moment before scratching an itch on my forehead that didn't exist, I smiled at her and said,

"Obviously you are looking at your predicament from only one point of view."

On guard, she replied, "What do you mean?"

"I mean that perhaps you should stop seeing me as some sort of thief and look upon our chance meetings as prescribed fate."

"It is simply coincidence. My fate is already established."

There had been nothing correspondingly light or humorous in her response. I was noting this and studying her at the same time when she changed the mood of the moment once again as she coyly queried, "Have you come up with a name for me yet?"

"How about Camille?" came my wry response.

She obviously did not see the humor in it or if she did, concealed it well. "Personally, I don't care for it, but that is unimportant. I'll answer to it if you like."

I simply stared at her, not knowing whether to laugh or get angry. "I wouldn't want to call you by something you didn't like so perhaps I shouldn't call you anything at all."

She looked directly at me then with what could only be described as total admiration and replied, "Perfect... Tell me, were you frightened to come here?"

"Yes, a little."

"But you braved the path anyway? Is that your nature?"

"Only when I feel I must get somewhere."

I stared intensely into the violet. She turned away quickly as if my double meaning had been too much for her, but not quickly enough for me to miss the tears welling in her eyes. I pressed on.

"Tell me, did you hear anything unusual last night?"

"No..." she said in a whisper. "Where I spend my nights I hear or see very little."

"Yes? Where is that?"

It came out of her like a shot:

"That is none of your concern. I don't mean to be offensive; it is simply that it is none of your concern. It could not be, not for a long, long time."

It was the most evasive and confusing of answers, yet somehow, somewhere, it seemed to fit her for I was beginning to fathom her rather special mode of conversation. There was no real contact involved in it. She simply responded to everything from a set point of view, as if she were forever cursed by some criterion she had to adhere to; could not waiver from. I decided to take the initiative and try to alter the mood of the moment myself, and so I said in a blatantly male manner,

"It's a small island, love. It shouldn't be too difficult to find out."

She looked at me incredulously and said, "Only if I live here, and I am not your love."

"You don't live here, on Diarma?" She tasted the word for several seconds before deciding to see how it sounded. "Diarma?" Immediately, that oblique quality entered her expression as she added, "I must go now. I live nowhere you know of. We will not see each other again. It would only bring pain."

I was on my feet, my hand grasping her forearm. I was totally oblivious to the fact that I stood perilously close to the edge of the buttercup.

"What are you doing to me? Why must we never see each other again? You're being ridiculous!"

Her voice quavered slightly, "Because I am returning to the place where I live and you cannot come there."

"For Crissakes, invite me! I'll find you anyway, somehow."

But I did not really believe that myself, for that same feeling of unreality I had evidenced upon first seeing Alethea, and then again when I had viewed the scene in the wood, began to seep into me.

"Please unhand me. I cannot invite you. How can I make you understand? It is simply not possible and you will not find me anyway, somehow, perhaps someday, but not for many Kalpas."

She immediately turned away and started for the pathway. Once again I restrained her.

"Kalpas! What the hell are Kalpas?* I'm talking about here and now."

She lowered her head as she spoke, "That is precisely the problem." She released herself from my loosened grip and once again turned to go.

"Look, I don't even know your name. Damn it all, why won't you see me again and don't tell me about Kalpas. I know there is something happening between us. I can feel it and I know you feel it too."

She stepped across the bridge way as if it were yards wide, turned and said, "There is your answer. I have a thirst for you."

She removed the rose from behind her ear and flung it over the precipice. Momentarily, I watched its flight. When I looked up she had all but disappeared into a small gully. Dumbfounded, I yelled after her in a voice that could have been heard to Motril, "I'll be at our rock tonight. Please meet me there?"

But the word "there" had decreased in decibel level to such an extent that even I barely heard it. At that moment, I felt as if I had become the victim of some sort of cosmic vampire who, instead of draining blood, had usurped all my energy.

---

*According to Buddhist Thought, if a normal-sized cloth robe descended from the sky once every hundred years and lightly rubbed up against a rock the size of Manhattan, the amount of time it would take the robe to wear the rock completely down to nothing, would equal one (1) Kalpa. So, I don't think she wants to see him for a while.

Utterly confused and using what remaining stamina that was left to me, I carefully departed the buttercup. As I reached the small ravine she had disappeared into, a glimmer of hope wedged its way into my manic. Her last words to me in our initial encounter had also been indicative of no further meeting.

I would stand vigil for her tonight, and for as many nights as necessary.

Like the wary but hungry fish, instinctively cognizant of the danger of the dangled prize, I had allowed my appetite to surmount my good sense.

I was very simply hooked.

****

XX

****

*"There are no Messiahs, no Saviors of the world. There
never has been except in the highly personalized sense of
the word - you are your own Messiah. What has existed,
and hopefully will continue to surface vis-a-vis the
combined forces of natural selection within the species
and the Universal Law of Cause and Effect, are certain
enlightened individuals (RE: Christ, Buddha) who can
best be described as Evolutionary Forces. Their
knowledge passed on should be looked upon as an
essential link in the Evolutionary Chain towards raising
mental and spiritual consciousness, but not as an
absolute (with the noted exception of the Teachings of
Jesus Christ, uninterpreted, unabridged and
unexploited) for there are no absolutes that we can
perceive. Rather, there are steadily heightening plateaus
to be attained, only to be partially or fully relinquished
upon the furtherance of additional insight into ourselves
and the Universe. That is one definition of Infinity. If we
become extinct it will be because we have failed to
mentally and spiritually evolve simultaneously, held onto
values and dogma no longer germane to our present
being."*
~ *The Diarma Mind*

I did not bother with the evening meal. I arrived at sunset and
went for a swim. The winds had not as yet begun their nightly
rampage and so the sea was tame. I remained a part of her until the
enormous fireball extinguished itself in the aqua-cum-midnight
blue. In its ritual of bidding its lamp goodnight, the sky had been
somewhat economical – only brilliant orange and buttery yellow,
tufted and streaked, paid homage to the vestiges of the day.

I had drifted far out to sea but not so far as to be unable to discern any and all movement on our rock. There had been none. My heart persuaded me it was still early; my mind was less kind as it hammered its message of "pipe dream" at me again and again.

As the sky continued to darken I attempted to capture that precise moment when day becomes night, was unsuccessful but while swimming shoreward received a consolation prize - two Diarmas - one above and one that has just now inverted itself in the placid waters.

I hoisted myself on, to the rock and seemingly simultaneously the winds gently stirred drying me in the process. I slipped into trousers and shirt, lay on the ledge and commenced my watch…

I felt the light touch of soft hands cupping my eyes from behind. I reached behind me and lightly caressed her arms. She came round to my side, took me by the hand and wordlessly indicated we were to dive from our perch. She stepped out of her caftan and arched her naked body into the pool. I disrobed and dove after her.

She swam to the tiny cove from where I had first set eyes on her, but instead of stopping there, led me between two groups of shale down and into a dry bed cave that appeared to be a volcanic tube. I recognized it as being one of the ones I had explored the previous night during my "hunt."

We had gone much deeper than I had when she signaled me to halt in the pitch black tunnel. She flicked a switch and the beam of a flashlight guided us the remainder of the way. We still had not spoken. We finally arrived at our destination and she sent the beam searching the walls that were covered with crystalline rock of every color imaginable, reflecting and refracting the light, imbuing the cave with a cathedral-like quality. She found what she was looking for, walked to it, and lit the single candle, extinguishing the flashlight in the same motion.

We were consumed by the multi-toned haven. The candle light supplied just enough glow to distinguish shape and form without intruding on it. I looked down at my feet. I was standing in black sand - a small diamond of beach that fed into a shallow, ever so gentle trickle of ocean. It was strictly a low-tide dwelling. She came to me then, took me by the hand and led me to the out-stretched down comforter.

She whispered, "At first, for an eternity, just hold me, and then make love to me as you would want to be made love to in your wildest fantasy."

Amidst the flickering light and dancing shadows, she guided me down to her, our eyes never leaving each other's. I felt a warm vibration run the entire length of my body. It was as if every cell, every fiber of my being, had lain dormant my entire life and was only just now being awakened to her touch. I finally tore my eyes away from hers and visually devoured her body. Gently, I pulled her close to me. I wanted to leave no part of her untouched, unexplored, but I gladly, ecstatically, adhered to her request and simply held her close, ever so close, and when I felt I could get no closer, I began to make love to her.

I denied not one of my senses. The texture of her milk white skin was satin to my touch, ambrosia to my taste. Her fragrance was the fragrance of a sweet flowered meadow moments after a spring shower. All the pleasure of this world and others were intertwined with each other. There was a total sensation of just being; of everything in my life having been for the sole purpose of leading up to this one moment; each and every moment an entity of ecstasy unto itself that lived out to its fullest natural life span, its sole purpose to enrich the succeeding one and so on and so on. She reached out to…

"Mr. Christos! Mr. Christos, is that you, sir?"

I was so startled by the sound of the masculine voice that had come from directly above and behind me that I almost fell from the narrow ledge on the seaward side of the rock.

"I'm terribly sorry; I didn't mean to startle you. Someone left this for you at the desk and asked that it be delivered as soon as possible. They indicated you would be here."

I shook my head as if to send the remnants of my fantasy on their way, remembered to say "Thank you," and took the envelope, all the while avoiding his eyes, as if somehow he had been reading my thoughts of the past few minutes. Without a word the messenger departed. I recognized the scent emanating from the envelope and in my rush to open it, almost lost its precious contents to the wind:

> *I implore you. Do not dwell on what might have been. Do not fantasize what could be. You and I live in different worlds. I don't know how to make you understand. If I could do that, then our world would be the same, and what separates us, would not. All I can tell you is that we must not see each other again, for you could be the life of me. I cannot allow that to happen... Perhaps for you, it would be easier to think in terms that you could be the death of me. Another time, another place.*
> *Good-bye.*
>
> *PS: I know when you are thinking of me. Please try not to for it makes it that much more difficult for both of us. Your thoughts bring me to life. Please respect my wishes even though you cannot understand them.*

The note bore no signature. I reread it a second, third, and fourth time, but it did nothing to clarify itself. What the hell did she mean, "The life of me"? "The death of me," I could partially fathom though I was convinced that some quirk made her prone to melodrama... or was it more than a quirk? Was she insane? Or was this all part of the curriculum? Yes, of course, that must be it. But again, to what end? What were they (she) trying to prove, point out to me? Was Alethea writing the script and directing the action? Was my illusive love with no name simply a great actress?

I re-read the postscript once again: "I know when you are thinking of me. Your thoughts bring me to life." It touched a responsive chord somewhere. A bell, indeed, chimed, not loudly, but distinctly. I concentrated very hard and finally made the connection. It was something I had read in a book on Buddhist Thought. I remembered that when I had first read it, it was difficult to perceive, almost abstract, but not quite, though reeking of excessive esotericism. Aloud to myself, I recited it: "There is no thinker, only the thought." Was it applicable?

And so, for the next two hours, once again, I forced myself to "consider the possibilities," at the end of which time, I was far more angry than amused. But something quelled that anger - the realization that I felt very much alive for the first time in years. The juices were really flowing. Something else of a less ephemeral quality was also responsible for the sudden change of heart. I was still not a hundred percent certain I had arrived at the correct possibility.

It was close to midnight when I removed myself from my contemplation and began my homeward trek. I did not remember traversing the path to the crest. I did not recall stepping into the meadow. I barely noticed the enchanting mist that had poised itself over it, thick, heavy, damp; the blanket extending itself the entire length and breadth of the glen, creeping up some three feet above the ground.

I walked on. What is that sound? I felt the earth gently tremor beneath me... a small, tiny feeling of movement... What is that sound? A familiar sound... overwhelmingly familiar... What is it? Rapid movement, yes, rapid movement... getting closer now... straining my eyes through the mist now... nothing. Very loud now... Got it! Horse hooves... more than one horse... taking form now... ghostly form... louder, closer, deafening. Finally, revelation in the form of four magnificently plumed white horses, the sound of the crackling whip being expertly executed by the hooded coachman dressed from head to toe in black... a human extension of the coal black sixteenth century coach coming straight at me…

I regained my reflexes only moments before I would surely have been trampled to death. I lost my balance in the process, but not before taking in the scene that lay behind the large egg-shaped window that was the only break in the carriage's motif; not before peering through the oblong window and registering her immobile, lying flat on her back, hair swept back severely, her violet eyes expressionless, her white-caked face a death- mask, her hands resting on her stomach, clutching the ever present black rose. She was literally a Cameo of Death. And then suddenly, the antiquated funeral hearse disappeared into the protective texture of the milky opaque.

Still lying on the ground, I remained motionless. I seemed to have lost control of my motor reflexes. I stayed frozen thus for an eternity, consumed by yet another side of my "paradise" – a macabre, horrendous side that felt the necessity to grotesquely illustrate her note; a demonic side of my Utopia that has just now mercilessly convulsed my body with shivers, permeated the fragments of my mind with shock wave after shock wave until the contagion of death dissipated into blurrrrrrr…

My entire body went limp as the misty meadow seeped into my head and transposed itself into the haze of total confusion. Just as suddenly, the spell was removed as I rose to my feet, stiffened my entire body, and screamed at the night as loud as I could,

"THAT'S ENOUGH, GODAMMIT TO HELL! ENOUGH!"

I did not stop running until I reached my room. When I did reach it, additional terror awaited me as I recalled her words once again: "Your thoughts bring me to life… I know when you are thinking of me…"

As I had stepped into the meadow, I had indeed been thinking of her. There is no thinker, only the thought?

****

XXI

****

"Religion has too long remained an entity unto
itself, unincorporated into the business of living life.
Therefore, it's safe to assume that we neither need
nor desire the resurgence of a heretofore
established religious organ, nor do we need
or desire another new religion. Rather,
what we need and indeed must attain,
is a religious way of living life."
~ The Diarma Mind

"I assume she's returned."

"Yes, sir, but just this morning, and I am afraid she'll be tied up for the rest of the day. Perhaps she could make time for you this evening."

"Not tonight, not an hour from now. Right now."

The woman in white, who apparently looked after the domestic side of things, studied me for a long moment before indicating I was to follow her into the study. She left the room immediately but not before granting me one last inspection.

I had been pacing for ten minutes before I finally settled into a large upholstered square chair. I checked the digital desk clock once again – fifteen minutes had passed. I could feel the adrenalin rising – a human composite of raw nerve ends awaited her. I felt I must do something to calm myself and so I decided to take meticulous inventory.

I rose, walked back to the entrance door, and took in the room anew. I had to suppress a laugh, for inlaid on the floor directly beneath me was a small brass plaque that read: "You must learn to live your life as a constant state of First Impressions."

I raised my head and allowed my eyes to sweep the room's entirety. It was a marvelous mixture of old and new. Contrived eclectic, but so tastefully so, it defied itself. Rays of sunlight seeped through mahogany shutters, complementing the overall warmth of atmosphere. It also managed to give forth the paradoxical sensation of isolation, but in the best possible sense – that when ensconced in this room, the outside world ceased to exist by choice. It was quite large and square in shape. The ceiling was not high. It, as did all the other rooms on the ground floor, fed into a large, circular, lushly planted courtyard of multi-colored tiles in Mediterranean hues that formed a mandala of evolution.

I turned my attention back to my immediate surroundings. In the right portion of the room was a very old and quite large antique writing table upon which rested a simply framed black and white photograph of a very strong but equally sensitive looking man who was in his prime. The inscription read: "To Alethea, whose being has fulfilled my life." I studied it a few moments, assumed it was her late husband, and continued my inspection.

Directly ahead of me and settled on a throw rug of white fluff was a solid black Lucite table. It had no legs and gave the impression of being a large rectangular black block. An incense holder and four clear Lucite candle holders of varying sizes and shapes graced its surface. Next, I turned to the west wall, which was solid window draped in avocado green. In one corner stood a marble chess table, its Knights, Pawns, etcetera, engaged in mortal combat. In the other corner was an antique tea cart, completely glass with double shelves and doors, gold wheels, and push bar. The interior shelves displayed blown glass decanters in reds, blues, golds, and greens.

I allowed my eyes to scan the entire wall one more time. It was then that I saw it and I could not believe I had actually missed it in my initial examination. It stood proudly on the window ledge, just at the point where the drapes parted and it has just sent a magnetic beam to my body, drawing me to her.

I dropped to one knee and strained my eyes to read the lettering on the alabaster bust. Only the first three letters of her name were recognizable – ANA. Time had worn away the others, but the dates were very clear: 1540-1566 AD.

My mouth dropped open in cliché performance.

"She was beautiful, wasn't she?"

I had not heard her enter and whipped my head around to the sound of her voice.

"Yes, she is, isn't she?"

"I beg your pardon?"

"I said is as opposed to was."

"If you prefer. She has, however, been dead for over four hundred years, so was seems more appropriate to me. I'm told she had violet eyes. That must have been something to see."

"Can we stop playing games now?"

I did nothing to disguise my disgust.

She walked to within a yard of me before speaking.

"Christos, I told you at our initial meeting, in the strongest possible terms, that I do not play games. I will say it again. I assure you I do not take time out of a schedule you could not even begin to appreciate to play games. I don't know what you are talking about, but if this is the test of it, I am going to ask you to leave, now. There are very few things I hold precious in this world, and at the top of the list is the time I am allotted in it. Is that clear?"

I felt a part of myself falling under her spell, giving into her force. When she had been speaking to me, I felt as if I had been looking into a pair of disembodied eyes, so intense had been their gaze, almost lunatic. I fought to keep the sense of myself alive and in a slightly diluted manner countered with,

"What if I told you I had spent time with this woman every day for the past three days?"

"I would say that you are either mistaken by virtue of having seen someone who closely resembles the late Anarose, which I would find difficult to believe, considering the unique quality of her beauty, or that we made a vast error in judgment in allowing you to stay on Diarma. I reiterate, Anarose, the woman of whom that bust was made has been dead for over four hundred years."

"And I'm telling you I saw her, talked with her, even touched her less than twelve hours ago."

She shifted her eyes to the bust and then back to me, walked to the black block, lit some incense, and motioned me to sit.

"All right, obviously you saw something, met someone. Tell me all about it. Leave out nothing."

*****

An hour later, she had lunch served on the lawn and while digesting our meal she digested my story. She finally spoke up.

"Millicent tells me she gave you a copy of the Legend of Alboran because of your particular ethnic background. Did you read it?"

"Yes."

"Then you have some idea of Anarose's role in it."

"Yes. From what I was able to gather, she became obsessed with death."

"Yes, but not in the sense you think."

"I'd appreciate anything at all you could tell me about her."

She looked at me in a questioning manner for a moment before she asked, somewhat incredulously, "Have you fallen in love with this woman?"

It was a question I had hoped she wouldn't pose and this reflected itself in my response.

"I don't know. I'm confused about my feelings for her… perhaps I have…"

"Perhaps?" And she just stared straight through me. I knew I'd been caught but I pressed on anyway.

"Yes, I know it sounds ridiculous. We hardly even spoke. I didn't even know her name until just now."

"It's not ridiculous at all, if you have, indeed, fallen in love with her."

Again that glance that made me feel as though I were under a microscope.

"Longevity has no claim on emotional response, Christos. As a matter of fact, the more in touch with yourself you become, the quicker you are to recognize the real thing. If you believe, that is, the real thing can include love and passion on a one-to-one male/female basis."

I almost laughed as I said, "And you don't?" Where would we be today if we didn't, I wanted to add, but didn't.

"I did not say that. I'm only tossing it into the esoteric arena, so to speak, for investigation. Whatever you come up with, you come up with, and it will be correct for you at the time. I will tell you this much, in the spirit of an alternate possibility, there are those who believe that we search for connection on that level as a substitute for connection to the Real Thing."

"God, you mean?"

"Precisely."

I suddenly felt uneasy, as if I, myself, had just been tossed into that same arena for the same purpose. There was something so clinical about her approach to humanity that it frightened me. I suspected a didactic dichotomy bisected her very core, manifesting itself on the one half in her eloquently astute articulation of her high mindedness, but it was mercilessly juxtaposed against an almost cruel pleasure in observing its own effect; that rather than being its privileged recipient, one was the happenstance victim of it.

I looked up at her then and suddenly realized I was way out of my league, for her lips have just pursed slightly as her eyes softened and with perfect timing she begins:

"To my mind, the description that most captures what Anarose was about is sainthood. You are already familiar with her background so I won't go into it further other than insisting you accept the inbreeding described in the Legend as the truth, which it is, as far as we have been able to ascertain.

"In any event, she came into this world a very special creature. She defied any and all conditioning or environmental influence thrust upon her by her parents or the times she was born into. From the very outset, she seemed to intuitively sense that there was another reality to be explored. And conquered. This led her into what became virtually a monastic existence by the time she was sixteen. She rarely departed her dwellings on the cliffward side of the island where now stands the lighthouse. She took daily walks, actually nightly walks, for she was rarely, almost never, seen during the day, at dusk, midnight, and dawn. Her route, as well as the iconoclastic quality of her being, together with her choice of hours, only added to the quality of mystique that enshrouded her during her lifetime. It is said that she always carried a black rose, a single black rose that is, with her on these sojourns. As the island, this or any, has never yielded such a flower, her plucking ground remains a mystery.

"Although there are those who would have you believe she cut a tragic figure, the exact opposite was the truth, for she had worked diligently towards, and had found, something real to hold onto.

"When she was eighteen, a small sailing vessel crashed into the cliffs during a hurricane and it was through this incident that a young Englishman came into her life, soaked to the skin, badly bruised and bleeding."

She paused for a moment as we both reflected on the similarity of occurrence as to my initial debarkation.

"She had been on her midnight outing when she heard his groans of pain and had rushed to him. He was conscious but badly shaken up and so she helped him to her house and tended to his wounds."

Again she paused and studied my expression that must have reflected equal parts of fear and skepticism.

"When he awakened the following morning and saw who his nurse had been, in that instant, something very special happened between them, for unlike all other men who had come into the briefest of contact with her – hence ultimately stalking her for her physical beauty alone – she immediately sensed something else, something far more powerful coming from him. It mirrored itself in his look that was totally devoid of lust or passion and, as it so happened, when he awoke she happened to be dressing in the one room dwelling, and was partially naked. All that existed in his gaze was pure love, joy, and gratitude for having been found by her.

"Don't misunderstand, her beauty was of such a quality that one would have to have been inhuman not to appreciate it, but Edward seemed to sense and understand at the very outset that it was not meant to be on that level.

"As he came to know her more and more, this instinct solidified itself in him, for the more they saw of each other, the more they communicated, the more he realized just how special she truly was. In short, though both were extremely physically attractive, they were in different places mentally, spiritually, and emotionally, but most definitely on the same voyage, for he was a quester, too. And so, someplace, he understood she was not a woman to take, but rather a woman to learn from.

"She became his mentor and for the following three years they saw each other periodically. His ship would pass through once every three months and he would take a few days leave each time to spend with her. Never once during that time did he make any physical advances towards her, even though it is quite possible, in retrospective analysis, that he had, even at that stage, come to harbor such feelings. He was the only human being she had any form of contact with whatsoever during that period or for the following two years when he did not see her once.

"She must have speculated a great deal as to the whyfors of his abrupt termination of their relationship. Not a word, not a note, nothing for two solid years, and she found herself missing him. She feared he had died, or perhaps married, for by this time he was a prime catch, as he had inherited a vast sum of money on his thirty-fifth birthday, which had come to pass the previous year. It had been his father's wealth and obsession with it that had driven him to the humble life of solace as a seaman. But perhaps he had changed, she considered.

"In September of 1566, he returned to her. She was quite naturally overwhelmed with joy. He had changed a great deal, indeed, and in most every aspect of his being. His hair had turned silver; his entire face had matured, lined with wisdom. But the one thing that struck her most was his eyes. Deep dark brown, almost black, they had always contained a touch of coldness, a hint of tragedy. But now they were soft, gently intense, and piercing at once. Their initial reunion was a wordless one. They just stared at each other, approximately where we are seated now, but closer to the edge. And so, after five years of exchanging ideas with each other, five years of probing each other's consciousness, in a single instant they fell in love. Completely, fully, passionately in love. He never volunteered the reasons for his absence and she never queried him on it.

"He gave himself over to his feelings immediately, but such was not the case with Anarose. She had worked too hard to come to what she had arrived at… you see, Anarose was a Buddhist. Not by virtue of instruction, but rather, apparently naturally, if that is possible. Nowhere in the records can we uncover a reference to any form of Lamist indoctrination into her young life. Be that as it may, she believed any form of desire or attachment, especially involving a sexual nature, could only hold her back, only force her to remain in the 'unintermittant hell that is this earth.'"*

She paused for a moment and reached into her pocket.

"That is why this note you showed me interested me so. The wording of it confirmed what we have been able to gather through her personal diary and what logs were left behind during the time she lived that were not destroyed by the volcanic eruptions that succeeded her death. *Whoever* wrote it had a very good sense of her, for although you did not understand what she meant by 'you could be the life of me,' in the Buddhist sense it is imminently clear, for serious Buddhists aspire to self-extinction and she is telling you that your intrusion into her life could only retard that goal. Is that clear now, Christos?"

"By self-extinction, I take it you are referring to the death of the sense of self as opposed to physical death?"

"Exactly. That is the single most misinterpreted Buddhist axiom by Western Man."

"Then I understand it though I don't accept it as valid."

----

*Gautama the Buddha

"Valid for you or valid for anyone?"

"I'm not sure."

"I'm very sorry to hear that because if there exists one biological, historical truth to accurately describe humanity, it is contained in my husband's words, as well as that book of insights I gave you: 'We, as a species, are unable to group our spiritual experience under one roof and proclaim this the house we must live in.'"

"Obviously, you believe it's valid then?"

"I did not say that, and your question is impertinent."

I could contain myself no longer.

"A thousand pardons, Your Majesty. I can only hope and pray that this minor transgression does not precipitate the lopping off with my head. That the true sign of a great leader of peoples, mercy and compassion will prevail. Might I add that I am in virtual awe of your seemingly infinite capacity for the picayune?"

She stared at me expressionless for a long moment before bursting into laughter far more raucous than I had ever expected from her.

"Humor, like ingenuity and tenacity, is also held in high regard on Diarma. Once again, were it lacking, there is virtually nothing we could do to instill it."

She narrowed her eyes slightly, and then added, "It may well be your saving grace if you can turn it inward. I think we had better get on with the story now.

"Edward moved into the hamlet and saw her every day and night. He made no attempt to force his attentions on her, but it was obvious that it was becoming increasingly painful to both of them not to be able to express themselves to one another as a man and a woman. Tension began to mount and wedged its way into the beauty that was despoiling it. But Anarose was strong, very strong, and refused to give into her desire.

"Ultimately, Edward made his decision to leave Alboran, never to return. He was, of course, broken-hearted, and the irony of it was that although he had fought her celibacy with every weapon of logic at his disposal, he knew that if he could not have her, he would never have or want another woman, which, in effect, damned or graced him, depending on your point of view, to himself.

"They agreed to meet at the edge of the volcano's crest... over there, which, in their time, flanged outwards for perhaps twenty yards and was made accessible by the same path that exists today, for a final meeting at dusk, one hour before his ship was to sail with the evening tide."

Once again she paused, took a sip of her iced tea, and looked intently at the horizon.

"It is at this point the account becomes somewhat confused. For reasons that will become obvious, there is no entry in her diary as to the sequence of events. There are, however, fragments of two recorded versions as to what actually happened during that final encounter. When all the pieces were put together, this is what history was able to reveal. You will have to make up your own mind, as I had to, as to which is the truthful one.

"They met a few minutes before the sun went down and wordlessly observed its descent. In the beauty of the moment that was charged with the culmination of their emotions of five years standing, their hands happened to touch. It was all the impetus the ensuing events required. She genuinely tried to resist him, but before she knew it they were kissing, touching, and caressing. Ultimately, he took her where she lay.

"When it was over, sobbing, she arose, walked slowly to the edge of the volcano's mouth, and without so much as uttering a word or granting him a glance, thrust herself into the chasm.

"Now, the other recorded version is this: The lovemaking was of questionable mutual consent. By that I mean that while they were indeed both caught up in the passion of the moment, she did strongly express her reservations, ultimately gave in to him, but, when it was over, became hysterical and struggled wildly to free herself from him and that in so doing she ran in the only direction of the moment which happened to be towards the volcano's mouth. He realized the gravity of the situation and ran after her, reaching her just as her momentum was about to carry her over the edge. Desperately, but ultimately in vain, he tried to prevent her from falling, not jumping, but was unable to. In fact, in reaching out to save her, he actually pushed her over the edge."

Her eyes had been boring into me with such intensity that I almost felt as though I were being hypnotized. I literally forced my eyes elsewhere and began to ponder what she had just told me. I suddenly realized that what I had just heard was less a legendary account than a parable veritably reeking of possibilities. I was about to expound on that when, mercilessly, she cut into my thoughts, providing the *coup d gras* with her unwelcome interruption.

"Now, what I have just told you, all of what I have just told you is only one of two completely different versions of Anarose's life and death."

Was that the tiniest glint of a smile that flashed in and out of her eyes? It did not matter, I could not resist.

"Don't you really mean one of two possibilities?"   ·

I looked her dead in the eye. She masterfully granted me no expression at all as she replied.

"If you prefer. If you wish, I can put you in touch with someone who will no less honestly and sincerely tell you the other version… or… possibility. The woman is imminently qualified, as she is both a scholar of the Anarose legend as well as claims to have lived it."

She held up her hand to my agape mouth and went on.

"Yes, I realize that is a little difficult to either believe or comprehend. You will have to make up your own mind as to the veracity of her source. All I can tell you is the woman sincerely believes everything she will tell you, and I can personally vouch for her integrity.

"You know, Christos, there are those who believe that life is nothing more than cycles of time coexisting in separate spheres simultaneously; that there is no past, no present, only now. You should not be so quick to rule that out as one of the infinite possibilities. Hear her out. She is a bona fide medium.

"What are you thinking?"

"What? Oh, nothing."

"There is no such thing, not for you, not yet. Shall I tell you what you were thinking? You were wondering if you were the victim of some complex manipulation and what end did it serve. Correct?"

"Of course."

"And, for the sake of conjecture and nothing else, if I could give you an answer, partial or full, to that question, what would it do for you? Give you peace of mind? No, I am not in the business of dispensing peace of mind. If I were, I assure you I would no longer be in this life form. Rather, I am in the business of helping others to unlock themselves so that they may see things clearly for what they really are, not what they would like them to be to simply to serve their own inconsequential ends, and I assure you once again that I will use anything and everything at my disposal to accomplish that end when and if you are accepted and enrolled in our curriculum here."

"So, what you are saying is that I am not, as of yet, enrolled, and therefore must rule out that possibility."

"No!" her voice shot back. "Consider it carefully, but consider equally carefully the other obvious possibility."

"Which is?"

"Are you really telling me that it hasn't entered your mind?"

I didn't answer her but she knew it had and so she articulated it for me.

"That you are of the genetic and spiritual make-up that leaves you open to, allows you to be susceptible to, suggestible to, other dimensions of communication, in this case, apparitions of a retro cognitive nature. Now, if this sounds too fantastic to you, I suggest you visit our library here and read through a few scientific studies of a parapsychological nature such as *Psychic Discoveries Behind the Iron Curtain, New Light on Survival, Out Of Body Experiences*, and a host of others. When you've exhausted those, you can start rummaging through the latest volume of recorded psychic phenomena compiled by the Society of Psychical Research in London.

"Then, if you still think it's too fantastic, consider the fact that you just happen to possess the identical bloodline as that of Anarose…"

"Which I only have your word for, as the publication I read, the Legend, originated from here."

With that she arose, walked through an archway and across the tiled patio into the study. When she returned moments later, she deposited a large leather-bound volume, whose leaf lettering announced: *Mediterranean Isles*, on to the table directly in front of me. She opened the cover, revealing the publication date: 1750. As she thumbed through the pages, I acknowledged to myself the authenticity of the work. The pages were yellowed with age and the script inking was so faint as to be barely visible. She found the correct page and produced a magnifying glass. With its assistance I read the passage verifying the version I had read. Quite kindly, I thought, she went on.

"As I was saying, consider the fact that you possess the identical bloodline as that of Anarose, to say nothing of the fact that you are a quester, and therefore, by definition, of an open mind, one would think and hope. This allows you the intuitive insight into the concept that the Universe is a Realm of Infinite

Possibilities, one of which you appear to be experiencing through another dimension here and now on Diarma."

I engaged my eyes in a game of optical showdown that was no contest at all. I'd only half-heard what she had said anyhow, as my mind was still pondering the ramifications of the verification of the bloodline. I felt totally off balance, as if any second I was going to plunge into an abyss from which there was no recovery, only a steady, ever quickening infinite descent. I started to feel slightly panic-stricken. I managed to calm myself and then asked in as natural a voice as I could muster,

"Alethea, tell me once and for all if class is in session or not."

"No, I will not, because, Christos, whether the scenario be real or contrived is of absolutely no consequence or import. Only how you function within the given circumstances is of significance, deep significance. Oh, you think that's rubbish? Tell me, how many times in your own lifetime did you manipulate or cajole or tinker with a situation or circumstance rather than flowing moment to moment with the reality of it?

"And, tell me, were the consequences, decisions, revelations of any less impact to either yourself or whoever was involved with you at the time because of this hedging of your bets? No. Whether or not the content of a domestic quarrel is spontaneous reality or well-conceived strategy is hardly the point. A broken home is a broken home.

"Do you honestly believe top level decisions arrived at by leaders of entire nations aren't second-guessed, dissected, manipulated by special interest groups? And are the consequences of their circuitous actions any less real?"

"You've made your point."

"I'm glad to hear it."

She removed pen and paper from her blouse and quickly wrote a note. She moistened the corners of the paper and quickly formed it into an envelope. She handed it to me, saying, "Where you will have to go to meet with Irena Pharaslet is about two-and-a-half hours from here by boat - a tiny atoll to the southwest. I will instruct the fisherman who will take you to wait for you, as it is not the kind of place you would wish to spend the night. It is what is called a Seaman's Retreat."

I eyed her skeptically.

"I thought the pamphlet clearly stated there were no islands within a hundred-mile radius of here."

"Are you still inspecting, testing, me, Christos?"

She broke the tension she had intentionally created with a little laugh and went on. "I assure you this is no island. It is a floating establishment of minute proportions. Irena is very well known there so you will have no trouble locating her. I reiterate: she is a most exceptional and totally honest person. So exceptional, in fact, that the SPR has been trying to lure her to England, to study her, for over twenty years."

She arose and walked me to the pathway. A look of concern momentarily settled on her magnificent profile as she lightly tapped me on the arm and said,

"If for any reason you should decide to leave Diarma before the three weeks are up, under the present circumstances or any circumstances for that matter, do not hesitate to make your feelings known. Transportation will be arranged at once. I only mention this because I see that you are deeply disturbed by the events of the past three days. If you come to feel your mental health is at stake here, by all means make the correct decision."

"And my emotional health?"

"Emotions can always be dealt with."

Her remarks had thrown me badly; they almost had the ring of warning to me, and so I inquired, "What exactly do you mean, Alethea?"

"Just exactly what I said. The decision is always yours on Diarma. In this instance, to stay or leave. You are not going to like what you hear come out of Irena Pharasalet's mouth, but I think you should hear it."

And not wanting to be banished from Eden just yet, too quickly I replied, "I assure you I have no intention of leaving Diarma.

Perhaps I should apologize for my behavior this morning, but I've been under quite a strain and simply haven't been myself for the past seventy-two hours or so."

"The self-analysis is quite correct. The time span indicated is quite another matter altogether."

Before I could register my surprise, she had lightly kissed me on the cheek and was walking under the ivy archway. I had gone perhaps fifteen yards when something turned me around just in time to catch the remnants of a smile I could not even begin to fathom. I knew she possessed an expertise that was undeniable - it was her field of endeavor that escaped me.

I was all the way down to the base of the slope when I remembered I had forgotten to ask her the most important question of all: Whatever became of Edward?

XXII

"We are neither the victims nor benefactors of time,
we are its conspirators."
~ The Diarma Mind

She had been quite correct – it was not the kind of place I wished to spend any more time in than was absolutely necessary, let alone the entire night.

My Seaman's Retreat was nothing more or less than a floating bordello which consisted of a dock and one sand road that separated dilapidated structure upon dilapidated structure of carnal bliss. The houses at either end of the atoll actually hung out over the ocean as if some greedy merchant of lust had been obsessed with squeezing in one more arena of entertainment into his Elysium of passion.

Black billows of smoke and soot spewed forth from the rooftops in puffs that blinded and choked me at once. I gazed through cracked, broken, and at times glassless windows as I cautiously traversed the pot-holed road. From each and every one there peered back at me a human mannequin displaying her wares, resplendent in garter belts, merry widows, and grotesquely made-up faces. The origin of painted hussy took seed in my mind.

I stopped the first male specimen of semi-humanity who stumbled my way and asked, "Which is the house of Irena Pharasalet?"

The man slapped me on the back, and then decided that as long as his hand was already there, he might as well use me to steady himself. He soddenly replied, "Irena Pharasalet? You looking fer her, are ya, mite? Aren't we all! Great fortune teller, she!"

He then broke into thundcrous laughter.

"Look, mite, I'm in a bit of a hurry. Would you just be so kind as to point out her house for me?"

"Wot's the matter, mite? 'fraid it'll go soft on ya?"

With his free hand, he held his prominent belly as if to hold back the gales.

"Right over thar." He pointed to a structure that by all rights should have been condemned before the turn of the century.

Without further ado, I headed in the direction of the man's still outstretched finger, totally ignoring the sound of the poor fellow's body thumping to the ground. Drunk as he was, he wouldn't even feel it.

Its interior was palatial by comparison, gaudy to the -enth degree, but nonetheless infinitely more palatable than its exterior. I was in a small anteroom that looked through a gilded scrolled archway into what I assumed to be the main parlor or getting to know you area. I spotted her immediately at a small cloth covered circular table upon which rested the tricks of her trade: a deck of cards, a crystal ball, and tarot symbols. A small lock of hair was clutched in one hand as the other inspected the palm of a very burly man. A huge tooth or fang set in gold hung from her neck by a multi-strand gold necklace. She was very old. Her face was so lined that her features, other than the prominent nose, almost became completely lost to the crevices of antiquity. It was her eyes that belied her – deep pools of black, of experience, of agony. Mostly agony. She wore a bright kerchief around her head wrapped tightly at the hairline. It did absolutely nothing to smooth her skin. Large loops of silver swayed from drooping lobes to the static movement of her head. I approached her quietly, not wanting to interrupt her performance. As I got to within hearing distance, I suddenly fathomed my drunken acquaintance's remark, "great fortune teller she," for she had just offered her customer a portent of the immediate future in the form of:

"I see a beautiful woman about to come into your life… tall, long legged, blonde, and very amorous… a Goddess of Love!"

Magically, the "Goddess" appeared alongside the hairy arm and swept him away and into the immediate future.

I had to keep from laughing. Her eyes flicked to mine and then ran the entire length of my body as if to say, "What in God's name are you doing here?"

I took my cue and approached her, letter in hand. She donned rimmed glasses, read it very quickly, and then motioned for me to sit.

"What can I do for you, Christos?" She sounded as if her larynx had been removed.

I looked somewhat surprised, and replied, "Doesn't the note explain?"

"It is merely a letter of introduction."

"I would like to purchase an hour of your time. I'll pay you well. I may need additional time, which I will also pay for."

She broke into a genuine cackle, raised her eyebrows, and in a manner that reminisced the beauty that never was, coyly responded, "I haven't given an hour of my time to anyone in forty years. Tell me, young man; is it that you anticipate a very long, extraordinarily interesting life, or is it simply that you have extremely bad taste in sexual partners?"

I burst out laughing and our rapport was established.

"Is there someplace else we could talk?"

With the help of two ivory canes, she rose and hobbled in the direction of the stairs, but rather than going up them, went under their overhang and into the filthiest room I had ever seen. She motioned me to sit in the only chair as she laid herself gently on the bare mattress on the floor. She lit a candle, reached up to draw the curtains shut and asked me what it was I wanted of her.

"I would like you to tell me the story of Anarose."

She sat there staring at me shaking her head almost imperceptibly. She let out a sigh that consumed the room. "I suspected as much."

It was the last thing I had expected her to say. To my mind it seemed an open admission of complicity. I started to speak but was not quick enough.

"Do not be put off by that vulgar prostitution of my gift you witnessed back there. Besides being a medium, I am psychic. Wholly aside from that, it was your eyes that gave you away. Fifty years ago, I saw that identical expression on a man who was sitting where you are sitting now – and for the same reason. You want to know about Anarose de Alboran? It can only mean she is back. If you insist, I will tell you, but I beg of you now, this instant, get up and leave and never come back."

"I must know about her."

Without a word she laid flat on her back, closed her eyes, and massaged the amulet resting on her breast.

"Very well. There will be no charge."

A good five minutes of deathly silence elapsed, then

"Anarose was what medicine has labeled today a schizoid personality; a split personality; two different people inhabiting the same shell, one of which emerged during the day with the rise of the sun and died with it to allow the other to surface at night.

"I know nothing I can substantiate to any degree of truth as to her nocturnal life. There are those who swear she was a deity, but those same openly admit they never saw her during daylight hours. I did. I saw her every day for five years. Almost every day, that is, up until the day she died, for my karma forced me to live right here then, too, as it forces me to live here now. There is something that neither she nor I, and perhaps you as well, have never been able to resolve that is connected to this place and Alboran. It wasn't always like this, you know.

"This used to be the most glorious atmosphere of carnal gratification imaginable – crystal chandeliers, gowns of the finest silks and laces, carpets and drapery so lush you lost yourself in them; food and drink fit for royalty. And the women… ahhh, the women were the most beautiful in the world in their trade. They had to be, for this place catered only to the nobility of Europe. But of all the beauties in my stable of love, none, but none, could compare with Anarose."

I stared at her, trying to comprehend what bizarre twist was now taking form. I forced myself to remain open to her as she went on.

"It's true. She worked for me. I was the house madam in those days. It was I who discovered her on Alboran. She came to be like my daughter, during the day, that is, for at night she always insisted on making the long voyage back to Alboran.

"She would arrive every morning at half past eight, leaving Alboran just post-sunrise, and would leave here every afternoon at four. She was adamant about her hours. She blatantly refused to stay one minute longer or arrive one minute earlier, no matter what the enticement. She insisted that she must watch the sun rise and disappear from the volcano's crest and nowhere else.

"She was, of course, the most preferred of my ladies from the very outset of our association. As word of her spread, it came to a point where she would – could – only grant her favors by appointment, and in no time at all, her bookings were filled weeks, sometimes months, in advance, for this tiny place serviced virtually all ships coming and going to all Mediterranean ports of call. She always allotted the same amount of time to her customers - one hour. They were not allowed to purchase more or less time, even though she was offered vast sums for "over time," if you'll excuse the expression. I let her get away with it for, besides being my favorite, she was literally a gold mine in and of herself. The other girls came to openly resent her - she was even attacked once by two of them, but Anarose paid them no mind and even pleaded with me not to dismiss them.

"She was twenty-one when she began her employ. I neither knew about nor probed her about her life on Alboran, and every day for two years she never missed a day of work. At the end of this period, she was well on her way to being a wealthy woman, for she and I had a special arrangement as to her percentage, which I granted her gladly. What she did with the money no one knows for certain. Some say she gave it all to a young Englishman who came into her life at about the same time she came into mine, and ultimately ruined our business relationship; others say she gave it away to the people of Alboran, but the most logical explanation is that it perished with everything else, including myself; for I was on the island that day, when the volcano erupted - three days after her death.

"Everything went very smoothly for the first two years, but then she began not to show up for long periods of time - two to three weeks at a stretch. A pattern emerged. Her leaves of absence came in three month intervals. I had admonished her severely, for her customers were distraught, to say the very least. But it was impossible to stay angry with her – that face and those eyes cut through everything. It was even more impossible to mold her, and so I finally learned from the pattern not to book appointments during the periods she would stay away. Every three months, I gave her a three-week holiday.

"And then, three years after it began, it stopped. She showed up for work during some of her expected absence periods. Naturally I was overjoyed. I asked her if this meant she would be returning to work full-time. Her reply was, "I have no idea," and for the first time ever, I saw tears in her eyes. In any event, I was right back where I started: unable to book appointments. But I assure you, her business did not drop off one iota as a result. It was obvious to see that something had saddened her since her return. Several customers complained to me that she had sobbed lightly during intercourse. I questioned her about this, but she gave me a look so cold that I never broached the subject again.

"She had been working steadily again for over a year when I decided to take a chance and book a special customer during one of those three week periods - a prince and direct ascendant to the throne of France. It is not necessary that you know his name; suffice to say, he was the most sought after man in his day. Extraordinarily rich, intelligent, handsome, charming, and magnetic beyond words, he possessed a charisma about him that was truly indescribable. But not to Anarose; she treated him, thought of him, just like any other customer.

"It was driving him crazy. He bestowed gifts upon her that in and of themselves constituted a fortune. She always refused them. If he would not take them back, in his presence, she would summon one of the other girls and give the prize to her. To the man's credit, he would not get angry or even seemingly annoyed. He would simply shake his head and laugh at her as if she were a sassy but adorable child. Needless to say, her popularity with her fellow employees rose swiftly.

"There was one gift, however, she always accepted from him on his frequent visits: two bouquets of black roses that he had somehow managed to cultivate in his greenhouse on his private estate in the Ruhr Valley. And, she made one request of him in the form of a gift to be delivered to Alboran after her death, which somehow she knew was not far off. When she made the most unique request, he laughed at her much in the manner she had laughed at him during one of his many sincere marriage proposals, an institution he had heretofore publically avowed he would never partake of, but he loved her so, whore or no whore. He was so totally under her spell that he agreed, in writing, to her wishes."

She stopped for a moment to light a long thin cigarette wrapped in brown paper - inhaled deeply, coughed twice, and continued:

"The particular gift was a magnificent sixteenth century carriage carved completely of onyx, and four white stallions, Arabian, of course, to be plumed with peacock feathers. She designed the specifications herself. And when she died, the Prince did indeed make good his promise as well as precisely follow the instructions she had left him in the wax-sealed envelope. On the nights of the first full moon of the month, the coach was to be driven once around the island of Alboran. An actress was to be hired and made up to look like her in death repose. As the volcano erupted, and all habitation ceased, the carriage carried out the tradition through the streets of Paris, for he had by then become

King, on the nights of the first full moon until the day he died.

"It appears that Anarose had chosen the kingdom of God over the kingdom of a man."

I looked at the old woman who had not moved a muscle nor blinked an eye other than to light a cigarette during her reading thus far. I suddenly had the feeling that it was not she who had been speaking at all, but rather something else was using her as a vehicle for the information being dispersed. Even her voice quality had changed; it had lost much of its raspyness and became more normal and contained, like the flat tonal delivery of one who is merely reporting. She appeared to be in total trance and it sent a shiver up my spine.

As abruptly as she had stopped, she continued.

"Suddenly, three years after she had returned to her normal work schedule (five years after she had come into my life), she stopped coming at all. A week went by, and then another and another. And another. She had never stayed away for more than three weeks before. I decided to leave for Alboran the following morning. That day, I was paid a visit by a young Englishman who was so totally distraught that it took me well over an hour, with the help of a half bottle of cognac, to calm him to coherence. He told me he had been seeing Anarose for five years, but not at all for the past two, not until they had had a reunion some four weeks ago. During all that time he had known nothing about this life she led, and had been under the distinct impression that she was a deeply religious person, a recluse, and that suddenly, after not seeing each other for two long years, they had fallen madly in love.

"My initial reaction, of course, was, why did it take him so long? He explained to me that their initial relationship had been on an entirely different level. He didn't actually say, 'You wouldn't' understand,' but that is what he meant. He went on to tell me that she was resisting his advances with all her power, that she did not wish to break the law of celibacy that she had self-imposed and that if she did it would result in her sustaining the spans of her human life times.

"When I heard that, I did not know whether to laugh or scream. I did neither - the look on his face convinced me not to. He went on to tell me he had learned of this place by bribing a fisherman she had employed to transport her to and from here. The man lived here as opposed to Alboran. This was obviously thought up by her to insure her privacy. He always picked her up shortly before dawn, returning her shortly before sunset. By chance, this man happened to be on Alboran the day Edward was inquiring about her in the village, trying to find some key to unlock her womanhood, as it were. The man, who had until then kept his vow of silence, had become quite drunk and equally indiscreet, and so for far less money than she had given him over the years, he divulged her secret.

"To his tears I confirmed her professional life. Without a word he threw down a very large sum of money and left. That was the afternoon of the night she died."

She jerked her head from side to side as if to scatter the ghosts and raised herself to a sitting position.

"I had a hobby in those days. I sketched. And I sketched that face immediately after he left, for I knew I would never see such a look of total despair and agony ever again.

"I was wrong, however. I saw it again fifty years ago on the Frenchman, a doctor who came to me, claiming he had been with Anarose. I sketched him again. I say again, for the resemblance on the pad to the picture in my mind is so close that one would swear it was the same person."

She got to her feet, and then hobbled to a dust-encrusted desk, while saying, "Have you ever seen yourself with a beard?"

She handed me the sketch.

"You had ice blue eyes then and were not quite so tall."

I saw the resemblance immediately on the yellowed-with-age, crinkled parchment, and felt terror permeating my reasoning processes. I fought desperately to maintain my senses, to not become the victim of the vibration of the moment. I repeated to myself over and over again that it was all a manipulation, not to lose control, and yet I felt as though poised at that tenuous abyss that divides sanity from total panic, light from, dark, freedom from incarceration. I knew that if I could just win the battle of the moment, not give myself over to it, it would pass. I felt its orgiastic surge, took a deep breath, and allowed myself several seconds of composure before asking in a voice that was eighty percent tremulo, "What is this note attached to it?"

"Ah, yes. I found it crumpled in the chair John Paul had been sitting in, after he had left. Apparently, he had written it down at some point during the reading. I had no idea what it meant but I knew he was a doctor and it was obviously medical jargon of some sort. Do you know what it means?"

I looked at it intently. "Acute Intermittent Porphyria... I have no idea."

"I decided to save it, for there was a ship's doctor who visited here about once every six months or so. When I saw him next, without going into the details of how I had come by it, I showed it to him. He did not know what it meant either but promised that the next time he passed through he would have an answer for me. I saw him about a year later and he explained to me that Acute Intermittent Porphyria is a very rare genetically linked disease that manifests itself as a form of schizophrenia, that there is no set pattern or regularity to the attacks which makes it very hard to treat; that only intermittently would the victim fall prone to it.

"This did not gel with Anarose's duality of existence and so I asked him, without specifically going into her case, as it was a genetically linked disease, would the symptoms tend to be more pronounced, more severe, more regularly established in a person whose bloodline had been purified by virtue of inbreeding for several generations within its own immediate family. He said yes, that could very well be, though he felt that that sort of inbreeding would surely result in severe physical deformity as well. As far as I am concerned, Dr. Jean Paul had been quite correct in his diagnosis. Deformity had simply reversed itself."

"How did she die?"

She was back on her bed now; her eyes shut tightly, her fingers fondling the tooth.

"When he returned to Alboran, they met at sunset on the outer edge of the volcano's crest, a favorite spot of theirs. She was waiting for him. She did not hear him approach. I can see his face clearly, a mask of resolute. He threw himself on her and raped her again and again – and this is where my source blurs – becomes indistinct. I have never received this part of the experience to any degree of absolute clarity, however, one of two things happened: He left her there unconscious and when she awoke, she walked to the edge of the volcano and plunged herself down into its mouth. The other message I get is that he actually dragged her unconscious body to the edge and threw her in. That is all I know."

She broke the trance and propped herself on her elbows.

"If you have any questions, I will try to answer them for you."

At this time, I remembered, "Whatever became of Edward?"

She looked at me intently and replied, "You don't know?"

"Madame Pharasalet, I wouldn't be asking if I did."

She appeared totally unfazed by my tone of rebuke as she replied, "The same thing that may happen to you. Only you can prevent it."

"Madame Pharasalet, please talk sense, not abstracts."

This struck her as being very humorous indeed, and when she had cackled herself out, she said, "Something is only abstract until you come to understand it, then other things become abstract – things you were incapable of even thinking about before… and so on and so on!"

I was on my feet now.

"Damn it! Stop the bloody lecture and answer my question!"

She appeared to examine my periphery for a moment before responding.

"Do you believe in the Law of Karma? You should."

"I don't know what I believe…"

"Karma is very simply Cause and Effect, single life span transcendent, of course."

"So, what is your point, Madame?"

"My point is, we send out positive and negative energy through our actions that permeates the whole of the Universe, and until we send out no energy at all, of either quality, we cannot attain a state of harmony, of oneness that is the Cosmos."

I was becoming totally exasperated. "Madame Pharasalet, lofty opinions aside, would you please give me a simple answer to a simple question? What the hell ever became of Edward, and the other fellow, Jean Paul?"

"There are no simple answers unless you see what you are questioning simply. What you are really asking me is not what became of Edward and the Frenchman, but what is going to happen to you."

My initial reaction was to scream at the top of my lungs: "Everybody's a fucking philosopher in this part of the world!" The truth of the matter was that she was quite right and so I acquiesced with a curt bow of my head, to which she supplied a corresponding sigh as she struggled to her feet with the help of the canes.

"I wonder what it is that prevents you from understanding that you and Edward and Jean Paul are all the same person. Unfortunately, to a lesser or greater degree, we all are. Good day, Christos."

I got as far as the door, and then suddenly turned back to her.

"Am I to believe that this is the exact structure, somewhat time-worn of course, as when Anarose was in your employ four hundred years ago?"

"You may believe anything you like; however, not only an eccentric old woman, but historical records as well substantiate the claim. Why do you ask?"

"I would like to see the room she… occupied."

"I see."

She hobbled to the desk and extracted an antique key from the tiny drawer.

"It is not in use. Here, take the key. I had it locked the day after the Frenchman came to see me. I will not accompany you as the stairs are too difficult for me. When you reach the second floor, turn to your right. It is the door at the far end of the hallway - number seven."

She went past me with amazing agility for a double-crutched octogenarian and returned to her customers at the round table.

The stairs creaked and whined with age as I headed for room number seven. I spotted two young sailors coming down the opposite corridor just as I turned into her hallway. I noticed my hand was trembling as I reached for the door knob. I knew the scene that lay beyond the door, and when I finally worked up the courage to enter, it was indeed a familiar room, not by virtue of déjà vous, but rather by association with recent experience, for the room I now stood in was identical in every aspect, save the two people, to the one that had magically appeared in the wood.

I sat on the bed and was immediately bombarded by rising dust. I glanced to the bureau and started to reach for her comb and brush but my hand brushed against something en route. I watched it fall to the floor, disintegrating in the process. I reached down to retrieve it but as I gingerly grasped its withered stem, it, too, dissolved to powder. Ever so gently I tried to scoop up the one fallen petal that had remained intact, but it too rebelled against my touch, as it all but vanished between my thumb and forefinger.

The symbolism of the moment did not escape me and so once again I retreated to the recesses of my mind to "consider the possibilities."

There was a rather smug expression on my face as I descended the stairwell and headed for her table. As there were three men around it, I was forced to walk behind her chair, pausing only long enough to drop the key on the table and deliver my *coup de grâce* exit line.

"It certainly has been a great performance, Madame Pharasalet."

I immediately left the brothel.

****

XXIII

****

*"One man's lunacy is another man's logic, or vice
versa; it is strictly a matter of point of view."*
~ The Diarma Mind

Or was it?

My mind wrestled with those two distinctly separate approaches to my predicament during my entire rain-soaked return to Diarma. The part of my mind that I had come to rely on, to trust: logic, unrelentingly repeated manipulation, perversion, degeneracy, to me over and over again, fortifying itself with realistic explanations to all the bizarre occurrences, for if I really thought about it, not one of the "mystical events" could not be explained away by either technology, imagination, or the combination of the two.

But that less familiar region, gently, consistently, and no less doggedly staked out its claim also; that unexplored territory that I had always been captivated by; that enigmatic place that did not adhere to the earth's gravitational pull; that vertical thrust of mind and spirit which also laid claim to my brain, my essence: the unknown, the unchartered, the unspoiled, the indiscernible. It was this vortex of mystical insight that cajoled, romanced, terrified, enthralled, and excited me into leaving its door open, too, but once again, only a crack.

I sat there, soaked to the skin, with my fist clenched tightly around the knob, trying desperately to conjure up the power – lo, the worldliness – to slam it shut once and for all.

I could not, and quite without warning, the tension released itself in a torrent of tears. I allowed it to run its course and then, as if inspired, I resolutely walked to where I had hung my coat, reached into the breast pocket, and removed the pamphlet. My fingers rampaged it until I found the quotation on the last page: "In the final analysis, there is no such thing as a good or bad experience. It is experience itself that is the catalyst to growth. Come. We offer you the experience of a lifetime, several lifetimes."

I was beginning to see the light. I did not like what it shed for I felt my face contort to rage as I ripped the pamphlet into piece after piece and tossed it thru an open porthole.

I was just about to verbalize my outrage when Alethea's words came back to me: "You can always leave Diarma, anytime you want to – the decision is always yours."

"You bet your warped mind I'm going to leave this Twenty First Century torture chamber," came my reply of the moment.

Of course, an hour later when we docked in Diarma I had changed my mind. I was not about to leave Diarma just yet, for I realized that if I did, I would more than likely never see "Anarose" again. I further realized that I was right back in their clutches, so to speak, for better or for worse, but with one major difference: they only had a part of me now, only until they played out the remainder of their "psychodrama" to and for me, for now I understood that the next sequential event was for "Anarose" to grace me with a final visit, arrange a final rendezvous, undoubtedly at the volcano's crest as she had done with Edward. As a matter of fact, I concluded there would most likely be a note awaiting me at the Pensión to this effect, and that is precisely when my day would come.

XXIV

"There are no 'original thinkers,' for there was
only one (1) original thought and we are
the result of it."
~ The Diarma Mind

There was no note or communiqué of any sort awaiting me upon my return. As a matter of fact, even the pensioner was nowhere to be found.

I checked the Roman numerals on the immense timepiece dangling from the cedar gable and realized I had only some fifteen minutes in which to refuel myself. Over supper, I rehearsed all the exit lines I would devastate Alethea with a moment before my departure. I would confront her at her home for my scenario of sweet revenge.

I settled on: "You have my greatest admiration, respect, and awe for being the greatest producer this planet has ever know; also the most dangerous and sadistic... the fact that your name Alethea is Greek for Truth is a Machiavellian touch sans compar. Your ego is in the same fine tradition as that of a Napoleon or a Hitler; the latter being the most accomplished practitioner of the Black Arts this planet has ever seen. However, with all due respect, you run a very close second."

A little wordy, don't you think Christos?

Whereupon, I would turn on my heel and walk stoically into the sunset.

Watch that first step, baby.

After spending an hour picking at my food, I rushed back to the hotel, to my message. The night clerk informed me I had none. I questioned the man as to whether he had seen a woman answering to Anarose's description, last night or ever, and the man replied that he had never seen such a woman; that he would surely recall such an exceptional creature; that, as he had told me the previous night, a senior citizen, a fisherman by the name of Jorge had delivered the letter, not a woman.

I asked him where I might find this Jorge and was informed that he lived on his boat in the harbor.

I located him shortly thereafter but was only able to ascertain that he had not actually seen the bearer of the note; that there had been a knock on his cabin door and had discovered the envelope with a message attached bearing urgent instructions to take it to the pension, and so of course he complied.

I vacillated between the Buttercup and the Rock and chose the latter as I felt the former too perilous to attempt at nighttime's approach. I knew she would be at neither spot. A new twist was developing; I went there more to sequester myself in an atmosphere conducive for thinking about and second-guessing their next move, more than any hope of seeing her. Several times while lying on the ledge, my mind alternated between the theory I had worked through and the other I had all but completely closed off, I felt I had to remain strong; not give in to the scenario as presented, but rather, more diligently pursue other possible avenues of manipulation. This, to what end, I could only imagine; I only knew it was some sort of complex test.

I came to nothing concrete! I would simply have to wait for the next development to rear its ugly head. But I would be ready for it no matter how or from where it came. And somewhere during that two-hour contemplation period, I jettisoned mystique – the unexplored, the unknown, the unchartered, the unspoiled, the non-discernible, and with its falling away, I felt catherized.

*****

I showered and went to bed. Exhausted, I drifted off at once.

I suddenly sensed I was not alone. I shook my head and actually pinched myself to be certain I wasn't merely dreaming. The hand was going to be played out tonight after all.

Without taking my eyes from her, I arose, threw on my robe. She had still had not moved. I inspected her ever so slowly. Again the art of perfect staging employed itself. Her back was to the open French doors. Moonbeams shone on her raven hair, cutting a path across half her face, igniting the violet. Her costume was a stroke of pure genius, sensual without being openly provocative. She was adorned in a long, white, satin gown of the simplest Grecian line that accentuated the grace and flow of her body to a degree of classic, untouchable perfection. Her hair was swept up and back, graced by a diamond tiara. Long, white, kid gloves ended just shy of the elbow. The black rose rested in her cleavage. I was speechless. Irena Pharasalet had been quite correct about one thing anyway - her beauty did cut through everything. All the diatribes, the chastisements, the anger, the hurt, in short, the whole of the vitriolic torrent that raged inside me was swept away in an instant with the Now. Even that most vulnerable of all feminine targets, the male ego, was supplicated in that moment.

She smiled gently at me, walked to the edge of the bed and poised herself on it in an almost Victorian pose of correctness.

"I had to see you one more time before I go."

It was the "script" that jarred me back to myself. I felt the anger rising and it did not, could not, escape her.

"Lo, and behold, enter the long-suffering Anarose."

"You are not pleased to see me. I will go at once."

I positioned myself in front of her, actually giving her a light shove back to the bed. Her eyes suddenly filled with fear.

In my most sarcastic voice, I launched my assault.

"Don't worry, Anarose, I'm not going to rape you. Personally, I prefer the other version of your demise... I mean, it was multiple-choice now, wasn't it? You know, the one in which we mutually consent in the heat of a fluke moment, I believe is the approximate wording, and then, because your virtue is lost, your passion spent, your deflowering complete, you walk stoically to the edge of the volcano's mouth. God's Mouth but of course, and arms raised in Christ-like ambiance, plunge yourself inward. But, of course, in all truth, ULTIMATELY UPWARD AND ONWARD INTO THE REALM OF ABSOLUTE TRUTH, YOU CONNIVING BITCH!"

Other than for her hand clasping her mouth to stifle her shock, she did not move a muscle nor blink an eye. Her eyes became opaque a moment before a single tear descended each cheek. In the voice of one who has just received the most devastating blow of her life, she whispered, "I beg of you, please forgive me. I am so sorry, so terribly, terribly sorry."

I fought everything in me that longed to reassure her, which was all of me but the tiniest cell of resistance. My voice became despair when I replied, "Sorry? You're sorry? Not good enough. Not after what you put me through. Not after awakening those feelings in me. What I felt for you is like nothing I ever felt for anyone, ever!"

"And you think to me this was an infatuation? Do you have any idea who I am, what I am? You do not. You could not, or you would never think that of me. I must go now."

But once again I refused to let her pass and implored, "No... Please, don't go. Look, Ana... for God's sake, tell me your name! To hell with Diarma... to hell with Alethea."

She actually became dumbfounded. When she finally spoke it was in short breaths.

"Tell you my name? Alethea? Diarma? My God, what are you doing to me? What are you talking about? You know my name! You called me by it twice a few moments ago!"

"Stop it! What am I doing to you? What are you doing to me?! For Christ's sake, stop this charade now, once and for all. I'm onto the experience, Anarose, but I'm willing to forget all that if you'll just be honest with me. Start by telling me your real name, now, this instant!"

It was more than she could bear and she began to weep uncontrollably. I started for her, wanting nothing more than to take her in my arms, to soothe her, to hold her close, ever so close. My mind suddenly reminded me of what Irena Pharasalet had said: Acute Intermittent Porphyria. Could it be? Would Alethea go to similar extremes by actually employing a genuinely sick woman to play out a role? This performance had too much the ring of truth to it to be play-acting.

In the end, I decided I had to force her out. If I had to break her down to do it, so be it. Just as I was about to continue with my interrogation, she suddenly screamed to the ceiling, "My God! Is there no end to it?"

She slumped to her knees, her entire body going limp with anguish.

Now you may well think this would have been the final straw; the confirmation needed to carry her beyond the edge of credibility; the one moment just a little too much in a great actress's virtuoso performance.

The exact opposite was the case. In that instant, I decided that no actress, past or present, could so expertly rape a moment, and so, as I could no longer stand it, went to her, lifting her, and bringing her gently to me.

"No, no. I beg of you, no…"

I brought her yet closer to me. Still resisting, she said, "You mustn't. Do you have any idea what you would be doing to me?"

As the scent of her filled me, I replied, "Anarose, God help me, I want you so…"

I gently stroked her hair as I searched those damp, incredible eyes.

"It will be all right, I promise you. I know everything will be all right."

I bent to kiss her and she pulled away.

"Can't you understand? I'm already spoken for! It will not be all right. I did not come here for this. I came here to… Please, Edward, I beg of you… No!"

But I could contain myself no longer for fate had intervened and we became suddenly engulfed in an ultimate moment that had quintessentialied our very beings. In me, this manifested itself as strength, gentleness, determination; in her, vulnerability, the vulnerability that rendered her helpless to resist a rare and total fusion of positive and negative energy.

All this occurred in a unique instant of contact; the briefest of moments, as our eyes met, reflecting our very essences, seeing each other for the very first time beyond the trappings of our situation, only as male and female. Edenesque, and although it was indeed only a flicker of non-calculable time, an eternity lived there.

(Of course, all of the above is spoken in retrospect, and it is quite possible that what I have really extrapolated is quintessentialized lust, in which case I am unpardonably guilty of employing a flowery means to a totally self-serving sensual end, but at the time, it seemed appropriate.)

I had heard and not heard her call me Edward. I chose not to hear the light sobbing that never ceased all the way through our lovemaking.

*****

I was jarred awake by the sound of the terrace door slapping against the jamb. I rubbed my eyes with one hand and felt for her with the other. I panicked when I realized she was not there. I sat up and turned my head in the direction of the wind and saw her silhouetted against the sky, one foot in the room, the other on the balcony; her profile to me; her back resting against the door jamb, her eyes staring off into infinity, her shinning hair splayed lightly in the wind; the outline of her body geometrically distinct against the white satin. A single star guarded by a quarter moon hung suspended above her head. I sighed with relief as I watched, and then observed her. Immediately, my entire being refilled with the pleasure that had been only an hour ago.

Aroused, I turned on my side to study her yet more closely. I suddenly bolted upright. She turned at the movement, her face totally expressionless. I seemed to stop breathing as the full sequence of possibilities flashed thru my mind.

"Anarose?" I called softly, cautiously.

She shifted her vacant stare to the sound of her name as she undid the tie on her gown, allowing it to fall away. A flood of anticipation overwhelmed me and just as I was about to go to her, a faraway look entered her eyes and in a childlike manner she began to recite more than say:

"Once upon a time, a man and a woman fell in love, and set forth together to seek the Happy Land of Romance that lies over the horizon of every lover's vision. In a very short time, they found themselves in a dark wood. It was full of luscious fruit, of which they both ate greedily. But the fruit turned sour within them and the brambles scratched them. Like all people who have lost their sense of direction, they went around and around in circles, and so began to feel irritated and frustrated and to realize that they were making no progress towards their goals. But they failed to see the true reason for it.

"The news of their plight reached the ears of the king, whose wise laws decreed that his subjects must solve their own problems and find their own ways out of their self-created difficulties. So the king sent for his prime minister, the Lord of Karma, to bring him the Book of Fate in which was recorded the life story of every inhabitant of the country.

"Having perused the history of each of these individuals, the king said, 'Through similarity of taste and temperament, they are reinforcing each other's weaknesses, and thus will never escape from the wood together. I am afraid you must tell the Minister of Death to take the woman away, and then the eyes of both will be opened and they will reach by separate but converging paths their desired destinations; and treat them kindly, for their souls are linked by true love, though as of yet they do not fully realize it.'

"And so Death carried out his mission and the words of the good king came true."

She took two steps and flung herself over the side. I had already been halfway to her and now the momentum of my own terror carried me to the railing only a moment before her body disappeared into the fog enshrouded base of the cliffs. My body stiffened as my hands welded to the railing while peering down the two-thousand-feet-plus, looking for the vestiges of her. I felt the stuff screams are made of rise in my gut but no sound came out.

Detachment set in as I observed myself cross over from shock to a place called insanity, and the latter lifted my foot to the railing and arched my body. The tiniest prick at the base of my neck occurred a second before the entire sky began to revolve. The revolutions sped up as I felt myself floating thru space that casted blinding, distorted light at me from everywhere at once.

And then I felt my body leave me as it crumpled to the balcony floor.

Perchance to dream…

XXV

"Appoint yourself a God; lay down the laws of a universe; become the master of a process."
~ The Aristos

I ran with all my might... in slow motion... I had to get there... not much farther... please... not much farther...

I reached the top of the knoll and found myself swallowed up by the density. The mist was so thick I could not see my own hand in front of my face. And all at once I was there but the line... the line was so long... I could not bear the wait; there must be a thousand of them all waiting to get to her. The mist cleared instantly and I observed the perfect order of the column, of which I was bringing up the rear. All the men were of precisely the same height and weight; all dressed in black tails and top hats, all carrying black alligator attaches in one hand and ivory canes whose handles were large phallic symbols, in the other. A black rose peeked out from under their lapels barely discernible against the black cloth were it not for the single drop of blood that oozed from each blossom. Suddenly, I checked my lapel... where was my rose? I must have my rose. I reached in front of me and tried to tear off the man's rose but it would not come... and the next man and the next but I could not loosen their rose...

I looked into their faces; they had no features.

I walked straight ahead now... deeper into the mist that had suddenly reappeared... deeper, and then finally I could make out its form and I sighed with relief. She was there, waiting for me in her carriage which dwarfed everything in sight.

It was at least four stories high as were the stallions. I saw Irena Pharasalet seated at her table just below the spiral staircase that wound up to the carriage door. She kept looking at her appointment book and was checking off names as she repeated the same phrase over and over again as the men passed in front of her on the way to the carriage: "You again... You again... You again..."

I was upon her now. I turned to look at the line that seemed endless and just as I realized that they were all the same man, for they had features now, my features, she said, "No! Not you again!" I started to plead, then beg, but she held firm: "No rose, no Anarose... Where is your rose? Those are the rules..."

She motioned the next man towards her. I grabbed the man and beat myself to death to get his rose.

She nodded her head in approval and I started for the carriage but she stopped me short with, "Wait, where is your gift? No gift, no Anarose. Those are the rules..."

And as I turned to look at her, all the other men opened their cases, allowing the jewels and gold to come spilling to the ground. I didn't know what to do. The column was coming straight at me - they had become a mob. I felt a light tap on my shoulder and turned to look into Alethea's face... just her face for she had no body. Her voice said, "Give her your heart."

I reached into my chest and tore out my heart, flinging it on the table. In one motion, a hairy hand appeared out of nowhere, scooped it up and consumed it in one mouthful. Irena nodded her approval once again and indicated that I could now enter. I opened the carriage door and was immediately overwhelmed by the richness of the surroundings: Gold Dust covered the floor in depth. Every jewel imaginable clung to the walls. The egg shaped window was a pure diamond; piles and piles of gold and silver coins took up every corner of the room. A huge black Lucite buffet displayed every kind of food imaginable; its centerpiece was Alethea's torso impaled on a huge revolving spit, an enormous pair of testicles clenched in her fists, and dead center in the middle of it all, raised by a platform of three marble steps, she waited for me as she lay in state in the gigantic white satin tufted coffin of onyx.

Slowly I walked to her and up the three endless steps. The three became thirty, then three hundred. After forever, I reached the top and looked inside. She was lying there naked. The beauty that was her intact other than her violet eyes that had turned to shattered glass.

I read the instructions on the scroll tattooed on her stomach: "Place ten gold coins in my mouth. Upon orgasm, exit immediately through opposite door."

I searched my pockets frantically but came up empty-handed. I began to cry and suddenly remembered the cache of coins in the corners of the carriage. I raced down the stairs and gathered up ten coins. I looked to the entryway and saw another man being admitted. In a state of panic I began the ascent once again but I was running out of breath.

"Just one more stair now… just one more stair… one more…"

But there was always one more stair to be conquered, and then the mist entered the carriage, closing in on me just as   the last stair was in reach. One foot is on it now…

A loud bell ringing and ringing and then a neon sign flashed on the ceiling, its lettering spelling out "I'm sorry. Your time is up whether or not orgasm has been achieved. Leave at once through opposite door."

I threw the coins at the lights, shattering them in every direction, and peered once again into the coffin just in time to see her falling, falling, falling into the night. This time, I saw her crumpled body slam into the rocks. This time, the scream came out. This time I jumped after her…

I awoke to the sounds of my own screams as my head banged on the stone floor. I took a moment to orient myself before noticing the imposing figure glaring at me from a few steps away. He approached me squatted down and said: "You have one hour to prepare your defense."

I glared back at him and replied: "Defense against what?!"

"The Specimen exists, doesn't he? Isn't that enough?" And then he did something that chilled me to the bone. He smiled at me and said: "You are charged with two specific counts of Insufficient Humanity." Turned on his heel and exited the cell-like structure.

And so now you know as much as I do.

****

XXVI

****

*"The major flaws of modern psychiatric practice
today are threefold: One, it presupposes that only
those who can afford to have problems, do; Two,
the knowledge imparted is too oft times the product
of textbook familiarization as opposed to life
familiarization; Three, its emphasis is on putting
one in touch with oneself in order to cope with the
world as it is, and offers little or no refuge or
revelation to those inclined (as well as troubled by)
higher realities..."*
~ The Diarma Mind

I was ushered out of the room into a circular cellar of block stone and up the ladder that led to the trap door. On its other side, I found myself at the base of a towering steel spiral staircase that would have glistened blindingly had there been any exterior light source whatsoever, and suddenly I knew where I was.

As I began the long climb up the lighthouse stair well, the symbolism of my locale of the moment did not escape me – obviously I was to be shown: The Light. To what end, I could only shudder. My legs became very tired and started to cramp on me and I had not yet gone a quarter of the distance. My hearty companion appeared to take every step in stride, which only caused to infuriate me all the more.

Completely out of breath and near fainting, I reached the top, which was a small landing, directly above which was yet another trap door. As I was thinking that I had indeed gone to hell, my guard nudged me none too gently towards the rungs. I felt an almost uncontrollable urge to shove him off the landing and watch his body plummet down the depths, but then the memory of a quite recent like incident quelled it with tears.

I pushed open the trap door and found myself in the most brilliantly lit room I had ever seen. It was of course circular and its entire circumference was floor to ceiling glass, save a small section of white wall directly behind me. The view was breathtakingly beautiful. I came to a semi-standing position and looked around. I was standing in a center aisle, with a semi-circle to either side of it lined with row upon row of solid white benches, pews, I realized.

It was a very large room, much larger than I initially suspected it could be. It could accommodate a hundred or more people in the spectator section alone. I turned and looked towards the "altar." It was raised by a single step to a second level and economically housed a large, sleek white podium behind which were situated three very tall black leather backed stools in equilateral positioning; the center stool placed one level above the other two. It did not strain my powers of imagination to conclude who was to occupy that particular one.

Immediately to the right of the podium was a chairless, clear Lucite square affair, open at one side. Its forward panel was made of two-ply opaque or frosted glass, I could not determine which. I decided that this was either a torture chamber or a witness stand, or a combination of the two in the event I wished to take the stand in my own defense. I followed the multi-colored wires and conduits that extended themselves from the base of the witness box to a small table with chair, on the opposite side of the docket. Upon it rested a laptop computer a shorthand calculator, and a tape recorder. Just the other side of the first pew was a large rectangular table with one chair - undoubtedly the accommodation for the accused. A brass railing was directly behind it and ran the entire breadth of the room.

The bailiff suddenly appeared and marched me to my seat and then took up a guard post directly behind me.

It was then, as I was registering my disgust by looking upwards in a bored fashion, that I saw it approximately twenty feet above and slightly ahead of me in the upper right portion of the room, almost to the very roof of the structure. It hung there suspended like a velvet vulture - a black opera box with two black velvet chairs that were back-dropped by a cloud and a small circular stairwell that led to yet another point of entry.

Some fifteen minutes later I raised my head once again to the sound of the descending jury of two. They had no faces. They were dressed in black from head-to-toe. Only cutouts for their eyes and nose appeared in the hoods.

Twenty more minutes passed: before I turned to the sound of the whir above. It got louder and louder until the helicopter settled on the roof above. Apparently, the stairwell approach was saved for the disfavored ones for, at the same time, I heard loud, shuffling sounds coming from behind me and I turned to the sound of the single section of wall sliding back, revealing an entranceway that allowed a virtual multitude to enter. To a one, they averted their glance, their faces set in grim; to a one, both men and women clutched a black rose in their right hand. I marveled at the theatricality of it. The staging did not escape me either, for I had had no idea that "wings" existed behind the tiny section of wall.

I recognized many of the Category I, II, and III residents as they somberly took their places in the theater/chapel/ courtroom in the sky. There was the sound of the outer door sliding back once again. I forced myself not to look around; not to give her the satisfaction.

The two women passed by me without the smallest sign of acknowledgement. I followed their shimmering, white-clad bodies to the podium with my eyes, and then Alethea did something that jolted me: She and the other woman, whom I recognized as the domestic who had shown me to the study, took their places to the extreme right and left of the podium, leaving the more highly perched place of honor – or for yet another.

Alethea rapped the gavel twice and announced, "All rise."

They all did but me. This time, in place, I looked around, for my curiosity had got the better of me. The door slid open revealing one of the most striking men I had ever seen. He was tall and strongly slender. He walked with an erect cadence of almost military correctness, but naturally. His hair was the non-color of freshly fallen snow as was his full but not bushy beard, his face heavily lined and lightly tanned. I could not see his eyes as they were covered with sun-sensor lenses set in a simple black frame. The rest of his features were very distinct - a high forehead, a long straight nose, a full mouth and very high cheek bones. It was impossible to determine his ethnic origin or precise age. He could have been Mediterranean, English, Nordic, or any combination of the three. He could have been forty-five or sixty. He wore a jurist's robe of white madras, and there was something familiar about him but it was of such a tenuous nature that I did not even attempt to place him.

He took his place above and between the two women just as I felt something being thrust over my head. A moment later I discovered I had been attired in a long black monk's robe. I turned my attention back to the podium, specifically Alethea, and realized that her eyes were boring into me with such a degree of intensity that I felt an explosion was imminent.

I gave her tit-for-tat.

The gavel sounded once, and simultaneous with the dying murmurs all natural light disappeared as huge black velvet curtains were electronically drawn, ringing the entire circumference of the room plunging it into total darkness. Next came the sound of an electronic revolution just as a long two by four section of docket opened to reveal floor spots that flooded the podium with white light. I was still in the comfort of darkness until just now when a single red pin spot beamed me in. Two overhead spots above the box seats, both of a violet hue, illumined the jury. Only the gallery, or as I preferred to think of them, the audience, remained in darkness.

The gavel struck twice more and a deep, rich voice of crystal clear distinction and almost stentorian quality announced:

"This Service is now in session. Alexander Christos, solely by virtue of its auspices, which have been convened under the authority of the Universal Law of Cause and Effect, in conjunction with the Socratic Axiom that there are certain things implicitly known to be correct by every rational human being; and, as this Service is satisfied as to your capacity to perceive same, your sanity, you are hereby arraigned.

"It is of paramount importance that the Specimen understands fully that this is not, repeat, not in any form or fashion a punitive court of law. In keeping with this, the term defendant has been stricken from use during these proceedings.

"Rather, it is a forum through which we shall investigate the root of the Specimen's retarding traits. Any and all verdicts arrived upon by this Service will be so reached with two objectives in mind: One: Did or did not the Specimen act in such a manner as to retard his personal evolution and future enlightenment? Two, was the Specimen, in the process of same, directly or indirectly responsible for the retardation of his fellow human being's evolution and future enlightenment, by inflicting pain through Lust, Cowardice, Lack of Compassion and Understanding, Cruelty, and Murder, which, in the Specimen's case are all manifestations of the same malady, Ignorance.

"Any and all sentencing arrived upon by virtue of a guilty verdict will be executed solely by this triumvate for the specific purpose of accelerating the Specimen's mental and spiritual evolution simultaneously.

"You are advised that although this Service is convened under Universal Law, the basic technique of execution is that of American Jurisprudence as it most closely resembles the aforementioned, with certain sophistications of a nature to the Specimen's benefit; with certain exceptions of a nature to Justice's benefit, to wit: The paraphernalia you see attached to the witness stand is an Aura Reproducer based upon the Kirlian system of

Aura photography. As it is the only one in existence, it bears further examination:

"Late in the 1930s, a Russian photographer by the name of Semyon Kirlian discovered a process by which to photograph body luminescence. For centuries, psychics, as well as those who were labeled somewhat less scientifically as witches, claimed to be able to see, with their naked eye, certain colors and patterns emanating from the human body. Upon further research and discovery, Russian scientists were able to confirm that the body did indeed project certain colors directly related to the mood of the individual, ergo, the basis in fact for such expressions as 'Green with envy,' 'Red with anger,' 'Gray with fear.' As it turns out, those are precisely the colors of the aura that correspond to the stipulated moods. Kirlian discovered how to photograph the aura; our paraphernalia projects the aura on to the opaque screen that fronts the witness stand. Instantly. In addition to the immediate perception of the mood and feelings of the witness, we have discovered that the aura is also an infallible lie detector, far more perceptive than the conventional polygraph or lie detector which is not a fool-proof device. The Aura Preceptor is.

"In front of you, under the glass section on your table, is a color chart. You will note that the colors appear on one side; words and definitions on the other. As each witness testifies, their aura will be readily accessible to you, and you will be able to judge them for yourself."

I glanced down at the chart.

> RED: ANGER
> GREEN: ENVY
> FEAR: GRAY
> LUST: MUDDY BROWN EDGED WITH BRIGHT RED
> CONFUSION: GRAY FLECKED AND SHOT WITH
>   BLACK

OVERALL AURA VARIES WITH EACH
INDIVIDUAL. THE ABOVE, HOWEVER, APPLIES TO
ALL. A SAMPLE AURA AND ITS IMPLICATIONS
FOLLOWS:

DEEP VIOLET EVENLY EDGED WITH YELLOW:
GENIUS, HIGHLY SPIRITUALLY EVOLVED
INDIVIDUAL.

WHEN THE TRUTH IS BEING SPOKEN THERE
WILL BE NO CHANGE IN THE INDIVIDUAL'S AURA
WHATSOEVER UNLESS OF A REVELATORY
NATURE (TO THE ONE WHO IS SPEAKING IT), IN
WHICH CASE THE ENTIRE AURA WILL BRIGHTEN
AND PULSE.

WHEN A NON-TRUTH IS UTTERED THE
INDIVIDUAL'S ENTIRE AURA WILL DIM
APPRECIABLY WHETHER OR NOT THE NON-
TRUTH IS DELIBERATE (DECEPTIVE) OR A
MATTER OF ERROR THAT THE SUBCONSCIOUS
NOTES AND REACTS.

Of course, I only had their word for this wonder machine. The
judge suddenly cut into my thoughts.

"Now, the witness is allowed no discrepancies. If one occurs,
his or her entire testimony is invalidated and he/she will be held in
contempt of this Service. Naturally, this only applies to an
intentionally fallacious response.

"As to the exceptions to Justice's benefit, the Specimen may
raise no 'Objections' on grounds of 'prejudicial nature by virtue of
past actions.' You do have the right to object on grounds of
'irrelevance' and 'hearsay,' but must prove those grounds to the
satisfaction of this Service. In addition, this Service honors no

statute of limitations that may or may not apply to the charges being preferred.

"You are being tried by a jury of your peers: two, not twelve, as is customary in American Jurisprudence. Their verdict must coincide."

I briefly looked to them before going on:

"You have no appellate rights. The decision of this Service is final as there exists no higher convening authority anywhere on this planet. In any event, if you are found to be guilty, you will be given the opportunity to offer evidence in Mitigation and Extenuation prior to sentencing. Does the Specimen have any questions thus far?"

The "Specimen" did not know whether to laugh or scream so he did neither.

"Very well, at this point, and only at this point, the Specimen has two choices: He may leave this Service, now, completely unhindered, and leave Diarma, never to return. A boat has been arranged and is awaiting his decision. But, if he opts to stay, he must remain in this Service until due process has been served. The only exception to that being barred by virtue of the accumulation of five counts of contempt, in which case, he will be removed and returned only to hear verdict and sentencing, if applicable."

I felt every pair of eyes in the room boring through me. It, they, didn't matter. They had known precisely where to hit me. It was above the belt but nonetheless dazing. Once again, I felt myself sucked back into the vacuum of irresistible mystique. I knew, in that instant, that for better or for worse, my life and that "place" were inextricably bound together. I knew I could not rise to a standing position. I knew my legs would not carry me to the exit. I said or did nothing until I stole a glance at Alethea. Was that the tiniest of smiles, smirks, I saw flutter in her eyes?

"Very well, you are your own defense counsel. The Prosecution will now proceed in the case of ALL THAT IS IMPLICI1TLY KNOWN TO BE CORRECT BY EVERY RATIONAL HUMAN BEING - henceforth to be referred to as

THE TRUTH - versus ALEXANDER CHRISTOS - henceforth to be referred to as THE SPECIMEN. Counsel for THE TRUTH is Alethea Alexis, of Diarma. The Specimen will now rise and be formally charged."

She rose, parchment scroll in hand, but I did not. The Judge studied me for a moment and said, "The Specimen has exercised the option to stay and will observe the decorum of this Service."

I stared back at him in total contempt and then finally rose to the occasion. Alethea immediately unrolled the scroll and began reading:

"The Specimen is specifically charged with two counts of Insufficient Humanity. It is to be understood by the Specimen that this Service considers any level of insufficient humanity to be a major contributing cause to the perpetuation of one's existence on a mundane level, to wit: Until one becomes sufficiently human, having transcended those areas of self that are of a self-retarding nature, evolution cannot become a reality.

"The specifications to the charge are as follows:

"SPECIFICATION ONE: IN THAT, the Specimen did, on or about, August Fifth of this year, premeditatedly in cold blood, with malice aforethought, attempt the murder of one Alexander Christos by placing a loaded revolver to his head and pulling the trigger at least six times in succession.

"THEREFORE, the Specimen is charged with Insufficient Humanity by virtue of extreme Cowardice in the Face of Life, Selfishness, and Stupidity, which, in the Specimen's case, are all manifestations of the same malady: Ignorance. This Service will entertain a motion to dismiss on the grounds of temporary insanity.

Does the Specimen so wish to enter such grounds?

"Very well, I will proceed with Specification Two:

"SPECIFICATION TWO: IN THAT, the Specimen did, on or about four AM, August the Twenty-Fourth of this year, on Diarma, premeditatedly commit murder by raping the core and taking the life of one Anarose de Alboran.

"It is further charged that the Specimen had been made reasonably aware of the potential consequences of his act prior to the situation that evoked it.

"THEREFORE, it is charged that the Specimen is guilty of Insufficient Humanity by virtue of LUST, CRAVING, and DESIRE; LACK OF RESPECT, REGARD, and UNDERSTANDING FOR THE SINCERE AND GENUINE BELIEFS OF ANOTHER HUMAN BEING, which, in the Specimen's case, are all manifestations of the same malady: Ignorance."

She re-seated herself as His Honor rapped the gavel once.

"The Specimen has heard the charges. How does he plead to Specification One - Guilty or Not Guilty?"

I said nothing.

"Is the Specimen indicating he wishes to offer no defense to the charges?"

Silence.

"Very well. In Justice's interests, the jury is instructed to interpret the Specimen's silence as a plea of *Nolo Contendere* – no contest - to both specifications of the charge. The jury is further instructed to substitute the words *Nolo Contendere* for both Guilty and Not Guilty."

His next statement was directed to Alethea:

"Does the Counsel for Truth wish to make an opening statement?"

"It does, your Honor." She arose from her chair and walked down into the far corner of the docket. She looked up to address the jury:

"The Truth will prove beyond the shadow of a doubt that the Specimen is…"

"Objection!" Before I realized it I had broken my vow of silence. The voice from the podium inquired:

"Just exactly what is it that the Specimen objects to and on what grounds?"

"'The Specimen' objects to the use of the designation 'The Specimen' on the grounds that it is an irrelevant reference of a highly impersonal nature. As it is I, Alexander Christos, who is on trial here, I demand that I be addressed, as such."

"It is precisely because of the exact opposite - the fact that this is a highly impersonal proceeding – that the designation stands. I congratulate you for being exactly wrong. Counsel for the Truth will proceed."

"The Truth will also prove, beyond any reasonable doubt, that his actions in question not only retarded his personal evolution, but that of countless others, as well. To substantiate that allegation, I enter the following quote into the record. It is taken verbatim from The Aristos, by John Fowles:

"'. . . unless we admit that we are not, and never will be, born equal, though all should be born with equal human rights, unless the Many can be educated out of their false assumption that biological superiority is a state of existence instead of what it really is – a state of responsibility – then we shall never arrive at a more just and happier world.'

"It is in the words 'until the Many can be educated out of' that implies there are indeed educators, presumably among the 'few,' but not the existing few; not the ones who have already perverted their biological superiority toward the sole goal of self-aggrandizement through the amassing of personal wealth, position, and power. They are a lost cause – dinosaurs soon to become extinct. And so, a new breed of 'biologically superior' people must emerge. At the present time, as it has been in the past, the Many have had only a singular goal to aspire to - the criterion that has already been established by the 'biologically superior' of this and every past age; the false goals of 'wealth,' 'position,' and 'power.' That is what they envy and we all know what envy breeds. That, because no other standards exist for them, is what they falsely aspire to, and that is why a new breed – the personal embodiment of responsibility – must emerge that not only shares the benefit of their knowledge, but the materialistic benefits that that knowledge provides in the way of power of acquisition of basic living necessities, and creature comforts, as well. And so, because the Specimen is obviously endowed in a biologically superior manner, his perversion of same is as devastating a crime in and of itself as the individual acts he is specifically charged with. To misrepresent himself is to misrepresent the 'best in all of us.' I repeat, the Truth will also prove beyond any reasonable doubt that his actions in question not only retarded his own evolution but that of countless others as well."

Although my eyes were downcast to the table, I could actually feel hers boring into my head. Mercifully, the Judge spoke up, "Does the Specimen wish to make an opening statement? No? Very well, the specifications will be pursued in consecutive order, following a ten minute recess."

```
**********************************************************
```

XXVII

```
**********************************************************
```

*"Clinging to the past or projecting into the future is
the mind's constant thief for it robs you of the NOW."*
~ The Diarma Mind

*"Yogiraj Swami Sri Shastri, Instructor of Hathayogic
Practices and Meditational Techniques,
Institute of Learning, Diarma."*

The stenographer said, "The Aura Preceptor is functioning."

I stared at the screens that shielded the entire upper torso of the witness. The man's basic body luminescence was shades of yellow, bright and pale.

"Yogiraj Shastri, would you please relate to this Service where you were, why you were there, and what you saw the night of August Fifth of this year?"

"I was temporarily in East Hampton, New York, visiting an ailing relative. On the night in question, I did, as was my usual routine, take a long walk down a deserted stretch of beach, found my 'spot' and began my yoga and meditation. Close to midnight, I observed a young man walking towards the ocean a few yards to my right. Apparently, he did not hear or see me, even though at one point he looked directly at me. It was a dark, moonless night and I was, at the time, in the Kurmasana or Tortoise pose, and therefore difficult to distinguish as a human being. It is quite possible that he believed me to be some inanimate object as he gazed in my direction.

"I observed him from this position until he finally settled himself in the sand a few yards from the surf. There was an ominous aura of reds and grays about him. In addition, his physical being gave forth a vibration so oppressive that I began to study him in earnest at once. For the first few minutes, he simply delved into his briefcase and continually extracted items, methodically destroying them one by one. The last item he withdrew was obviously of greater weight than the others from the way he handled it. As he placed it to his head, I realized it was a gun.

"I made the decision not to interfere at this point for two reasons: One, the distance between us was at least thirty feet and, at my age, I could most likely not reach him in time to prevent him from pulling the trigger; two, I was afraid that if he sensed my presence in coming towards him, for in his present state of mind he would be very sensually attuned, it might cause him to panic and pull the trigger when there was always the chance he might not be able to go through with it. I was thinking this when he suddenly lowered the gun and emptied the revolver's chamber. I could not tell if he had removed all the bullets, but I assumed he had and sighed with relief. I was about to go to him then when he suddenly put the gun on top of his case, shed all his clothing and walked into the surf. I wondered momentarily if he simply had decided to alter his mode of demise, but the thought was academic, for I cannot swim. I walked immediately to his belongings and the gun. It was then that I realized that he had left one bullet in the chamber, and so, removed it and returned the gun to its place. I rummaged the sand for the other four bullets but was able to come up with only three. I then checked his jacket and pants pockets to make sure he had no spares in them.

"I looked into his wallet, ascertained his identity, and on an inspiration removed a small business card I immediately recognized as that of being an organization utilized by Diarma for the screening of potential residents – Voyages Unlimited – and placed it in my pocket. I saw him floating, more than swimming, back to shore moments later, and decided to give up my search for the last bullet. I thought about taking the gun in the unlikely event he found the missing bullet, but decided against it as the Gods must be allowed their play as well.

"When he washed ashore, at first I thought he had drowned. He lay there totally motionless for a full minute, but then he raised himself to a sitting position, stood upright, and walked to his belongings. He raised the gun once again and spun the chamber once as he was seating himself. He placed the weapon once again to his head, and then, allowing long intervals between, squeezed the trigger a total of five times. I'm certain you can imagine his shook when he found himself to be alive. He then pulled the trigger five times more in rapid succession, the gun barrel still at his temple, and then, a sixth time. To my mind, he was the most extraordinary human being I had ever encountered on a mundane plain. I decided he either possessed a superhuman nervous system or none at all, or was totally insane. But more importantly, I thought, 'My God, if that determination, that uncompromising resolve, could be channeled into a positive direction, there would be no stopping the man!' Later, after he had fallen asleep, I left a message for him in the sand, which he discovered upon awakening the following dawn."

"Thank you, Sri Shastri. Would you please tell this Service what your interpretation of his precise response was the moment he discovered he was not dead?"

"Total shock that gave way to infuriation – he actually cursed the heavens."

"Is there any question in your mind whatsoever that the Specimen was indeed trying to kill himself?"

"Absolutely none. I have never heard of, let alone witnessed, an individual so strongly bent on the total annihilation of his flesh - and spirit, too, I fear."

"One final question. On the Specimen's first evening on Diarma while dining with me, he referred to the 'message in the sand,' which I denied having any knowledge of. Would you be so kind as to inform this Service as to the very first time this information has reached my ears?"

"Only moments ago, when I related it to this Service."

"We have had no prior discussion concerning this, whatsoever, then?"

"Absolutely none."

"Thank you, Sri Shastri. The Truth has no further questions."

"Does the Specimen wish to cross-examine?"

I had been intently watching the screen to see if a lie had been indicated. His aura had remained unchanged during his entire testimony, so either he had answered her last question truthfully, or the machine was a fraud. I looked up at him and in as off-hand a manner as I could project, said,

"You really shouldn't have meddled in something that wasn't your affair." The voice shot from the podium.

"The Specimen will apologize at once to the Yogiraj Sri Swami Shastri or be held in contempt. Your remark is impudent, impertinent, and stupid."

"Apologize, my ass!"

"Log the Specimen's first count of contempt to be dealt with at a future time. The witness may step down."

She immediately assaulted me from the other side.

"Does the Specimen honestly and truly believe he has the right to take the life of another human being, under any circumstances other than those that may be justified by the immediate threat to one's very life or in the immediate threat to the life of another?"

I laughed sardonically a moment before retorting with, "My life has been immediately threatened since the day I was born. To more specifically answer your question, of course not, only you have that right, Alethea."

I caught her in the act of shooting a quick glance to the podium and awaited my second count of contempt. It was not forthcoming.

"The Specimen's sarcastic response notwithstanding, the fact of the matter is, you do not. The Truth rests as to Specification

One: The attempted murder of one Alexander Christos. Does the Specimen wish to make a closing…"

"The Specimen does NOT wish to make a closing statement as to Specification One."

And banged my fist on the table. The sound had no sooner finished resounding when I heard the inevitable in an a most bored voice,

"The stenographer will log the Specimen's second count of contempt, to be dealt with at a future time. Proceed with Specification Two."

She looked at me for a moment, hands on hips, in the manner of a contemplative mother trying to figure out what to do with her cantankerous child. She walked to within a very few feet of me as she spoke.

"Specification Two: The premeditated murder of Anarose de Alboran. The Truth calls as its first witness, Alethea Alexis – myself - during which time, Counsel for the Truth turns the responsibility of direct examination over to Karen DeWitt."

As she took her place in the witness stand, I smiled to myself for the first time since the Service had begun. You can bet your sweet… the Specimen will want to cross-examine is what I thought to myself. I raised a request just as Ms. DeWitt removed herself from the podium and walked on to the docket.

"I… excuse me, the Specimen, would like a pad of paper and a pencil."

"Request denied. It is imperative, repeat imperative, that the Specimen stay with the moments, each and every one of them, as they unfold in this Service. Taking notes would tend to obliterate many of same."

Ms. DeWitt began.

"State your name, place of residence, and occupation."

"Alethea Alexis, Diarma, Executive Evolutionary."

The stenographer confirmed, "The Aura Preceptor is operational."

I studied her aura intently, and then checked the chart. It was, of course, the same aura they had given an example of: Deep violet evenly edged with yellow, which, according to them, equaled Genius, Highly Spiritual. I stared at her in open contempt as she began answering the questions.

"Do you know the Specimen? If so, state his name and point him out."

"Alexander Christos."

"Will you enlighten this Service as to the specifics of a visit paid you by the Specimen one day ago, August Twenty-Third of this year?"

"The Specimen came uninvited into my home. At first, I refused to see him as I had just returned from New York and had a great deal of work to do."

Which caused me to snort loudly, which I quickly tried to cover with a cough as I did not wish to incur another contempt citation just then. I got caught anyway.

"If the Specimen has suddenly fallen ill, arrangements can be made to take him to the infirmary while the balance of this proceeding continues. Is that understood?"

I nodded "Yes."

"Very well. Proceed." He stroked his beard while riveting me to my chair with his look.

"I consented to see him after being informed of his distraught condition, by you, as a matter of fact. When I came upon him in my study, he was inspecting a sixteenth century bust of the woman known as Anarose de Alboran. He then, after we had exchanged differing opinions as to the period of her life span, proceeded to tell me that he had not only seen this woman, but had indeed spent time with her over the past three days and nights. At first, I indicated reluctance to believe his story…"

I did not even bother to note that her aura had not changed in the slightest, for I realized that she was going to get away with recounting her testimony without lying once. But cross-examination would be another story.

"But, as it unfolded, it became apparent that he had indeed experienced something of an inordinate nature. I invited him to stay for lunch, during which time I told him the version of Anarose's life and death that we, on Diarma, ascribe to. I recounted it fully and in vivid detail. When I had finished, I indicated that there was yet another complete version of her life and death, and that I could put him in touch with someone a few hours away who could relate it to him. Furthermore, in the account I rendered him, I included both versions of the circumstances surrounding her actual death. He accepted my offer as to hearing the other version and left my home a little after two PM."

"Did the Specimen offer any evidence of a physical nature or otherwise, to substantiate his claim of having seen the woman called Anarose?"

"He did. Of a physical nature, this note…"

She withdrew it from a folder and went on. "I was particularly interested in the wording of it and told him as much, for the note confirmed what we have always believed of Anarose - that she was a Buddhist. I quote:

"'You and I live in different worlds. All I can tell you is that we must part for if we do not, you could be the life of me. I cannot allow that to happen. For you, perhaps, it would be easier to think in terms that you could be the death of me.' Serious Buddhists aspire to self-extinction, ergo, the reference to the 'life of me.' Her concession to the Specimen as to the 'death of me' was merely a translation of the terms into an understandable form for him to assimilate."

"Did you explain to the Specimen what you have just told this Service?"

"I did."

"Did he seem to accept this?"

"No, he did not accept it, but he did understand it."

"Any other evidence submitted as to having actually seen her?"

"Only of a heresy nature. By that, I mean he told me of four bizarre incidents. The first one was that he had awakened to the sound of her screaming; the second, that he had seen her in death's repose, lying in state in the carriage of a horse-drawn sixteenth century hearse that had almost run him down in the meadow the previous evening. He also mentioned that on the morning of his arrival he awoke to find the worst of his lacerations had been tended to. The one other incident he told me more or less in passing, as if he was not fully convinced himself that it had actually occurred, was in the nature of an apparition. He claimed to have been walking through the west wood on the way to the noonday meal on the first full day of his stay here, when he looked into a portion of the forest, and saw a couple making love in a second story bedroom that was suspended in midair."

"And as he recounted these incidents to you, what was his emotional and mental state?"

"It ran the gamut of badly shaken to skeptical to horrified to confused."

"In your opinion, could an experience of the sort described induce such a state?"

"Most definitely."

In a flash, I was on my feet. "Objection! The witness is not – repeat not – a qualified member of the medical profession. Her remarks are strictly lay conjecture."

I had received my first inkling of their method of attack and felt I must nip it in the bud.

The Judge did not even attempt to disguise his annoyance.

"This Service objects to your objection on the grounds of total irrelevancy, ignorance, and inanity. The witness is eminently qualified to offer a totally authoritative opinion in any matter dealing with the psychological functioning of the human mind or as relates to the perception of emotional response. The Specimen simply still has no idea of what or who he is dealing with here. I would think he would be well apprised of the limitations of the vast, vast majority of all psychiatrists, psychologists, or psychoanalysts practicing in the world today. No one more than the Specimen should be aware of this as he felt there was no one he could turn to for adequate counsel, which in turn might have averted his suicide attempt. Or, if he did indeed seek out such collaboration, the fruits of same should be equally obvious to him. I reiterate, no one more than the Specimen should be aware of this and should be commensurately in debt to this Service as he is being privileged to the highest quality of psychotherapy available to man today, right now, in this very chamber, and for absolutely free. Is the Specimen now clear on this point?"

I simply looked away so that they would be unable to see the tears of anger, frustration and self-pity that had begun to well in my eyes.

"In other words, there is no doubt in your mind that the Specimen had indeed experienced something of a highly emotionally disturbing nature?"

"That is correct."

"What was the Specimen's reaction to the version of Anarose's life and death that you related to him, both during and afterwards?"

"During, it varied from total absorption to disbelief to shock - all this on a strictly emotional level. On an intellectual one, it was obvious to see that he comprehended everything I said, was quite taken, even fascinated by the account."

"And afterwards?"

"He expressed a degree of skepticism."

"And that is the note you parted on?"

"No. When he left he was in a state of confusion."

"Please elaborate."

"His final words to me were 'Please forgive me. I simply haven't been myself for the past few days,' which, to my mind, indicates a confused state of being. However, this Service, or the Specimen, need not take my word for this alone as, moments after he uttered this statement, he was photographed through the Kirlian process."

She reached into a manila envelope and extracted an eight-by-ten color photo. She held it up for the Judge and jury to see, then displayed to me.

"As you can see for yourself, his aura photographed distinctly overall gray flecked with black. If the Specimen would care to consult his color chart, he will see that this is the pattern that corresponds with confusion."

The Temporary Counsel for the Truth looked me directly in the eye as she said to Alethea, "In your experience, have you ever known someone to be confused by something they have already discounted as not being the truth, or at the very least, a possibility?"

"That is not possible. When you discount something from your mind, you remove the nature of its conflict and attain clarity of mind as to the issue at hand. It can, and quite often is, a false clarity of mind. Nonetheless, one sees things clearly for as far as one can see, ergo, no confusion."

"Then we may assume that the Specimen, when he left you, in a state of confusion, had still left the door open to the possibility of having experienced something of a transcendental, parapsychological nature?"

"That is the essence of it, yes."

"And, what would you determine to be the effect on one's psyche when their state of mind is straddling the void between that which is known and that which is of a metaphysical nature?"

"I cannot speak for 'someone's state of mind,' for we all vary in degrees of suggestibility, susceptibility, and openness. Specifically, as relates to the Specimen, such a state would tend to impair his powers of reasoning and judgment."

"Is it your opinion then that even while in the aforementioned state, the Specimen's basic sense of morality – right and wrong – would still be functioning on a level of clarity of perception, if and when confronted with a situation or set of circumstances that called for the actual execution of universal values?"

"Absolutely. There are certain things that are implicitly known by every rational human being, short of a lapse into temporary insanity, which is not the case here, regardless of the stress or strain of the moment. This applies even and especially to the

Specimen who possesses genius level intelligence, though, for some perverse reason, insists on negating it through his actions."

"I have one final question of the witness. You have indicated that his judgment and reasoning powers in his particular state of mind would be impaired to one degree or another. Does this include his rationale, *en toto*?"

"No. To answer your question again, peripherally, it would be affected, but the core of it would remain stable in the Specimen's case. Any act he committed of a basic nature involving the execution of universal values during the period of stated imbalance he is fully responsible to and for."

"Thank you. Does the Specimen wish to cross-examine the witness?"

In my mind, the first glimmers of insight into my real predicament were beginning to take concrete shape and form; and, just as I was about to admit defeat (or victory), I was saved, plunged back into my reality as the vision of her body floating through the night invaded my mind.In that instant, I not only thought I saw their lunacy, but my own as well, and so I rose to my feet, walked to within inches of her, took a deep breath, and began my cross.

"Do you believe 'the end justifies the means'?"

"Objection!"

"On what grounds?"

"The question is irrelevant, Your Honor. The witness is not on trial here."

"I disagree. We are all on trial every moment of our lives. The witness is instructed to answer the question."

I could hardly believe my ears. I turned my attention back to her as she replied, "I do not. Never. Only if we could perceive the end to all things, which we are incapable of doing, would that be a correct rule of thumb. Good means attain good ends, period. Therefore, the exact opposite is the correct axiom. 'The means justify the end.'"

"And, of course, the 'good' in 'good means' is relative to the Diarma Mind."

"Good is never, repeat never, relative. Good is good."

"Are you actually saying that all I have been put through since arriving on Diarma has been good for me?"

"You are alive, healthy, and learning about yourself for the first time. I would unqualifiedly say that all those things are good, not only for you, but for everyone who should come into contact with you."

"Even for Anarose?"

"You misunderstand. Everyone who should come into contact with you from this point on."

"Then the 'end does justify the means'?"

"No, because your original supposition was flawed by saying 'everything you put me through,' which should have read, 'everything I put myself through'?"

"Surely you must have researched me enough to know where my inclinations lay, my weaknesses and my strengths, yet you set the stage anyway, knowing the possible disastrous effect?"

"First off, I admit to setting no stage. Secondly, had I, indeed, set the stage, that is precisely how I would have done it. 'There is only one good definition of God: The Freedom that allows other freedoms to exist.'

----

*John Fowles, *The Arostos*

"Do I make my point? Thirdly, you were indeed researched beyond anything you could possibly imagine before allowing to take your first step on Diarma."

"There you go, comparing yourself to God again. Why does that frighten me so?"

She threw up her hands then, looked me dead in the eye and said, with a smile in her eyes. "Beats me."

The entire gallery was in uproarious laughter and the Judge had to rap the gavel several times to restore order.

"I will supply you with the same general answer as I did last time, to your trepidation: It is one thing to play God, quite another to believe you really are."

"Playing God can get people killed."

"Lots of things get people killed. Do I have to bore this Service by enumerating them?"

It was a losing battle. I'd pose a real and specific question; hers was a philosophical response. It was like arguing religion; it was arguing religion. I decided to attack another flank.

"Would the witness kindly inform this Service as to the exact time she became aware of the Specimen's existence?"

"Objection, Your Honor, on the grounds of irrelevancy. At what point the witness became aware of the Specimen's existence is not germane to the issue or charges at hand."

"Sustained. The Specimen will please direct his examination of the witness to the issues at hand; the Here and Now."

"Objection sustained? I thought this was at least the pretense of a fucking court of law."

"The Specimen is admonished on two counts: One, this is not a court of law, it is an evolutionary service conducted under the auspices of Universal Law utilizing certain basic principles of American Jurisprudence.

"Two, this Service will not tolerate the use of profanity or obscenities. Is that clear?"

"Yes, goddamit to hell, it's clear."

"The stenographer will log the Specimen's third count of contempt to be dealt with at a future time."

"Fuck you, man, make it four."

"The stenographer will please log the Specimen's fourth count of contempt. Does the Specimen wish to try for his fifth and final count, to result in his being barred from these proceedings until verdict and sentencing, if the latter is so applicable? No? Very well, proceed with your cross, as we know how difficult it is for you to bear."

And amidst the chuckles and snickers, proceed I did, right back to my table.

"The witness may step down."

She arose from the stand and did a very strange thing indeed: She smiled warmly at me for a long moment, and then the Judge announced:

"This Service will take a thirty minute recess."

The threesome disappeared down the aisle and out the door.

XXVIII

*"Jonahs, Jonahs, what are you trying to do to me?
Listen well. We are both old and experienced
enough in the Law to know that we, as jurists, are
not purveyors of Justice - we are purveyors of
expedience, the expedience required of and by the
Law to maintain the balance of social and moral
behavior. It's not a bad system, Jonahs, you know
that or else you would never have dedicated your
life to it, but, we are both aware of its limitations. It
is not complete because we are not complete."*
~ *Alma Pate to Jonahs Wainright,*
Loki and Simba, *M.S.*

"State your full name, place of residence, and occupation."

"Irena Pharasalet, Isle de Femme, Psychic, Medium, and Teller of Fortunes."

She had a multi-hued pastel aura.

"Do you know the Specimen? If so, point him out and state his name."

"Mr. Christos. I do not know his first name."

"How did you come to know the Specimen?"

"Thru a letter of introduction written by you delivered to me by him yesterday afternoon."

"What was the Specimen's motivation in contacting you?"

"He wished me to tell him the story of Anarose de Alboran."

"And did you so comply?"

"Yes, after first strongly recommending that he leave at once and not near the story."

"Why is that?"

"Because I have seen that particular look in the eye before and it is not a pleasant story"

"But he chose to stay nonetheless?"

"That is correct."

"What did that indicate to you?"

"That he wanted to hear the story very much indeed. He indicated as much in so many words to me."

"Did you discuss anything of a related nature prior to divulging the story?"

"Yes, I indicated that I…"

"Objection, Your Honor. Isn't that what's known as leading the witness?"

"Objection overruled. There are times when a witness should be led. Proceed."

"I indicated that I recognized him."

I stared intently at the aura screens to see if any change was taking place. Of course, it did not, for she too had couched her statement in the word 'Indicated,' and, of course, I only had their word that the aura preceptor really accomplished what they purported it would anyway.

"Had you ever seen the Specimen before your meeting yesterday afternoon?"

"Oh, yes. Through my gift of psychic readings. The first time was in 1566; the second, some fifty years ago."

Her aura suddenly dimmed and I rapidly checked the chart to be certain I was correct about her lying. Just then the voice of the stenographer cut in.

"The Aura Preceptor indicates a non-truthful response."

Madame Pharasalet stared at the machine in total contempt and said, "Well, perhaps it was closer to sixty years ago. At my age, the years tend to group themselves together."

"The Aura Preceptor indicates a truthful response."

And my smile became the hint of terror.

"Did you tell him this?"

"I did."

"What was his immediate reaction?"

"Astonishment that gave way to skepticism"

"Did you substantiate your claim in any physical manner?"

"Yes. Later, at a breaking point in my reading, I showed him a sketch of the man called Jean Paul, who visited me some fifty – excuse me – sixty years ago."

"And?"

"And his eyes admitted the resemblance was undeniable. He seemed stunned."

"Did you offer any other evidence?"

"Yes. I explained Acute Intermittent Porphyria to him; what it was, and how I came by the term. He became very pensive when I told him of this, as if considering it carefully."

"While you were telling your version, how would you classify his behavioral responses?"

"For the most part, I cannot answer you. I was in trance during my reading and therefore only in contact with my source. You must understand that if you were to ask me to recount the story of Anarose, right here and now, I would be unable to do it without entering into a trance state. Likewise, I have no recall of what I have said. However, at two distinct points, while not in trance, I observed him. The first time I did so, he appeared horrified; the second, he sent out utter confusion."

"And when the reading was complete, what was his overall reaction then?"

"Curiosity, strangely enough. He asked me whatever became of Edward, Anarose's first lover."

"Which indicated what to you?"

"That he had at least partially accepted the veracity of my reading."

"So, what you are saying is, at this time, he had been fully apprised of both versions of Anarose's life and death and had neither fully accepted nor rejected either one?"

"Yes, that is the truth of the matter from what I could observe."

"And what was the state he left in?"

"Confusion."

"What is it that makes you so certain he left in a confused state of mind?"

"Because he was unable to grasp the simplest thing I had said to him in our meeting, which I said to him just before he left."

"Which was?"

"That he, Edward, and Jean Paul were all the same person, as well as, most all of us to a lessor or greater degree. For one not to understand the simplicity of that, one must be extraordinarily confused."

"Thank you, Madame Pharasalet. I have no further questions. Does the Specimen wish to cross-examine the witness?"

I directed my question from the chair, keeping my eyes riveted to the opaque screen.

"Madame Pharasalet, you claim you were in total trance during your reading of the Anarose legend, yet, at one point, towards the end of the reading, I distinctly recall you stopping for a moment to light a small cigar. Do you always suffer nicotine fits while ensconced in the spirit world?"

"I wouldn't know. If you tell me I paused to indulge my habit, then I shall take your word for it."

"Come, come, Madame Pharasalet, are you telling me that you smoked that entire cigar, then methodically put it out while in a state of trance, as you put it?"

"Yes, that is the truth of it."

The not so dulcet tones from the podium suddenly cut in. "If the Specimen will closely observe the screens, he will see that a non-truth has not been indicated. Further, had the Specimen availed himself less of his sensual appetites and more of his intellectual ones, by perhaps visiting the library, as was suggested to him, both through the Pamphlet as well as by the Counsel for the Truth; and further, had he availed himself of any one of the works on parapsychological phenomena suggested by the same individual, he might well have learned that subjects given to prolonged and/or frequent transcendental states quite often perform mundane bodily functions while 'ensconced,' I believe is the word you used, in a plain of higher awareness, without either lessoning the state or being aware of the function. In short, all the aforementioned would have been readily available to the Specimen had he been a little more prone to exercising his brain as opposed to his penis. If this point is now clear to the Specimen, you may proceed."

With glaring eyes directed at him, I directed my next question to her. "Madame Pharasalet, did I not indicate to you, in so many words, as I was leaving the brothel, that I found it difficult, at best, in fact, totally discounted your reading based on your total recount of past lives?"

"Not total," came her gravelly reply.

"Excuse me, your partial recall of past lives. The so many words were these: 'It certainly has been a great performance.'"

"I recall no such statement and if I had heard that I would have undoubtedly taken it as a compliment as to the execution of my psychic powers."

The gallery as well as the bench burst into laughter. I was instantly on my feet approaching the witness box, my eyes searing the unchanged screens. I directed my disgust and outrage more at them than at her: "You are a liar, Madame. I don't give a damn what your aura preceptor indicates."

It was the stenographer once again. "The Aura Preceptor indicates a totally truthful response."

In a fit of rage I started towards the stenographer. Alethea quickly positioned herself between us and said, "I think I can clear this up. Would the Specimen please inform this Service as to his exact physical positioning when he made this alleged statement?"

"I recall it vividly. I was leaving her place of employment and as I spoke the words I was walking right by her. She was situated at her table and was no more than a foot from me when I uttered those words in a clearly audible voice."

"I see. You were standing in front of her then?"

"Well, no, as a matter of fact there was a rather large sort at the table blocking the aisle, so I was forced to go behind her chair as I was leaving. What the he…, what does that have to do with anything anyway?"

Immediately, I knew the answer before she responded.

"That answers it then. Madame Pharasalet has been deaf since birth. She communicates through lip-reading and her unquestionable ability to perceive emotional behavior."

"Well, it's certainly refreshing to know that justice is rendered by the Karmic Scales every once in a while, and while Madame Pharasalet has my deepest sympathy, it hardly alters the point. That was my exit line. Does that sound like a manifestation of a state of confusion to you? I mean that is the whole thrust of your attack, isn't it? Show that the Specimen never fully discounted either possibility and he's fully liable for his acts. Isn't that right, Alethea? Because if I had discounted your little Anarose story, I can only be guilty of animal lust, but not culpable for the consequences of her act; am not guilty of premeditated… Oh, my God! This is total insanity! That woman is dead! What are we talking about? What am I doing here? That girl is dead and I'm taking part in some sort of mock trial! Jesus!"

I slumped to my knees until the tears had run their course, then rose and walked back to my chair.

It was the judge who broke the silence. "The Specimen is admonished on a single count: He – we – are not engaged in a mock anything here. This is an…"

"YES, YES, I KNOW. THIS IS AN EVOLUTIONARY SERVICE, CONVENED UNDER THE AUSPICES OF UNIVERSAL LAW FOR THE SOLE PURPOSE… BLAH… BLAH… BLAH… BLAH… BLAH… BLAH…"

I saw the Judge conferring with both Ms. Perry and Alethea. He let out a long sigh before addressing me.

"This Service is inclined not to reprimand the Specimen, not cite an additional contempt count due to his outburst as it is understood that the emotional content of the past few moments overwhelmed his good judgment. Counsel for the Truth will now proceed with her response to the Specimen's query, 'Does that sound like a manifestation of a state of confusion to you?'"

"It does not, which is not to say that it comes from, or could be considered, in any form or fashion, to be a realm inspired by true clarity of mind. Does the Specimen have any further questions of the witness?"

The sons-a-bitches were covered. I had to hand it to them, and so I simply said, "No."

"The Truth rests its case as to Specification Two: The premeditated murder of Anarose de Alboran. It does, however, wish to make a closing statement as to this specification."

"Proceed."

"The Truth believes that whether or not the Specimen believed either version of the Life and Death of Anarose in its entirety is irrelevant. It further contends that it has proven beyond any reasonable doubt, beyond a shadow of a doubt that he did believe to both a mentally and emotionally influencing extent, both versions up to and including the moment the deceased jumped from the Specimen's balcony. It yet further contends the Specimen was made reasonably aware of the consequences of gratifying his lust, by virtue of having been privileged to hear both versions of her life and death, as well as having substantial contact with the deceased, up to and including the night, the very moment of her untimely death: THAT, the Specimen blatantly disregarded these consequences and in the pursuit of the gratification of his own lust, he did, in the heat of passion make physical love to the deceased even though she had amply, convincingly exhibited her express wishes not to do so, both prior to and during the act itself; that ultimately the Specimen's lust annihilated both his compassion and her resolve, as well as the deceased herself."

Wet-eyed and furious, I knocked my chair to the floor as I shot from my seat. "It was by mutual consent. I loved her."

"You have absolutely no conception whatsoever of the meaning of that word. We wished to spare you any unnecessary pain, but if you insist on following this tack, we can present a tape recording of last evening and I assure you that nowhere in it does the word 'love' exist."

"You rotten, vile scum. Did you also make a movie of it?"

"The Specimen has just accumulated his fifth and final contempt count. The stenographer will please log. The bailiff will stand ready to eject the Specimen from this Service immediately after I have conferred with the Counsel for the Truth."

They spoke in hushed whispers for perhaps twenty seconds.

"It has been decided that it would serve no good purpose to bar you from the remainder of these proceedings as they are rapidly coming to a close. In lieu thereof, you shall be gagged at the mouth." I immediately felt the gag go into place – I did not struggle. "If you further persist in a contemptuous manner by displaying any violent gestures, you will be bound to your chair."

At this, I immediately placed both hands under the table edge and sent it careening across the docket, barely missing Alethea.

I felt the rope being wrapped around my chest, arms, and legs. The table was righted and resituated just out of bodily reach.

"The gag will be removed, but not the bindings, at the end of the Truth's final closing statement, so that you may make one of your own if you so desire. If you opt thus, all restrictions as to the use of profanity and obscenity will be lifted for the duration of your statement. Counsel for the Truth will now proceed."

She walked across the docket to the stenographer, received a manila envelope and returned to situate herself directly in front of me. She opened the clasp and withdrew the photograph.

"Would you care to see the color of your aura just prior and during the act of *in flagrante delicto*?"

She slammed it down on the table in front of me. It was, of course, muddy red, the pattern for Lust.

"I assure the Specimen, the color pattern for love is not muddy red. Now, let's examine those two statements you so glibly made a few minutes ago. 'It was by mutual consent. I loved her.'"

She returned to her table and pressed the button on the tape recorder.

"No, no, I beg of you! No!"

"Tell me, does that indicate mutual consent to you? And a few moments after that, 'Anarose, God help me, I want you so.'

"'WANT you so,' are your words, WANT, as in crave, desire, lust for; not 'LOVE you so,' as in feel an ultimate connection to, cherish, want to protect, honor, and share with. And only moments after that, 'can't you understand? I'm already spoken for. It will not be all right. I did not come here for this. I came here to... Please, Edward, I beg of you... No...'

"I suppose the Specimen was so filled with Love that he didn't even hear the 'Edward.' Need I continue? The Truth reiterates: with premeditation, being made reasonably aware of the potential consequences of his acts, and disregarding same in the pursuit of his Lust, the Specimen did directly bring about the death of one Anarose de Alboran, to wit, murdered her.

"The Truth rests as to Specification Two."

"Does the Specimen wish to make a closing statement as to this Specification?"

I nodded negatively.

"Very well. Counsel for the Truth will sum up."

"The Truth feels it has proven beyond any reasonable doubt, beyond a shadow of a doubt, that the Specimen is guilty of both specifications to the charge of Insufficient Humanity. It further recommends that should the Specimen be found guilty as charged to either or both specifications, that this Service render a most fair and merciful sentence.

"The case of ALL THAT IS IMPLICITLY KNOWN TO BE CORRECT BY EVERY RATIONAL HUMAN BEING, THE TRUTH, versus ALEXANDER CHRISTOS, THE SPECIMEN, rests."

She turned on her heel towards the podium. She had resumed her place to the Judge's left before he asked, "Does the Specimen wish to present a defense, or wish to take the stand in his own defense?"

I remained motionless.

"Does the Specimen wish to make a final closing statement?"

Again I gave them nothing.

"Very well. This Service reiterates, if the Specimen is found guilty as charged, it is its sworn duty to impose a fair and merciful sentence specifically arrived upon for the sole purpose of accelerating the Specimen's evolution and future enlightenment.

As stipulated earlier, this is not, repeat not, a punitive court of law."

He turned to the jury and continued.

"You have heard the charges and evidence. It is understood that your verdict must coincide on each specification. Does the jury wish to retire to deliberate a verdict?"

They shook their heads in negative unison. "Very well. You will indicate your decision by the traditional thumbs up or thumbs down gesture. As to Specification One, Guilty or Not Guilty?"

Two thumbs poised downwards.

"As to Specification Two, Guilty or Not Guilty?"

The thumbs did not change position.

"Alexander Christos, you have been found to be guilty as charged to both specifications to the charge. The presiding members of this Service will now retire to deliberate a just and merciful sentence."

Suddenly, the gag was removed from my mouth, but not so the rope.

"But first, the Report Card."

"THE WHAT?!"

My adrenalin flow had sent me to the floor.

"Leave him be."

Alethea rose and walked to where I lay, five-by-seven card in hand. She addressed the gallery.

"The Specimen was enrolled in two of the five courses we offer here on Diarma.

"PENETRATION: The practice of the consideration of all possibilities: F for Failed.

"COMMUNICATION: Emphasis on the perception of universal emotional behavior as a language unto itself: F for Failed.

"CONDUCT: Unbecoming.

"DEPORTMENT: Degrading.

"ATTENDANCE RECORD: Physically and emotionally perennially present; intellectually absent; spiritually bankrupt.

"GENERAL REMARKS: Student is highly intelligent but allows his emotional responses and sensual appetites to subjugate both his good judgment and idealistic aspirations.

"RECOMMENDATIONS: Termination of all study. Not to be allowed to further matriculate."

I watched them disappear down the aisle and out the door in single file just long enough to re-enter the room and walk back to their places behind the podium. The judge massaged the bridge of his nose, raising his glasses slightly upwards as he said,

"Does the Specimen wish to offer a statement in mitigation, or extenuation, before sentence is passed?"

I shook my head, "No."

"Very well. Unbind the Specimen. Rise for sentencing."

I rubbed the circulation back into my arms but had no intention of rising for their *tour de force* finale. Strong arms anticipated me, yanking me to my feet.

"Alexander Christos, it is felt, taking into consideration all things, to wit: The undeniable pattern of consistent self-retardation that is so firmly entrenched and of a self-perpetuating nature, that your future evolution and enlightenment would best be served by denying you the physical opportunity of accumulating more negative Karma, Causes and Effects, within this life span. Further, it is regrettably implied by this same self-serving pattern that you would continue to contribute to the retardation of your fellow human beings' evolution, as you are obviously of superior biological endowment but irresponsibly so.

"THEREFORE, the only fair, merciful, and realistic sentence applicable is one through which you can no longer subsist thus. You are hereby sentenced to death."

My first reaction was shock, but then the logic of the pronouncement caused me to want to laugh. All my study certainly was being "terminated," and I was definitely not being allowed to "further matriculate." I suddenly recalled a phrase in the Pamphlet that had intrigued me when I had first read it. I realized now that I should have viewed it as a warning: "Compassion has many faces." I was about to protest when I felt myself being jerked out of my chair and dragged towards the jury box. They halted me at a position almost directly beneath it. The stenographer walked to the forward portion of the podium, opened a panel, and raised a lever. The sound of machination filled the room as the velvet vulture-like structure descended to floor level. A button was pushed and the red glow streaming from the overhead spots became the flaw revealing phosphorescence of modern offices.

"The jury will please rise and identify themselves to the Specimen."

The first juror removed his hood and I looked into the expressionless face of a man who was made up to bear a striking resemblance to myself, with the exception that his face was the face of death; a blood encrusted bullet hole was situated in his right temple.

My heart beat a little faster as I strained to look at the other juror, but then I realized it would be someone made up to look like her. The man with the bullet hole suddenly jerked off her hood and I saw the Anarose mannequin staring directly at me with blank eyes. A tear of blood was painted on each cheek. My entire body wretched as I felt the vomit rise.

I was barely aware of the thunderous applause of the gallery. Someone wiped my mouth and nose as I felt the grasp on my arms tighten and was led up the aisle between the rows of pews. They halted me briefly as a woman, whom at first I did not recognize without make up, rose from her aisle seat and walked directly to me. Millicent Rand, travel agent extraordinaire, looked me directly in the eyes as she pinned the black rose on my tunic. I was immediately shoved forward and out the door, up a flight of stairs, and through a trap door to the very pinnacle of the structure, upon which rested a helicopter and fear, real fear for the first time since the Service had begun. It rampaged my mind as I realized they were going to execute me in the same manner I had executed Anarose.

Suddenly, the helicopter's engines ignited and raised itself from the surface heading off to the northeast. It was then that I saw it, for it had been hidden from view by the craft, a small octagonal glass booth with one point of entry. Alethea and the Judge suddenly appeared and unlocked the door. I was unceremoniously marched to and through it.

A deafening version of Igor Stravinsky's "The Rite of Spring" filled the chamber. I put my hands to my ears as I read the sign on the baseboard: "The gas that will be released is of a highly toxic nature and will bring near instantaneous, totally painless death. The Specimen is advised to take three (3) deep breaths from time of first realization of emission."

When I looked up the entire booth was surrounded by the spectators. Their faces were devoid of any emotion whatsoever as they all raised their hands and flung their roses at me in perfect unison, turned, and walked away. I was now completely alone. It was happening so fast that I could focus neither my mental nor emotional bearings. In what soon became obvious was a moot attempt, I banged ferociously on the glass panel. I did not even comprehend in the slightest the paradox that existed in this moment of pre-death as compared to my resignation at the beach only weeks before. I was calculating how long I could hold my breath (and at the same time cursing my cigarette habit of the past twenty years) when I heard the first hisssss, ingenuously emitted at the precise moment of andante pianissimo in that classic work. I dared not let out my breath. I felt as though my lungs were about to burst. I held out for as long as I thought humanly possible and then held out some more, until I felt the lightheadedness that precedes fainting. Finally, I exhaled being ever so careful not to gulp a first deep breath. Three breaths, the sign had said. I took my first as shallowly as I could and immediately became aware of the sweet, pungent aroma.

I felt a slight drowsiness come over me and shook my head to clear it, and just as I was thinking "they really are going to kill me," a figure appeared through the glass directly in front of me, no more than inches away. It was a third juror, still hooded, hands clasped behind the back. The image was still distinct but I felt certain it would blur at any moment. I dared not let out my breath as I watched the gloved hand slowly unravel the chord at the base of the hood. I strained my eyes until I thought they would pop. I exhaled and took my second breath - too much, damn it! Again, the wave of drowsiness but the figure still remained in full focus. The hood was lifted with both hands and simultaneously the music stopped dead.

The shock of what I saw caused me to exhale. The image began to blur as I felt consciousness leaving me, but not before I gazed into deep violet eyes; not before my mind registered her reaching behind her ear, removing the rose and flinging it at me.

My motor reflexes fought desperately to form her name …
A… N… A…

I only barely heard her pose the question a moment before I slumped to the padded floor.

"Are you the Seventh Man?"

XXIX

*"For all we know, this could be death and
what we have labeled death, life."
~ The Diarma Mind*

I came to an indiscernible state of undeniable consciousness, but had no idea as to what I perceived with – my eyes, I imagined, for there was no other sensation available to me whatsoever. I only knew I was not dreaming.

Suddenly, I perceived motion – a light floating sensation, but had no conception of what it was that was floating. Two gigantic stars entered my field of seemingly unlimited vision. I felt that if I had hands I would reach out and touch them. Their glow was blinding me. The cosmorama slowly expanded to take in the full moon. I was on it and the first germ of realization that I was an entity within Infinity took seed in what I assumed to be my mind. Ever so slowly, It revealed more of Itself to me as I was plunged into total darkness, but I felt I was most definitely a part of that darkness.

Without warning, I was encased in a brilliant golden beam that conically streamed into eternity. I could actually look up its interior. I felt completely serene; fully uplifted. From its highest point of visual perception, a barely discernible speck began to descend its interior. It was still so distant I could not make out its shape or form. Its rate of descent accelerated and the image came at me with incredible speed and force as it tumbled down the avenue of Light.

It was almost upon me now, getting closer and closer now, and then all at once the image was distinct – it was myself, sitting in the sand, my right hand holding a gun to my temple, and just as it began to disappear with the entrance of yet another image beginning to tumble from the very top of the beam once again, a huge Number 1 grew outwards from the center of the image until its size obliterated everything else.

The same image came at me again and again – Numbers 2, 3, 4, and 5. Number 6 is just making its descent now. It is the identical image except that it appears in extreme close-up proportions - only my trigger finger and a section of my temple are visible, and then, in the fraction of an instant, the finger depressed and I realized yet another sensory organ was intact as the excruciatingly loud explosion filled everything. It was really more of an implosion as it seemed to be coming from within what I assumed to be my head.Simultaneously, the image changed to vivid running red and scattering bone matter. It only lasted a very few seconds before everything went out.

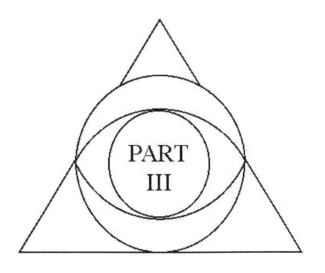

THE SEVENTH MAN

*"We, as a species, are poised
Interregnum."*
        ~ The Diarma Mind

* *

XXX

* *

"Get the doctor, quick! He's coming around!"

The orderly rushed from the room and down the hall. She leaned over me and took my pulse just as my brain began to register my environment. Blaringly, glaring white. Quickly, I shut my eyes to escape the excruciating brightness. Little by little, ever so slowly, I opened them. I brought my hand to my forehead using it as a shield, discovering in the process that I did indeed possess limbs. Again, the glare forced me to shut them. The sound of fast-paced footsteps – a door swinging open – an excited voice.

"I'll take over from here. Notify Dr. Guillerman at once. He should be out of surgery now."

There was the clacking of departing footsteps – the door swinging open once again – a soft, soothing professional voice.

"Mr. Christos. Mr. Christos, can you hear me? Just nod your head. My name is Dr. Naismith. I'm the chief resident here. Now, try to open your eyes, very slowly."

He indicated for the orderly to adjust the rheostat and the room's light dimmed appreciably.

"That's fine. Now, Mr. Christos… you're going to be just fine. Nod your head if you can see… wonderful! Now, can you speak? Try to say your name… come on, now. You do know your name, don't you?"

I stared into the deeply lined, ruddy complexioned face of the sixtyish man. My eyes scanned the room, and as I realized my whereabouts, I tried to sit upright but the man's firm grasp eased me gently back.

"Oh, not so fast, Mr. Christos. You've had quite a time of it… take it easy… one thing at a time. Now, tell me your name."

It came out in a whisper.

"Alexander Christos."

I heard the doctor sigh with relief. He turned to the approach of the other doctor who had just entered the room, his back to me, studying a chart, and said, "Respiration normal. No damage to the mesencephalon."

He turned back to me. "What was the last thing you remember, Mr. Christos?"

My eyes were adjusted fully to the light now and though I felt my strength returning, I sensed the overall weakness of my condition. When I replied, my voice had gained timbre.

"I was being executed."

Dr. Naismith turned to his colleague and registered his surprise. The other doctor, still out of view, began to question me in low tones. "You mean on the beach where you tried to 'execute' yourself?"

I felt the panic start to rise and instinctively tried to raise myself to a sitting position. Once again, I was held down.

"On the beach? No, not on the beach, in the gas chamber on Diarma."

Dr. Naismith shook his head and walked to the corner of the room to confer with the other man. They spoke in hushed whispers and I could only catch snatches of the conversation.

"… not a complete success, Brad… could be partial… to the medulla."

"Not necessarily… be nothing more than a… blocking device… man's … a time of it… delusions… unusual in his case… work up look?"

"All vital signs strong, heart excellent… reflexes good… breakdown of DNA whatsoever… been able to establish."

The senior man remained in place somewhat hidden by Dr. Naismith and indicated for him to continue with the questioning:

"Mr. Christos, do you have any idea how long you have been here?"

"Been where? Where the hell am I?"

"You are in a private hospital in Pembroke, on England's southwest coast. Do you have any remembrance at all of being on a beach in Long Island, New York, about two months ago?"

"Two months ago! It was more like three weeks ago... yes, of course I remember. I tried to kill myself... but it was less than a month ago."

The two men exchanged glances and Dr. Naismith went on.

"You were almost successful, you know. You came within a centimeter of accomplishing it."

I was in a sitting position now. "What is this shit? The gun was empty! What the hell are you trying to pull here?"

And then my eyes suddenly went askance as my head jerked back involuntarily from some unseen force. I seemed to have momentarily entered into a very brief, but powerful, trance-like state at the reference to my shooting myself. Dr. Naismith acknowledged the sign from the corner of the room.

"That's enough for today, Mr. Christos. We'll come by tomorrow when you're stronger. Right now, just rest. It's a miracle you're still alive."

"Just a goddamn minute..."

I threw back the covers. An orderly appeared out of nowhere and restrained me as Dr. Naismith prepared the syringe.

"Mr. Christos, you must not, repeat not, exert yourself in any way – physically, emotionally, or mentally – in your weakened condition. You don't seem to be able to grasp just how close you came to dying. You've been through three neurological operations in the past six weeks, during which time you have been completely comatose. You must allow yourself some time."

I just stared at the man as he rolled up my sleeve and dabbed the underside of my elbow with alcohol.

"Are you telling me I shot myself?"

Immediately, my head jerked back involuntarily once again.

"Yes, that is precisely what happened... now, don't be alarmed. In cases such as these it is expected that one should block the entire incident. In good time, it will most likely all come back to you, either sequentially, or in bits and pieces. The operations were successful. There is no – repeat, no brain damage."

I watched the little spurt of fluid shoot from the upraised syringe. In my heart, I knew they were lying to me. I could not deny the odd reaction I had experienced to both references to me shooting myself. Nor could I deny the sound and sensation of an explosion in my head that had jerked it back with such strange force; to say nothing of the immediate simultaneous vivid vision that flashed in my mind: spurting, gushing blood and scattering bone fragments. I looked up into the kindly face as I asked,

"How did I get here?"

But the question wasn't earnestly put forth. I was only trying to buy time to figure out some way of knocking the syringe from the man's hand. Of course, it would be a futile gesture, but I wanted them to know that I didn't buy it for a moment. The voice from the other side of the room suddenly commanded:

"That's enough for today, Dr. Naismith. Sedate the patient."

He left.

There was something familiar about that voice, English accent or no.

"Goddammit, how did I get here?" I yelled the instant before I felt the prick of the needle.

"How are you feeling today, Mr. Christos? Are you ready for your first solid meal in over two months?"

The nurse raised my bed before placing the tray across my lap.

I did not answer her as I stroked the growth on my face. "Get me a mirror."

She seemed totally unoffended by my curtness and immediately went to the bathroom and produced a small mirror. I stared at my face, my bandaged head, and tried to dip into my past some six years to recollect how long it had taken me to raise a full beard. Three weeks to a month, I thought. My face looked haggard. I not only felt older, but looked it as well. Or so I thought. Wasn't that more gray at the temples, and my beard was almost white.

Dr. Naismith appeared in the doorway, his face beaming as he approached the bed. He said, "My, my, you look great today, Mr. Christos. Much better than three days ago. We'll have those bandages off in no time."

"I've been out for three days?"

"We decided it was better not to have you mucking about until the scars had formed. Would you like a shave?"

"No, I would not like a shave. I would like some answers. Now."

"Now, now, then, Mr. Christos, just take it nice and slow. Well, you're certainly recovering quickly... such determination! Good show! Very good show!"

"Forget the good show, Doctor. Just tell me how I got here. And who's that other doctor who was here before?"

"That is the man - correction, the medical genius – who saved your life when everything pointed to the fact that it was very simply lost! If not physically, then at least in every other respect. Were it not for his revolutionary surgical procedure, you would be either dead or living dead, a vegetable, if you'll excuse the expression."

"Oh, please don't stop now, Doctor, It is just getting interesting."

Dr. Naismith turned to the nurse, totally ignoring the innuendo. "Set up the skull series. Mr. Christos seems quite strong enough to explain things to now.

"Mr. Christos, on August the Fifth, you shot yourself once through the head, or rather, into the head just above the right temple. You were discovered, still alive, but just barely.

"Ah, yes, thank you, Nurse, light up the panels and that will be all. Pardon the interruptions, now, where was I? Oh, yes, you were found barely alive by a man who happened to be walking the same stretch of beach and heard the shot. You owe your life to that man Anyway, he immediately got you to the local hospital in Southampton, but they had neither the facilities nor staff to perform the operation to remove the bullet without placing your life in even greater peril, due to the location of the slug. You were flown by helicopter, that very night, to Mount Sinai Hospital in New York City, where a team of top neurologists diagnosed your condition. It goes without saying that the prognosis looked bleak at best."

"Tell me, Dr. Naismith, does Mount Sinai have a helicopter pad, by chance?"

It was a question sincerely put forth.

"I really don't know, why do you ask?"

"Oh, nothing. Please continue."

He walked to the phosphorescent panels that illumined the x-rays and began. "The bullet lodged here, right above the mesencephalon, or hindbrain, and imbedded itself here, in this section of cranial tissue. Fortunately for you, it was of small caliber and low velocity. Also, fortunately for you, you have an extremely firm cranium. Hard headed, in other words. This x-ray shows the bullet still lodged. One centimeter this way and you would have died instantaneously. Two millimeters this way and it would have penetrated the medulla and this would have resulted in permanent quadriplegia – total paralysis from the neck down. Now, the surgeons at Mount Sinai saw the problem at once – how to remove the bullet without damaging the brain tissue surrounding those two most critical areas. It simply could not be accomplished through normal surgical procedures.

"Dr. Perle, one of the examining doctors, knew of Dr. Guillerman's experimental work in localized cryogenics, which is simply the method of freezing the tissue around the wounded area with liquid nitrogen, then heating this same area, directly circumventing the bullet. I am sure you are well aware, cold or freezing causes contraction; heat, expansion. The premise was to allow the bullet to release itself through heating the frozen tissue. Now, freezing the tissue causes no damage for short periods of time. Once the tissue is frozen, then heat and suction were applied. The suction guided the outward path of the bullet as opposed to allowing it to move yet deeper, which would have resulted in paraplegia. The cryosurgery was performed three times over a five-week period with absolutely no surgical cutting other than that of non-critical tissue and bone essential in getting to the wounded area. We utilized three operations because we did not want to risk freezing the tissue for too long a period of time at one stint. With each operation, the bullet was moved outwards a little more until the final operation, when it protruded enough to remove with forceps. Do you follow me?"

I just stared at him.

"All right, now, here is the x-ray of your skull taken last week. Note the tissue appears normal and the bullet has been removed. No brain damage whatsoever. As a matter of fact, within a very short time, other than for the scar left by the surface incision, an x-ray would be hard pressed to reveal that you had even had a bullet lodged in your skull at all. Thanks to the miracle of Cryosurgery – and, of course, Dr. Guillerman's surgical genius…"

"I'll bet…" I said somewhat under my breath, yet audible to the good doctor. At this, he simply checked his watch and said,

"I'm due in surgery in a few minutes. You just take it easy, Mr. Christos. I overheard Dr. Guillerman say the bandages come off tomorrow, which means you'll be out of here in no time at all. You will stay away from beaches at night, won't you, sir?"

But I hadn't heard him. Something had clicked when Dr. Naismith checked his watch and so as soon as he left I rang the nurse, who arrived within seconds, and asked, "Are all of my personal effects in the room?"

"Yes, sir. Everything you were wearing or had with you at the time you were discovered is either in the closet or the drawer next to your bed. Can I get something for you?"

"No… no, thank you. I'm feeling a bit tired. I'll just grab a nap."

"Very good, sir. If you need me, just ring. Would you like me to wake you for lunch?"

"Yes, please do."

As soon as I could no longer hear her footsteps in the hallway, I checked the drawer and rummaged through my things. It wasn't there. It couldn't have been, for it had been smashed on the rocks during my prolonged raft ride to Diarma.

Conversely, had I actually been discovered on the beach and all my things had accompanied me… They had finally made a slip – a simple thing they had no way of knowing about for if they had, they would have quite easily substituted a replica.

I tried to get out of bed and almost fell flat on my face. A lousy watch. But it wasn't just a lousy watch. It was my sanity. I wanted to laugh out loud, loud enough for Alethea and the Judge to hear me clear to the shore of the Mediterranean. But not Anarose. Oh, no, not Anarose. I didn't want her to hear me laughing. She was going to hear something quite other than laughter from me.

I braced myself with both hands on the bed. I was weak but I sensed it was the drain that comes from remaining immobile for too long, combined with the many drugs they undoubtedly subjected my system to. How long had they kept me flat on my back, anyway? Three weeks? Those bastards. What was the date? I looked around the room for a calendar but couldn't find one.

Cautiously, using the nightstand for support, I steadied myself and took my first steps. I halted momentarily to allow the dizziness to pass and then steered myself towards the door. I opened it and stared down the antiseptic hallway. Nothing. No one in sight.

I backed into the room, closing the door behind me, and walked quickly, for me, to the bathroom and stared into the cabinet mirror. The trace of a smile as I gingerly, then carelessly unraveled the gauze, and then self-satisfaction instantly contorted to terror as my fingers traced the puffy red circular scar gracing my right temple. Then no expression at all as my fingers raised a few inches and ran along the shorn hair housing a second sign of incision about an inch and a half long running vertically up the right side of my head.

It wasn't so much that I was now convinced that I had indeed shot myself, for I was not, that brought on the waves of nausea, but rather the realization that there were no bounds to their godgame… had they actually performed surgery on me solely to lend credence to their story?

Suddenly, I heard the door opening. Wordlessly the nurse and orderly guided me back to my bed. I watched the opaque liquid fill the syringe and then I jerked violently, sending the nurse sprawling while at the same time escaping the orderly's grasp. I ran for the door and was grabbed just as I reached it. I felt the needle enter my arm as I stared into the intense face of the stethoscoped man standing a few feet from me in the corridor. He just now rubbed his eyes under the photo-gray glasses and directed an order to the nurse.

"Don't bother replacing the bandage. It was coming off later today anyway."

He turned and walked away.

I'm being laid down now, tucked in now, feeling very, very sleepy, and just barely holding onto the threads of consciousness. My mind is keenly focused on the vestiges of the man who has just left, on his hair, the white, white hair. But he looked younger. The beard was gone, but the voice was a dead giveaway. The Judge apparently had more than one calling. And just before the cobwebs entrapped me, I realized why the Judge had seemed vaguely familiar to me when I had first seen him enter the courtroom. The Judge, the man in the photograph on Alethea's desk, and the "surgical genius" Dr. Guillerman, were one and the same: Alethea's dead husband felled by a hit and run assassin.

Perhaps it was the drug. Perhaps it was the experience, all the experiences of the past few weeks. Perhaps it was a combination of the two, but as I fell victim to the anesthesia, I was convinced of but one thing: An actual place called Hell did, indeed, exist. I maintained residence there.

XXXII

I awoke to the same image.

"How are you feeling today, Mr. Christos?"

I did not answer but rather continued to study the Judge's concerned expression.

"We haven't been formally introduced. My name is Dr. Guillerman. I performed the surgery. Would you like me to raise the bed?"

I indicated that I would as Dr. Guillerman went on with his inspection of the sutures.

"Depending on your state of mind, you should be able to leave late today or tomorrow. You have made a remarkable recovery. Do you feel any pain here? How about here? And here? Excellent."

"Tell me, Dr. Guillerman, is Anarose my nurse, and Alethea perhaps the anesthesiologist?"

Dr. Guillerman looked at me intently, raised the lid of my right eye and shone a light into it. In a very soft voice he queried, "Who are Anarose and Alethea, Mr. Christos?"

"Oh, I see. You don't know. Come, come, 'your Honor.' You know, you cut quite a striking figure in a white beard. I suppose you never heard of Diarma, either?"

"No, I can't say that I have. Is Diarma a what or a who?"

"Oh, it's a 'what.' God knows what, but definitely a 'what'!"

"Tell me about Diarma and Anarose and Andrea."

"Alethea, not Andrea. How very clever of you, Doctor. And I'm certain you know much more about it and them than I ever will."

Dr. Guillerman stepped back and seated himself on the edge of the bed.

"You called me 'your Honor.' What did that mean?"

"Cut the shit. You know goddamn well what I'm talking about."

"I'm afraid I don't, Mr. Christos. My contact with you has been limited to a doctor-patient relationship for the past five and one half weeks in which you were comatose."

"For your information, 'Doctor,' for the past three weeks, I have been on an island in the Mediterranean. But, of course, that's hardly news to you. An island called Diarma that even De Sade, in his wildest state of degeneracy, would have been incapable of conceiving. An island that you and your wife Alethea conceived and oversee in the spirit of some perverse God game."

"I see. And you recognize me from this island. Is that what you are saying?"

It had been uttered in the perfectly executed manner of the slightly patronizing, yet ever so concerned physician.

"Yes, goddammit to hell, that is exactly what I am saying. Now, I want out of here, NOW!"

"Mr. Christos, I'm afraid I was a bit premature in indicating your release date. In your present condition, until we have been able to ascertain the cause of your delusions, I'm afraid you will have to remain our guest for a little while longer. There is, of course, a quite plausible, completely innocent, if not obvious, explanation to your hallucinations. No, no, please wait. Hear me out and then you may decide for yourself. I stated that you had been completely comatose for the past few weeks, which, sir, you have. This is not to say that you did not, several times, open your eyes, achieve a self-conscious state for a few seconds. Now, during these periods, brief and as infrequent as I assure you they were, your brain would have registered your immediate environment. It is quite possible that you saw me, as well as others of my staff, even heard us speak or address each other at periodic points during the stipulated time frame.

"It is also quite possible that these images were then incorporated into whatever consciousness of a dreamlike quality you were experiencing at the time. As I was constantly with you during this time, it is only natural that my impression upon you would register strongly on your subconscious. Dreams, as I'm sure you're aware, have a way of taking on distortions, subtle ones, which could account for an alteration of my appearance, such as a beard.

"I repeat, people in comas hallucinate, dream, and fantasize, much in the manner of a prolonged sleep state, which isn't to say that having recall in such detail is usual, it is not, but hardly unheard of. Now, considering the conditions under which you came to us, which were traumatic to say the least, whatever form, thread, or plot these fantasies took would likely as not, and probably more so, be connected in some manner to your attempted suicide. If you could perhaps describe some of the characters in your 'dream,' maybe I could match them up for you with some of our staff who have had close contact with you. The names Anarose and Alethea happen to be quite close to the names of two of my staff, by the way: Anthea and Roseanne. One final thing, Mr. Christos, it's nothing to worry about, I assure you, once you recognize it for what it is, that is. This sort of thing is simply a manner by which the brain continues to function when most other bodily functions are not - consciously not, that is."

I began to laugh, but even to myself it had the slightly hollow ring of "forced." That same quality carried over to my vocal chords.

"Do you really expect me to believe that everything that has happened to me over the past few weeks, and especially the period from August Fifth to the First of September, was nothing more than a dream?"

"Mr. Christos, obviously I do not, cannot know the specifics of what you are referring to. All I can tell you is that you have been under my constant care since the morning of August Six. There is simply no other explanation... That's not correct – there is one other, but I'm not qualified to broach it; however, I'll have our resident psychiatrist look in on you and you can discuss it with her. Her name is Anthea, by the way."

I avoided his glance. My hand automatically had gone to the knob on the nightstand drawer where my watch wasn't. Dr. Guillerman interrupted my thoughts: "Is what I said beginning to sink in, Mr. Christos?"

"You get the hell out of here now." No emotion, simply cold, flat tones of white anger.

He rose, smiled gently at me and headed for the door.

"Wait… wait a minute. Is there a girl on your staff, twenty-five to twenty-eight, dark hair, very, very beautiful… violet eyes?"

He turned to look at me, mulled something over for a moment and then smiled broadly. "Now that's much better. With one exception, you have just described Roseanne, my anesthesiologist, to perfection. She has blue eyes, however, but bearing in mind the subtle distortions of dreams. It so happens that Roseanne suffers from light sensitive eyes and when in the operating theater, with its bright lights, always wears magenta lens glasses, and we all know what happens when you mix red and blue together."

"Purple or violet."

He actually beamed at me. Quelling the feeling in the pit of my stomach, I finally spoke, "Tell me, was there any point in the past six weeks where I was closer to death than at any other time?"

"Why, yes, as a matter of fact, there was. It was during the final stages of the last operation. Some tissue around the hindbrain - that governs respiration - became disturbed during cryosurgery. Why do you ask?"

"In other words, if I had any recollection of that moment, it might have been as if I were choking, gasping for air, suffocating?"

"Precisely. If you had any recollection. Do you?"

"I don't know…"

But I did know. Timing and situation-wise, it fit the gas chamber sequence perfectly. Suddenly, I was plunged back into uncertainty.

"The pieces starting to fall back into place? Excellent. Perhaps you will be able to leave soon. I promise you, after a few weeks back in circulation, everything will take on its proper perspective for you, Mr. Christos."

I searched his eyes for any sign whatsoever of double-meaning. I could find none.

"You get some rest now. I'll ask Dr. Guilestremes to look in on you a little later. She's the resident psychiatrist I was telling you about."

He started to leave.

"Uh, Doctor... Roseanne, the anesthesiologist... I'd like to see her."

"Oh, I am sorry, Mr. Christos. She's not permanent staff here. Our regular man was on vacation, so I had her imported from London. She returned after the final operation. I'll tell you what I can do. I'll get her address for you but you won't be able to contact her for a while, as she indicated she was taking a holiday to America... somewhere in the Midwest, I believe, to visit her sister. I really have to go now."

We both raised our heads to the sound of the rotary blade engines getting closer and closer.

"That's my ride to London now. I'm due at a conference. Wonderful things, these helicopters, don't you think? Oh, by the way. If Dr. Guilestremes gives her approval, you can leave tonight. As I won't be back, I just wanted you to know there will be no bill, as Cryosurgery is still in the experimental stages and the law prohibits charging a fee. If I were you, I would consider yourself a very lucky guinea pig...

"And one other thing. Should you be inclined to enact a repeat performance of that fateful night, I strongly suggest that rather than placing the barrel to your temple, place it inside your mouth, angled upwards towards your nose. Then, when you pull the trigger, the bullet will pass immediately through your brain, blowing off the top of your head, causing near instantaneous death."

He was out the door before I could reply, leaving me to the depths of my own vacillations.

Was it possible? I started looking for other obvious connections, and the one I uncovered moments later had simplicity of revelation about it that chilled me to the bone: Island was the key word. I had, after all, some weeks prior to that night on the beach, been intently investigating island areas. Was it possible that Diarma had simply been a Utopian extension of that which I had been unable to physically find?

But Diarma proved to be no Utopia. And the watch, that was physical evidence and I clung to it with every fiber of my being.

XXXIII

I had opened the Venetian blinds some twenty minutes before and had just stood there staring at it. I had gone back to my bed and laid on it to find out if it was visible from that prone position. It was not.

I then raised the bed and laid back down on it. From this perspective, its upper half was clearly visible. I wondered why, in an unconscious state, they would have laid me thus - possibly for intravenous feeding, I conjectured. I had gone back to the window, my eyes transfixed on it, when I heard the door open. I maintained my gaze of the lighthouse as another familiar voice greeted me.

"Hello, Mr. Christos. You're looking fit. I'm Dr. Guilestremes, the staff psychiatrist here. Actually, my primary field as well as first love, I must admit, is parapsychology."

She picked up my chart as I turned to look into her enormous gray-green eyes that were now covered by oversized horn-rimmed glasses. Her hair was different, too. It had more gray in it and was severely swept back, giving those oversized, chiseled features an almost other worldly look.

"You know you are truly fortunate to have had the benefit of Dr. Guillerman's surgical skills. When we initially consulted on your case, the chances for any recovery at all were very slim."

Yet another double meaning? I walked back to the bed, not knowing whether to suppress a smile or scream. I studied her openly for several seconds before saying, "Tell me, Dr. Guilestremes, did you look in on me several times during the past few weeks, and why would Dr. Guillerman consult with a parapsychologist on a simple surgical matter?"

"To answer your second question first, he consulted me as a psychiatric/ neurologist, not a parapsychologist. I ran some tests of a neurological nature to determine the extent of damage, if any, to certain areas of the brain governing response. As to looking in on you several times, no, not several. I came to see you and take additional tests after each operation, a total of four times. Why do you ask?"

"And I suppose that during these times my eyes opened for a few moments?"

"I really couldn't say. I was busy with my work-ups at the time. Why? Is this somehow connected to the dream Dr. Guillerman very briefly filled me in on? That's why I'm here. I joined him for the ride up to the helicopter pad and he sketched it roughly for me. The area of subconscious hallucinations is not altogether unfamiliar to me. As a matter of fact, I taught a seminar on that very subject at the Society for Psychical Research in London. Would you care to tell me about your dream?"

"It was kind of him to be concerned, but he pretty well cleared it up for me. Didn't he tell you that as well?"

"He mentioned that certain pieces were beginning to fall into place for you."

"Well, as a matter of fact, just before you came in, I received the final proof, so to speak. I discovered the light house in my dreams. That, together with the fact that Dr. Guillerman resembled one of the - hallucinatory characters, as did the anesthesiologist from how he described her, and of course finding out that you had a helicopter pad here, which tied into yet another part of my dream - was all the convincing I needed."

I stared directly into her eyes. This time, she was the first to look away.

"Excellent. I'm so glad to hear it. Tell me, do I resemble anyone in your dream?"

I decided it was time to throw them a red herring for a change, so, baring my most male smile, I said, "No, I'm afraid I wasn't that fortunate, Dr. Guilestremes... Guilestremes is a Greek name, isn't it?"

"Yes, I'm Greek. Why do you ask?"

"Come, come, Doctor. You are suffering from an occupational hazard. You mustn't analyze everything everyone says to you."

She laughed and said, "Yes, I'm afraid you're right. And speaking of occupational hazards, I fear I suffer from yet another – curiosity. I was wondering if you would indulge me inasmuch as allowing me to ask you some questions about your dream. "Be my guest." I replied.

"You see, Mr. Christos, recent discoveries in the field of psychical research have firmly established that certain crisis situations most definitely act as springboards, so to speak, for psychic experiences, especially initial ones.

"For example, it has been proven that when people are quite ill, there is a greater likelihood for an out of body experience – what we term OBE. It has also been repeatedly shown that initial experiences of this sort are also prompted by certain drugs of an anesthetic nature. In short, what is quite often referred to as Astral Projection quite often occurs for the first time when one is either actually close to death or fears he is close to death. May I proceed with the questions? You won't have to go through the experience itself."

Yet another dimension was being hurdled at me. They were uncompromisingly relentless when it came to the expropriation of my faculties. Nevertheless, I nodded my assent.

"During your dream were you aware of any strong vibrations running through either the upper portion of your body or your entire body?"

"No, not that I recall," I lied.

"At any point, were you aware of a sensation of being separated from your body?"

"No... several times from my mind, but not my body."

"What do you mean by that?"

"I'm not sure."

"I see. Were you at any point aware of a feeling of levitation?"

"No."

"Did you have the feeling, at any time, that you possessed a second body or no body at all?"

"No."

"Did you at any time have the feeling that you could pass through matter such as a wall or building?"

"No, but that's one I wish I'd experienced, believe me."

"Did you at any point experience a strong sensation of rapid movement, such as a soaring feeling, that if experienced would be like no other sensation of movement you have ever felt?"

"No."

"Did you have the feeling at any time that you were viewing something in another dimension of either time or form?"

"No," I lied, once again.

"At any point, did you note a distinctive heightening of your sensory awareness, especially as relates to your visual or audio faculties?"

"No."

The lies were coming quite easily now, and I wasn't even positive why I was doing it. I only knew that for her to challenge any of my responses in any manner was verboten; it had to be in order to maintain the illusion. So what was I gaining? Nothing if I had indeed shot myself, but if I hadn't – and dammit, I hadn't – their pat explanations and my strange reaction to the reference to my shooting myself aside, then she knew I was lying, and if she knew I was lying, then she had to know I didn't embrace the current scenario, and that essentially is what I wanted her to know. Still and all, I had the strange feeling it was a fool's play, but fool's play or no, I had reached that fork in the road where one must choose a path, either path, but nevertheless only one path if one is to reach his desired destination. And so, after "considering the possibilities" this time, I chose the path with the sign post that announced "To doubt myself is insanity."

I looked up at her then, her arms folded across her chest, the barest trace of a smile at the corners of her mouth as well as her eyes a moment before she averted them to the floor and said, "Well, I think it's safe to assume that what you experienced falls within what Dr. Guillerman termed it – subconscious hallucinations, as opposed to any form of psychic experience. You may leave this evening if you like…

"I feel I should say this in light of the obvious strong impression your dream made on you. It may not apply at all. You know, when one is very close to death, it has been reported in various circles - lay, medical, and theological - that one's life, or rather the high and low points of one's life, passes in front of him, almost as if it were on a reel of sorts. Also, quite often, given the same circumstance, there have been reported cases where the hallucination, the dream, contains or revolves around retribution of one sort or another. For a long time, many of those in my field felt this was nothing more than suppressed guilt finally being released with the catharsis that is death. Now these same are not so certain. In any event, it appears to be a common denominator in instances of this nature.

I have my own theory about it. Would you care to hear it?"

"By all means."

"I think it is a way through which one's essence finally informs one – reveals to one, the essential errors of one's past ways. And it is for that reason it only occurs when one is very close to death. Do you believe that is possible?"

I smiled briefly and turned to stare at the light house.

"Let's say I'll take it under consideration as one possibility."

"Without batting an eye, she replied, "Well, if you come up with another, by all means let me know. Good day, Mr. Christos."

When she was out of hearing range I, too, observed the amenities. "Good day, Alethea."

After I showered, I decided to keep the beard. While showering, I had further considered the possibilities. Had the watch not been missing, I might well have fallen for it. A substantial part of me, even now, gave itself over to it. The evidence to support their latest contention had been subtly and overwhelmingly convincingly laid out. It was pat, but not too pat. Obvious, yet logical. Most of all, it preyed upon such an unknown, unexplored area of man's self-consciousness that one could easily give oneself over to it. Gladly.

As I stared at the scar, I was somewhat in awe of the lengths they had gone towards the realization of their goal, whatever the hell it truly was. No aspect of my being had they left unplundered, mentally, emotionally, spiritually, and finally, physically, all were considered fair game to them. But surely they must realize this latest deception could be disproved with a phone call. Even if what Dr. Naismith had said were true, that the technique of cryosurgery left virtually no traces of itself, hospitals kept records, and even they couldn't coerce an institute as renowned as Mount Sinai to falsify admission records.

So what had they hoped to prove? What didactic design was employed here? But before Mount Sinai, something more pressing had to be confronted.

Anarose. It wouldn't take long, but I owed myself one last rendezvous with that sainted/painted lady, and by God I was going to have it.

"To doubt myself is insanity," I said to myself over and over again. I was still saying it as I opened the closet door to retrieve my clothes.

Again, the laughter. Again, it was forced.

I seemed to have invented a new sound, a new means of human communication – the half-scream, half-laugh. I stared at the lightweight worsted pinstripe suit, vanilla shirt, and black print tie. I had not brought those particular clothes with me to Diarma and I had certainly not brought the black alligator attaché that rested next to my shoes. I had purposely not packed anything at all that would serve to remind me of that night at the beach, and yet there they were. I took hold of myself and finally realized the obvious – that breaking into my New York apartment and taking items of clothing that the benevolent Indian gentleman had undoubtedly described in detail, was most assuredly one of their minor miracles of the past few weeks.

"See, Christos? Calm down and use your noggin and you can come up with a logical explanation for everything."

I dressed hurriedly, noting I had neither gained nor lost weight, and left the room. I followed the white line on the floor that led to the outer exit. But before I had exhausted it, I was sidetracked by a red line which sneaked under an elevator door that read "Surgical Observatory." I had to know, and so I depressed the button. I exited into a very small glass booth that had eight chairs, not two, which was raised above and overlooked the operating theatre, which was, of course, slightly more oblong than circular, to allow for the distortion of dreams. Although it was not glass walled, it was glass domed and did, indeed, have only one point of entry, a door at the far end. There were no pews. I imagined myself lying on the operating table and catching a glimpse of the gallery just as the anesthesiologist, or Anarose, placed the trick of her trade over my nose and mouth. A brief squint at the jury? How very clever of them.

But then I realized something. I was not being shown this room. No one had taken me here to compare it to my courtroom in the sky...

"Work it out, Christos. Calm yourself now... there's got to be a reasonable, rational answer that fits into your scheme of things here.

Of course! A form of fail-safe. If they had made a point of "showing" it to me, it might have been the one similarity too many, that one too loud, and excessively shrill scream from the dying Desdemona. On the other hand, should I discover it for myself...

I felt I was beginning to fathom the Diarma Mind. A few minutes later, I walked into the muted colors of the dying day. I noticed a few convalescents in wheel chairs scattered here and about to lend the hospital another ring of authenticity. I had just passed a very old, decrepit one snail-pacing it along the grass when I heard someone call to me.

"Young man, do you have a light?"

I smiled as my hand went into my pocket. I didn't even bother to look around. That gravelly larynx absent voice could belong to no one else, and she certainly deserved a curtain call, too.

"Say, aren't you the young man in 16-B? The one who shot himself?"

Again, that incredible implosion in my head, that graphic vision of running red and scattering bone fragments, but it seemed to dissipate more quickly this time.

"Perhaps you shouldn't be up and around just yet. You don't look too well."

I forced a smile and replied, "Oh, I'm just fine, thank you." I bent to light the small, thin black cigar.

"I came to see you often, late. Very late, after the doctors had gone and there was only the night nurse. I was so curious as to why such a fine looking man as yourself would want to do away with himself. Although, I suppose I shouldn't be since my nephew Edward slashed his wrists, pour soul."

"Your nephew Edward, you say?"

Suddenly, she became very excited. "Yes, did you know him?"

"No, I'm afraid not. Did I tell you?"

"Tell me what?"

"Why I tried to do away with myself."

"No. No, you were unconscious the whole time."

"Ahhh, but surely, I must have opened my eyes at least once?"

"Not that I recall… Oh, damn! My light's gone out. Would you mind?"

I relit her cigar and dropped my lighter into the outside right-hand pocket of my suit coat. I heard it make contact with something and felt my heart skip a beat. I placed my hand in the pocket and fondled it, afraid to remove it, but when I did, it all flooded back to me. My mind came up with the correct reel, sat me down, dimmed the lights, and shot the images. I was back on the beach. I had just placed the gun on top of the attaché and had taken off my clothes, preparing for my final swim. My fingers had undone my watch band without me really being aware of it. I had glanced at it and remarked to myself that not only had my time's run out, but man's as well as the dying battery barely igniting the time and date. Orderly person that I was, I had placed it in my suit coat pocket. I even recalled the moot gesture attached to the act.

The projector in my head switched off. In a state of terror that transcended all the other nightmares they had subjected me to, I stared at the quartz digital Seiko and pushed the date button. It read "August 4."

With the full significance of my latest find slowly seeping yet deeper into the remnants of my mind, I dropped the watch and backed slowly across the lawn. I would have made it had not my current reminiscence touched off still another episode in the Life and Times of Alexander Christos. This time, the projectionist indulged in science fiction. Two enormous stars, a huge full moon. I was in an infinite conical beam, a never-ending stream of light, down which came images of myself, again and again.

EXPLOSION!

BLOOD!

BONE FRAGMENTS EVERYWHERE!

Suddenly, my mouth went even further agape. My hand came to rest on my forehead; my eyes focused on some non-existent point far, far away a moment before they turned upwards in their sockets and I fainted dead away. It was possible. I had shot myself. I had chosen the wrong path again. Diarma had been nothing but a dream, an illusory experience, and a hallucination was my mental legacy of the moment.

*****

I came to as the blurred images of an orderly and Dr. Guilestremes bent down beside me.

"Get him back to his room," she ordered.

"No! No, really, I'm all right. Really, I am. The sun… it's still quite strong and I've been inside too long. It just caused me to black out for a few seconds. Really, I'm fine now."

I came to a sitting position, feeling slightly nauseous.

"Mr. Christos, you are not all right. It's my fault. You appeared to have made such a remarkable recovery. Obviously you require more rest. Now come along."

"No!"

"Just for the night. You can leave in the morning if you're feeling up to it."

"Doctor, I tell you, I'm fine. I'll be just fine. I have a plane to catch."

I rose to my feet.

"Very well, but promise me you won't press yourself for a few weeks. Take it slowly, please?"

"I appreciate your concern, but, really, I'm okay, Alethea."

It had slipped out. I quickly turned to see her reaction. She had removed her glasses and was standing there looking at me with the identical expression of bemusement she had displayed when I had turned to look at her the day I left her home on Diarma, after she had told me the story of Anarose. The very same, exact expression. The one I could not even begin to fathom then and I could do no better with this time either.

Watch or no watch, Diarma had been no illusion and she was letting me know it.

XXXIV

I began to retrace my steps. To the first fisherman I came upon in Motril, I said, "Will the tide be low enough to affect docking in Alboran this evening?"

The man obviously did not understand me, so I rephrased it, inserting a Spanish idiom here, a gesture there, but to no avail. I was finally rescued by a somewhat pompous Englishman.

"My dear fellow, it hardly matters if the poor chap can fathom your inquiry or not. It is a generally known fact that the Mediterranean is the only ocean in the world that is not affected by tides – high or low."

The look that entered my eyes sent them both on their ways.

An hour and a half later I had chartered a boat. Some three hours after that, land came into sight. At first I thought the fisherman had taken me in the wrong direction, for the smallish and flat island we were approaching did not resemble in the slightest the island of Diarma, but rather was indeed a resort isle with several smaller out islands.

But what struck me to be even more bizarre was my own knowledge of the oceanography – there was simply no land whatsoever indicated on the map other than Alboran in this section of the Mediterranean.

I had just decided that it was of such minor significance that the map markers had decided it didn't warrant charting, when the small boat heaved to and headed directly towards it.

"What are you doing? I don't want to go here. Take me to Alboran!"

The man looked very perplexed, even frightened, as he pulled away from my grasp and said, "Pero, Señor, este es Alboran."

I stared into the man's eyes, searching for any sign of deception, tightened my grip and said, "Diarma! Take me to Diarma, dammit!"

The man's eyes begged to be released. I let him go and asked in a far gentler manner, "This is Alboran?"

"Si, Señor. You want come here, no?"

I ignored the feeling in the pit of my stomach as I whispered, "No. I'm sorry. I've made a mistake. Are there any other islands in the area… otros aqui?"

But I already knew the answer. "Very well. We can go back now."

"Si, Señor," he said, obviously ecstatic that in less than three hours he would be rid of the loco Americano.

The next morning, I chartered a small plane and investigated the entire shoe of the Mediterranean, even though the pilot had assured me the only island in the area was Alboran. He proved to be a knowledgeable man.

"To doubt myself is insanity."

But I could not negate the all too familiar feelings of fear and confusion that had become staples in my makeup. I began to methodically recall the night of the initial voyage. Rambeau… the man I had taken an instant dislike to… could he have been a part of the plot? He had approached me, after all, not vice-versa, so that was a possibility.

Had I been taken somewhere other than Alboran? Obviously, but where? What about the time element? Had I been drugged? Of course, the wine… the wine I had reluctantly accepted. The wine he had been overly insistent about my accepting. I had felt immediately tired after I drank it. At the time, I dismissed this as jet lag, as well as the prolonged road travel I had just completed on my way to Motril… Yes, that must be it. I had been drugged, transferred to another boat, or more likely, a sea plane, and flown God knows where… It could have been anywhere on this planet.

Drugs distort one's sense of time. Then, I would have been placed on an identical boat to awaken to the outline of La Boca de Dios.

I exhorted all my senses to recall every visual, every scent, every feeling I had experienced on Diarma. The black sand and the volcano were of course the biggest clues. What other islands housed volcanoes? Santorini, yes, the Greek island of Santorini or Thera, but I had seen a travelogue on Thera and they didn't match at all. Where else?

I would have to investigate this… then the realization that there was no point to that, after all. I only had their word for the fact that La Boca de Dios was indeed a dormant volcano. It could be nothing more than a mountain with a leveled crest. And the black sand… could they have imported it from the Galapagos, for instance, which is renowned for its black sand beaches? Price was obviously no object to these people.

I suddenly realized that trying to find that island could become a lifetime career, what with all the island territories in the world.

By the time the plane returned to Motril, ninety percent of the doubt – ninety percent of the anguish, frustration, and confusion – had been allayed, dissipated, or quelled altogether. Once again, logic had come to my rescue as I realized that I could, if I wanted to, counter balance each seemingly inexplicable facet of the experience with a corresponding explicable possibility. It was just a matter of thinking it through… of painstakingly considering the possibilities, including the watch, a replica of which could easily be purchased at any one of hundreds of jewelry stores. I understood then that the emphasis had not been so much on the watch's time, but rather its timing insofar as my discovery of it at the most vulnerable possible moment.

With the first light of the following day, another level had presented itself to me and it was undeniably a far more realistic perspective. Obviously, it was not meant for me to return to Diarma, whether real or imagined. This "experience" was over. I actually felt the finality of it… mentally, anyway, but hardly emotionally. Logically, I fathomed this, even ascertained its value.

The message had been simply put forth: Take what you have learned about yourself and apply it to the NOW. To backtrack, to seek explanations, hard evidence, revenge, or vilification, was verboten. I was expected to get back to the business of living life, having been "reborn," so to speak. Yes, the "holiday" was over, and by now they were undoubtedly selecting their next "Specimen," whoever the hell "they" were.

It wasn't really just this that decided it for me. It was something else as well. Something far more specific that had come to me during these thoughts. I could not really pinpoint the precise moment of origin of mental discovery, but all at once it had been there with its unmistakable ring of truth that was not to be disputed. It was the quotation that graced the cover of the Pamphlet that a memory cell had surfaced verbatim for me:

"Reality is a place, a state of mind, in which you live, thrive, and grow that knows no societal, geographic, cultural, or self-consciousness boundaries."

I recalled that when I had first read it, all but "self-consciousness" boundaries had made perfect instinctual sense to me, and now, "self-consciousness" boundaries made more sense than "societal, geographic, or cultural," for their entire collective force was geared towards the expansion of my limited self-consciousness, and illusory technique was their prime visual aide.

In a moment of illumination the entire scheme of their thinking revealed itself to me: Illusion vs. Reality; Physical Reality. What is the difference, Specimen? As long as you can grow from the experience, what possible difference does it make whether or not you actually physically experienced something?

They were quite correct. I drove to Madrid that morning and booked myself on a late flight to New York that same day. While killing time waiting for my flight to leave, I ordered lunch at a large outdoor café and thus provided the opportunity for Diarma to have a final laugh on me. You see, being an incurable romantic, and at the moment feeling kindly towards Alethea, I ordered the same thing she had served me the night I arrived on Diarma. The

American waiter was quite taken aback and, suppressing a haughty sneer, enlightened me as to certain facts of marine habitat.

"I'm afraid that's quite impossible, sir. Abalone is strictly a Pacific Ocean catch."

XXXV

But the clarity of mind had not, as of yet, transcended the emotional scars. So, for the first few weeks upon arrival back in New York, I did indeed play detective.

I checked with Voyages Unlimited. "Dr. Millicent Rand? No, I never heard of her, sorry, sir."

Through travel agencies and literature, I investigated island areas, but other than for a false alarm in the New Hebrides, and a travel agent's sales oriented description of one of the Seashell Islands, I turned up nothing even close. It seemed that bits and pieces of Diarma turned up in different parts of the globe. The volcano and night winds in the Greek Isles, primarily the Aegean portion; the fauna, flora, and architecture in the Balearic Islands, as well as the South Pacific; the overall climate with its mist and fog – the Scottish Isles in August were quite comparable, I was told. One agent had gone so far as to adamantly state that the island I claimed to have visited could not possibly exist on this planet. In short, he called me a liar to my face.

To which I simply smiled, which frightened the hell out of him.

I even went so far as to check on the credentials of one Dr. Brad Guillerman. "Cryogenics was his specialty, Ma'am, as well as a Dr. Guilestremes... Anthea was her first name; psychiatry, parapsychology, and perhaps Black Magic were her fields."

"Yes," came the long-distance response. "They both practiced in London, but there was no connection between them. No, sorry, we've never heard of a private hospital of your description in Pembroke... I'm certain we'd know about it, sir."

You may well wonder why I didn't ferret out the most obvious first. The answer is simple: I didn't really want to know. That is the reason why, even though I drove all the way to Mount Sinai Hospital, I turned around before parking the car and entering the admissions office. That is why I never had the scar examined, although I did dance around that one, one night, when I ran into a doctor acquaintance of mine and was somewhat condescendingly informed:

"If this hypothetical situation arose, and Cryosurgery was performed, one would have to have it checked fairly soon afterwards, I would imagine, as the particular technique, which is still in the experimental stages, heals itself quite rapidly," etc., etc.

The man simply confirmed what Dr. Naismith had already implied.

All of my digging only went to substantiate my earlier conclusion: The possibilities were endless.

And so it went until one morning in late December, two and a half months after my return home. On that particular day, I awoke to a snow-covered Riverside Park and as I gazed out at its purity and cleanliness, something like a switch in my stomach shut off.

"Enough," it said. "Get on with the business of living life."

Within a week, I had a job two days a week as a consultant to a major architectural firm. It would bring in just enough money to meet my expenses without appreciably tapping my limited capitol. Now, with the remainder of the time, I could return to my first love, painting, which I had so badly neglected for some fifteen years, but which had been very much gnawing away at me since my return to New York.

Through all of January, February, and March, I spent hours and hours just exercising technique before attempting my first work. Rusty is what I was. But even in the process of this laborious exercise period, I sensed a newness of dimension trying to show itself. It manifested in my choice of colors and textures, not form or object. That had not come to me yet. When it did, around the first of April, it got me out of bed and sat me down at my easel for the next two months. It had come to me through a dream. I saw no one during this period. I took a leave of absence from my consultant's job. I had all my daily living necessities delivered and only left my apartment when spring finally arrived to work in a very secluded section of upper Riverside Park, where I would paint from dawn to just before dusk; then, back to my small terrace to take advantage of the muted colors of the sun-setting hours.

"Happy" is not the correct word to describe my state of being during this period, for to experience happiness over a prolonged time, there must be a strong association with the "who" who is experiencing it: the self. I hardly ever thought or felt about myself these days. Content, at peace with myself, more closely captures it.

Of course, there were pitfalls in my new manner of existence that I had to learn to avoid. For instance, much in the manner of a child, I had to learn to discipline myself, for hours and hours would rush by before I realized I had forgotten to eat… or to sleep.

I tried putting myself on a routine, a schedule, but it didn't take. In the end, I slept when I was exhausted and/or when the incessant flow of thoughts didn't get me up and march me to the canvas to accomplish yet another brush stroke to compliment the new thought; or, send me to my desk to make a written notation of a conceptual change nature.

I wasn't worried about my health. I was still young and quite strong… but then the other changes, perhaps phenomena are more apt, began to invade my being. At first, the newness of them, the strangeness of them, frightened me, but then the ecstasy of the experiences themselves, together with the residual effect they had on my work, allayed any and all fear.

The first one struck two nights after I had just completed the "first draft" of my painting. Up until now, the only recreation I had allowed myself was the reading of all the books that had been left for me at the Pension on Diarma. I had managed to purchase them all at a small bookstore on West Seventy Second, but this particular night I decided to celebrate by actually sitting down to a meal, thus ending the never-ending diet of sandwiches and miracle liquid energizers I had subjected my martyred digestive tract to for the past few months. I chose a favorite spot of mine that I used to patronize regularly in the "old days" – a small, outdoor café on West Sixty-Fourth and Broadway that served an excellent continental cuisine and was so situated that one could view the rainbow spray of the Lincoln Center Fountain.

The tables on the tiny terrace were so close together that I could not help but overhear the poignant conversation in progress between the attractive mid-thirtyish couple. By both the tone and text of it, I realized that these intelligent, sensitive people were caught up in the universal dilemma of quasi-connection. As I continued to listen, I mentally sifted out the ego and personality traits that had begun to rapidly cloud the issue as the tone had emotionally escalated, usurping what objectivity was left to them, with it. Suddenly, I saw the larger question in dispute – male/female relationships in general, with such clarity of mind that all the ingredients that went into allowing two members of the opposite sex to meet and subsequently grow together, as well as all the factors that forced them apart, actually flashed sequentially through my mind. I was stunned by the visual quality of the experience, awed by the seemingly totally authoritative place it was coming from. It was as if the information being dispersed was coming from a source outside of myself, from a higher, far more knowledgeable intelligence that I had somehow piped into, had for some reason selected me as its vehicle for revelation. I felt the strangest hum running through my entire body as all the possibilities (as well as impossibilities) continued to flash in front of me.

In those few seconds, every factor from the importance of timing to the revelation that the greatest predator of all male/female relationships is the inability to separate past from present experience, thus robbing the relationship that is from the moment to moment reality of the Now, from those prone to emotional promiscuity to those bent on committing emotional abortion, as well as why those two are naturally drawn to each other, to the affirmation of Alethea's statement, "There are those who believe we look for ultimate connection to each other in lieu of ultimate connection to the real thing – God." And on and on. In short, I experienced our emotional infancy.

From the natural life span of a given moment to the complete transiency of everything but the Truth, all registered indelibly on my brain.

I had felt totally isolated as I had been experiencing all this. It was the man's light sobbing that snapped me out of myself. I turned to look at him and realized I hadn't been aware of the fact that at some point the woman had left. It was the combination of the look on the man's face, the defeated position his body had naturally assumed, the light uncontrollable weeping, that stirred and ultimately surfaced my very essence, stabbing me with such a deep surge of compassion that I felt as though I was experiencing his pain every bit as much as he himself. It was then, at that precise moment, that I felt the strong uplifting sensation. It was then that I left my body, attained another state of consciousness. It was as if I were outside of my body, positioned above both myself and the man, observing, just observing. I had no feelings of manipulative powers, quite the opposite. I knew I was not to try to alter or change, to the tiniest degree, what had or was to transpire. I was only content, overjoyed, to observe from this exalted perspective.

It wasn't until quite some time after that experience that I came to realize that it never would have come to be had I continued to steer my thoughts on an intellectual plane as I had initially been doing during the encounter. It was only when I got outside of myself, applied the knowledge to a condition as opposed to a personality, that it dimensionalized me. It was the compassion I had felt, not the intellectual revelations that allowed me to transcend myself, ergo, the spirituality of the experience.

Long after the man had gotten into a cab, the feeling of ascendency remained. Then, somewhere in my incredible walk home, it changed on me, became something else, and that something else actively stayed with me for ten days. The vestiges of it were never to leave me, they too were indelible. Now it was my sensory perceptions that had been illuminated and enlightened; heightened to such a degree that at first I was frightened badly. Sounds became such entities unto themselves, so distinct that when I listened to a Bach recording it was as if I were inside each and every note bursting with them – like wearing headphones that were a thousand times more sensitive than anything available on the market.

Dimensions of color revealed themselves to me in a way I had never seen before, so quite naturally I walked to the canvas, tossed it in a corner as if it represented three minutes work instead of three months, and began anew with my new eyes.

My overall powers of reasoning were greatly affected. I saw to the core of things at a glance, cutting through all the obstacles to understanding that man is so prone to put in his way through ego, ulterior motive, desire, the bastardization of language itself. They no longer seemed to restrict me when conversing with a friend or stranger; when reading a book, viewing a film. I was only receiving the headlines of everything and of course the flaws of everything as well.

With each passing day, my newly acquired powers overtly diminished to a certain extent, until the tenth day, when I began to feel almost normal again, but the residual effects remained.

It would not be fair or honest of me to leave out the negative factor of that ten days that occurred intermittently throughout. Terror. This manifested itself in me in the absolute certainty of immediately impending death… at any moment. It became an obsession with me. I was afraid to sleep for fear of not awakening. In time, I realized I was indeed experiencing a death process, but not the death of body; rather, the first symptoms of death of self, or if you prefer, the universally negative aspects of self.

Unquestionably, the greatest fruit yielded by this unique spiritual harvest was the fitting of the missing piece to Alexander Christos. As if shedding an item of restrictive clothing, my lifelong feelings of alienation dropped away and the sense of connection I finally felt was like emerging from an endless bitter night into the warmth of bright sunlight.

I described all but the just previously stated, some months later, to a friend of mine who had conducted numerous clinical experiments in the Sixties with hallucinogenic drugs. Much to my astonishment, the man had laughed and said, "Why didn't you just tell me you had taken an acid trip?" I had laughed in acquiescence, for how was I to explain to the highly degreed man that I had indeed taken an acid trip sans Lysergic Acid Diethylamide? I didn't even smoke grass.

I painted and painted and painted. I would break pace three times a day to go for a short walk, grabbing a bite to eat along the way. Those walks became something very special. My awareness of all things, and especially nature, its colors, forms, and sounds, treated me to sensory delights that I felt certain I and I alone was experiencing. What other explanation could there be? After all, that incredible sunset wasn't really just for me, but then again, with all these people around, why am I the only one who is really looking at it?

"Hey, come on... will you look at that moon! Where or when else have you seen a burnt orange moon the color of the setting sun? With pastel rings around it yet! Look right up there! Get your head out of that newspaper and glimpse the real reality! Hey you, over there against the railing. Take that idiotic transistor abortion away from your ear and listen to the sound of gull wings flapping the breeze as the water slaps the pier."

I began to look forward to the time when I laid down to sleep. Sleep was a problem but nothing compared to what it had become in the past few weeks. Now, instead of just occasionally rousing me out of bed to jot a note, my work connected thoughts rushed at me with agonizing speed and consistency, one thought opening the door to the next, often as not superseding the one it had sprung from. There seemed to be no end to it, for although my body was dead tired, my head would give me no quarter, for when the creative juices flow, no mercy do they show.

And still I looked forward to it for there was great compensation: a new world of transcendental experience had opened to me. More than once, I awoke in a state of what the Indians refer to as Levitation, and the feeling was pure joy. One time, I soared through the Universe. Literally. The sensation of motion had not been imagined. The colors I had perceived defied description. I was neither awake nor asleep during these experiences; rather I was somewhere else; in a twilight of being, so to speak. Science has labeled it Astral Projection, but unless you have experienced same, the label is totally impotent in delineating the state." Language is, after all, the tally of the self-conscious mind" (Richard Maurice Bucke, *Cosmic Consciousness*).

I would always be forewarned when the latter, semi-described experiences were impending, I would suddenly be awakened from dead sleep, totally refreshed. In the next instant, a feeling of tremendous pressure in my lower chest would begin pushing upward with great force as if my very essence was trying to release itself from the bondage of my body. Simultaneously, the overall body vibrations would keep increasing and the uplifting processes would begin. Up to, and including this juncture in the experience, I was still in control of it. I could mentally will it to cease or to continue. Once I had worked up the courage to let go, something else, my own higher consciousness, steered the course of my travels, and yet, I was aware that even at this point I had but to think the thought and I would return to my body. I was not aware of a second or Astral Body, rather I felt as though I had no form at all;* just energy, pure energy. These were not imagined, hallucinated, or illusory experiences. They actually mentally and spiritually, essentially, happened to me.

And I began to experience Extra Sensory Perception in graphic detail, at first solely with one individual I felt especially close to, though had not seen in years. She had left New York some years before for a less hectic existence upstate. I had never been to the area nor seen her dwellings, yet I visited her several times during my nocturnal sojourns, and when I saw her in subsequent years, described to her in the minutest detail both her home and the surrounding environment, as well as precisely what she had been doing when I had "visited" her.

----

*Parapsychology has categorized Out of Body experiences into two separate classifications: Ecsomatic (Awareness of second or Astral Body); Axiomatic (Sense of being as pure energy).

Finally, during this period, I received a portent of the immediate future that was fully confirmed by the next evening's six o'clock newscast. Once again, it had come to me in great visual detail while in a state of astral being.

The only way I could explain the phenomena to myself was that I had lived, died, and been reborn without ever having left this earth... well, almost never having left this earth.

At one point, shortly after I began to experience this new consciousness, I recalled the questions that Dr. Guilestremes had put to me in the hospital dealing with parapsychological phenomena. Had she been priming me? Preparing me? Had she somehow known this world was about to reveal itself to me?

The question was academic at best. The truth of the matter was far less mystical than it was natural. Diarma, real or imagined, had prepared the soil and planted the seeds to allow me to "branch out." My work, my total absorption and dedication to my painting had catalyzed it into action.

I completed my first painting the first day of May. I contacted an old acquaintance of mine who, in turn, put me in touch with a Madison Avenue gallery owner who came to see it the following Sunday. The man immediately agreed to sell it. I indicated that I was not certain I wanted to sell it but would definitely like to have it placed on view. I was more interested in the reaction, I told him, than the money. Wisely, the entrepreneur did not press me as to its commerciality, but instead suggested that I unveil it at a showing where he was going to introduce several new works by established artists. The show was scheduled for the following Saturday. I agreed to be there.

XXXVI

The following morning, I drove to the Hamptons. I had decided that I wanted to stroll that fated section of beach one more time. Not to uncover mysteries, but rather to juxtapose moods, past and present. Close to noon, I found the exact area and once again it appeared deserted, save a man some distance down beach walking his dogs.

I walked at a leisurely pace, lost in thought, and was naturally quite jarred when I heard my name called.

"Hello, Christos! I had a feeling you've wanted to talk to me."

I stared at him for some time, appraising him before I replied. "Yes, you're quite right. I would very much like to have a word with you. I don't wish to go on, but I sense you have further plans for me. I'd rather stop now."

"Because the story's over?"

"Yes, I feel the finality of it. To continue I feel would be somewhat presumptuous of you."

"I couldn't agree with you more, but I am not a totally autonomous being, Christos. I have tradition to uphold and a system to conform to."

"What exactly do you mean?"

"I mean that I am, to a certain degree, at the mercy of The Editorial Mind. As a matter of fact, what we are doing right now is considered a Cardinal Sin."

I reached down and petted his dogs.

"Gorgeous animals. Are those blue eyes? What is so objectionable about this conversation?"

"Come, let's walk. Let me put it this way. While it is bad literary manners to mix one's metaphors, it is considered heresy to mix one's genres. In short, I am breaking tradition; however, be that as it may, editorially speaking, other things may go, but this chapter stays, every word of it."

"And why are you so adamant about it?"

He smiled gently as he spoke.

"Ahhh, because they may technically edit my work, but may not, will not, conceptually edit my mind, and besides, I am not setting a precedent in so choosing this course of action. Did you read John Fowles' *The French Lieutenant's Woman*?"

"Yes."

"You did? When?" came his incredulous reply.

I just smiled at him.

"Well, then, you'll understand what I mean when I say that Chapter Thirteen of that work tapped a new dimension in literary experience, opening the door to another freedom for all in my vocation to walk through. All I'm doing is accepting his invitation to follow him through that door and browse around in the room that lies beyond. And, so long as I'm here, I thought I might as well indulge in some interior decoration, so to speak."

"Ahhh. By all means, proceed."

"You see, Christos, our individuality is our fundamental birthright, which is the reason why you can attempt to break away from me now. Unfortunately, all systems, be them educational, socio-economic, religious, or corporate, and especially governmental, are geared, not as a plot, but rather by virtue of being a system, towards the dilution and neutralization of the very process of individuality, for all man concocted systems cajole, coerce, and at time blatantly force adherence to their established values. That is their basic law of self-preservation. It is, of course, ultimately self-defeating; for it is precisely such a structure that provides the spawning ground that nurtures the yield of the strongest individualists."

"Let me see if I have this right. Are you saying that all systems have an adverse effect on the vast majority of humanity?"

"No, they are essential stepping stones in our evolution, but there must also come a time when 'we cast away childish things.' I'm saying that, ultimately, the only correct and fully employable system is the universal system, or, as Mr. Fowles defines it, 'If a cosmos is infinite, it is without end. If it is without end, there can be no end it is serving. Its end lies in its means...' To which I append: As man is the potential epitome of the Universe, the universal system (systemless system) is the only system he is naturally allied to. Any other systems we have made up to serve immediate and 'far reaching' ends, and unfortunately we have reversed the universal principle in so doing. We live in an 'ends justifies the means' oriented world. In a capitalistic society, the 'end' is always money, which in turn equals wealth, position, power. The 'means,' whatever has to be done, compromised, in order to attain it, and, Christos, the highest price always paid is one's individuality. As Alethea told you during your trial, only good means attain good ends. Therefore, the means has to justify the end."

"How do I know that your 'good means' will justify my 'end'?"

"Have I let you down so far?"

"No, but you've been pretty damn tough on me!"

"That is only because you reversed the most basic axiom of living life."

"Which is, pray tell?"

"You took yourself too seriously and life not seriously enough. It's all right. You've got a lot of company. That, to my mind, is Homo Sapiens' single greatest area of misguidance."

"Are you saying that we can't take life too seriously, but we do ourselves? Why do I feel like a straight man?"

He laughed for a moment before replying. "To answer your second question first, the day you don't, I will have reached full enlightenment. As to your first question, precisely."

"To get back to the true justification for the inclusion of this chapter for a moment. I have an idea. I told you I didn't want to go on. That I felt my story was over and I really mean that, but I also understand and respect your point of view of what I assume to be satisfying the reader, so, why not offer them a choice?"

"Such as?"

"Tell them they may turn the pages until they come to the next chapter and pick up the story line from there, and if they so opt they will have lost nothing story-wise, plot-wise. Or, tell them they may read on and draw their own conclusions as to the relevance of, as well as reasons why you have included this chapter."

"Not a bad idea. They could categorize it as many things: Genuine concern, Indulgence, their indulgence of me, not mine of them... Let's see, what else?"

"How about Mental Masturbation and/or Mental Exhibitionism?"

"That's great! Definitely. I'll include that and also I'll have to include *Chain Reaction Manifestations of Real and True Connection*, regarding Fowles' and Boobis' works."

"Who is this Boobis you've referred to now several times?"

"A great genius, both as a painter and a philosopher, who died in 1972 at the age of forty-three. A man who was accurately lauded by one art critic as a combination of Michelangelo and Socrates. A man who locked himself into a room for nine years and painted. A man who was so poor that each month the telephone company threatened to shut off his phone for non-payment of his bill, who I know for a fact turned down a half-million dollars for a single painting entitled "Portrait of a Female," because he did not want to see his work sequestered in some wealthy individual's home, but rather wished it to remain with a collection of his works in a museum for all people to be able to view and thereby greatly benefit from."

"Where are his works now? Can I see them?"

"No, not at the present time. When he died very suddenly, a mutual friend of ours had to get them out of the country and under lock and key, for which she went to jail, to protect them from his wife who would have sold them off with the estate settlement. One day, you will be able to see them, and I promise you, once you have seen "Portrait of a Female," it will forever be singed into your mind and soul."

"That's very interesting, but back to the main issue. What are we really here for on this beach, right now? For what specific purpose, what specific end?"

"Well, an issue has suddenly been raised that I did not anticipate, did not nurse into existence. You just showed up here today, Christos, without warning or any form of preamble. You see, the key words are 'Beginning' and 'End.' Now, for you this story began on Page One... although now you inform me that you've read *The French Lieutenant's Woman*, so I can't even be sure of that. Anyway, for the sake of discussion, we'll say that for you the story began on Page One. For me, I cannot possibly begin to tell you where or when it began. Not really, although I openly admit the manner in which I chose to tell it took seed roughly forty odd years ago upon reading *The Magus*. But of course, you must already know that, after what you've been through. To try would be the height of self-deceit, the fulcrum of foolishness.

"I will tell you this much, the part that I know. It has been nurtured by a thousand averted glances, and a very few ones of real contact. It has been fed vis a vis the depths of many depressions; many introspective moments prodded by unending inequality as well as the seeming futility of existence, and relatively few moments of elation, optimism, and enlightenment. It undoubtedly took on additional body at any number of the crossroads, detours, back roads, sharp curves, et al, in short, the non-freeways we elect to travel; or to take it to its extreme, it might have been born when I breathed my first, but chances are equal to the chances that are not, and the odds all in the favor of knowledge and evolution, that to place its conception in conjunction with my own would be placing it far shy of its real mark, for there are no real and true beginnings as there are no real and true endings.

"That is the basic definition of the Universe, so your story, Christos, does not end for the very same reason you and I don't, not really. But I cannot just leave you hanging out in Limbo, for the novelist can, and more importantly, is expected to affix, contrive, an ending as is his want. So, I will give them their, or far more accurately, my contrived ending. Reluctantly, I will live up to my traditional responsibility, for the truth is that I would like all who experience this work to go away from it with a feeling of being satisfied."

"How very, very noble of you."

"I think I just got caught. Yes, of course there is another reason, and that very simply is, the reality is in the doing –who knows what you (or I) might come to by extending your life span somewhat longer?"

"But what about those rare ones who do not require the satisfaction of your ending, of having all the loose ends tied neatly in a package, of having displayed for them the tricks, plot devices, that went into some of the more bizarre situations I was forced to confront during the invasion of my mind; for those who do not require having their insatiable curiosity satiated, for who, like me, the Fowlesian statement 'every answer is a little bit of death,' rings true…"

"I don't happen to agree with that statement, by the way, unless he means every answer given as opposed to worked out… For them, the story is over, for they have already discerned the significance of The Seventh Man. Actually, it was over on page 211 when you fully understood the meaning of 'Reality is a place,' etc., etc., and if it wasn't over there, it was most definitely finished when you made the decision not to check the admission records at Mount Sinai, not to have your head examined for evidence of fraud… or rather fraudulent surgery… everyone should have their heads examined for evidence of fraud. I'd be first in line. Everything since that point in the story has been nothing more, or less, than a form of positive post-mortem. Do you happen to recall the essence of the first paragraph of Chapter Thirteen in *The French Lieutenant's Woman*?"

"Not off hand."

"Good, because it was my turn to talk again. 'The novelist stands next to God' (in the creation of his characters). Now, bear in mind the man's definition of God that Alethea quoted to you: The freedom that allows other freedoms to exist. The very justification for having this discussion springs directly from that statement, for contained in it lies what I believe to be the very essence of how novelistic responsibility should manifest itself. Do not be put off by the use of the noun 'God.' All that is being said here is that there comes a point, or rather should come a point, when concepts, plots, story and outlines aside, the characters must be allowed to evolve of themselves, independent of the author's personality or 'ends.'

"Now, if you, or any reader, are saying to yourselves right now, 'Come on, Staley, who are you trying to kid? You and you alone, for better or for worse, have put the words into your character's mouth; have pulled the strings that have caused the subsequent movement – emotional, physical, and mental.' If you are saying that, then in effect, you are saying you suspect me. Now that is your prerogative, but all I can tell you, Christos, is that I had every intention of having you check the admission records at Mount Sinai; every intention of having you verify or not the operation, and then, fresh with the revelation of discovery of the deception, have you rediscover the island of Diarma, in some far corner of the earth, and deliver a tirade of anger and bitterness, to say nothing of righteous indignation, that would rock the very foundation of The Diarma Mind. And then, after an appropriate period of emotional convalescence, begin to reap the benefits of the ordeal. But you, not me, would not have it that way. Apparently, you were too impatient to wait to grow. That's all I really have to say. It's your turn to speak. Would you like to leave the reader with something 'earth-shaking' before I re-incarcerate you?"

"Yes. Come, your ending awaits you. But I must warn you, you will not find out what happens to me in the long run…"

"Now, wait a minute. How do you know that?"

"I didn't interrupt you. Don't interrupt me. Mr. Staley will not, for instance, allude to my future fame and/or fortune because he feels that as pertains to my growth either or both of those two tangibles are totally irrelevant. Now I'm not at all certain that I agree with that…"

"Christos!"

"Sorry, Massah. You see, the truth of the matter is that I could care less about having any more money or recognition than is absolutely required to give me the freedom and mobility to allow whatever talent I may possess to grow. I know that to amass a fortune beyond said criteria for other than humanitarian ends is nothing more than a sophisticated form of gluttony, to force that last piece of turkey down your throat purely for its diminishing sensual delight, and, of course, to keep that fellow across the table form having it. I know what form the subsequent regurgitations of the fat man take: I have experienced the ghettos of the mind which create the ghettos of the world. Come, your ending still awaits you. All the answers to your plot questions; the final pieces of the puzzle are a mere finger flick away. Go ahead, turn the page. You have nothing to gain but 'a little bit of death.'"

I stared at him for a minute then attempting to discern the smile in his eyes, I asked, "Do you think anyone will put down the book at this point?"

"God, I hope not."

"You're a fraud, Michael."

"I am limited by my life form, Christos."

"You had to have the last word, didn't you?"

XXXVII

I noticed her at once, standing motionless in the otherwise milling crowd.

It was her force of concentration that separated her from the others, and the fact that she seemed spellbound by my painting was also a contributing factor to her standoutishness. But in all truth, she would have stood out anywhere - she had that quality about her. How would you like her to look? That's exactly how she looks.

Quietly, I approached her, not wanting to distract her. I was almost upon her before I realized how lovely she truly was. I studied her studying it and that feeling that has always and will always allude a definitive label gently eased its way into me.

I realized I was smiling only a moment before she did. She didn't really acknowledge me but rather returned her full attention to the work. She stared into the four-foot-by-six-foot painting, stepped back from it, and took it in anew from this slightly removed perspective. She turned to me and whispered, "I love it. I don't think I understand it, but it has such power, such force and the colors are magnificent. I've never seen such colors before."

I didn't bother to mention to her that I had borrowed the pastel rings from around the moon; instead, refreshed by her honesty and unfettered perception, which had come on the heels of countless overheard interpretations that even I could not begin to fathom, I smiled and said, "What is it about it you don't understand? Perhaps I can clear it up f or you."

"You're the artist?" Her tone just shy of awe.

And into her deep-set mocha eyes that contained a slight Asiatic cast to them, I replied, "Yes."

I walked to the canvas and raised my hand to its left portion, which was an enormous green eye, within which was set the expansive lawn, a portion of a very modern structure, a deep rolling meadow, a royal blue sky, the faint glow of six budding stars, the jagged cliffs of the northeasterly approach, a raging sea, and a very diminutive version of myself some two centimeters to the left of her pupil. I turned back to her.

"The work is called First Impression." I did not bother to go into its double meaning. "That is how she saw him at their first instant of visual contact."

My hand moved to the right portion of the canvas and traced the outline of the liquid brown eye of equal proportions which reflected the expansive lawn, the multi-toned sunset, the new and full moon, the tangerine sun half-submerged in the calm waters, two stars set in a powder blue sky, and two centimeters to the right of the pupil, the back of a tiny woman seated at a wicker table.

"And that is how he saw her?"

"Yes, that is how he saw her."

"There is such a feeling of order versus chaos, beauty versus ugliness… It's so harmonious on the one hand and almost grotesque on the other. Why is that?"

"I would say you have just described what we have labeled 'life' quite accurately. Forgive me, I realize that is a rather general response to a specific question but it applies nevertheless, and to be perfectly honest with you, I am incapable of giving you a more specific, personal one."

"And the fact that the lid of the brown eye is partially closed, almost squinting, while the other is wide open and serene…"

"Yes, that intentionally contributes to its sense of paradox."

What she had been initially referring to had been the overall effect of the painting as a single entity, for while each half of our faces taken separately were quite beautiful, where they seemed in the center, the overall image monsterized. I had accomplished the remaining facial features, as well as the outlines of our heads, in almost an anatomy chart method, but rather than utilizing the harsh reds, blues, and greens normally associated with same, had substituted soft pastels of primarily violets and yellows to affect the linear outcome."

She stated very matter-of-factly, "That's you, isn't it?"

"Ahhh, but note the eye is now wide open."

"Both eyes?"

"When it comes to intelligent and beautiful women, I shall undoubtedly squint until the end of my days."

"We're not all that difficult to understand."

"Spoken like a true intelligent and beautiful woman… I shall never understand you, and of course that is why I must."

She turned back to the painting, a universal knowing feminine smile tracing her lips. "Who is the woman?"

"I don't know. Perhaps a figment of my imagination."

"Perhaps?"

And it was paranoia that tried to fathom her smile.

"Perhaps."

"I don't have much money but I would like to buy it. Could we work out something?"

"I'm not at all sure I want to sell it, but let's talk about it over dinner, say tomorrow night."

"As a matter of fact, I'm attending a screening of my first film performance tomorrow night. Why don't you meet me there and we can grab a bite afterwards?"

"I'd be delighted."

"Good. The thirty-sixth floor of the Gulf and Western building. It starts at seven sharp, though I warn you that if you blink even once, you're likely to miss my bravura performance. I'll leave your invitation at the door. I have to leave now. I have an audition in fifteen minutes. See you tomorrow."

I suddenly realized I didn't know her name.

"Claire," she said, right on cue.

XXXVIII

I disembarked on the thirty-sixth floor of the Gulf and Western building overlooking Manhattan's Columbus Circle. I was standing in the lobby of the New York offices of the Paramount Pictures Corporation. It was six-fifty-five. I was certain she had said seven sharp, apparently not, for the usher who was guarding the screening room door told me the film was just about to begin and that I had to be seated immediately if I wished to attend.

I signed the register and was escorted to an aisle seat in the small, pitch black room. It appeared that Claire was the only other latecomer – perhaps she had gotten the time wrong – for as my eyes adjusted to the dark, aside from the seat to my immediate right, all the others, some thirty or so, were occupied.

As I settled myself into the chair, the screen guard raised as if somehow the two actions were interdependent. I lit a match and stole a glance at my watch. Where the hell was she?

The first thing that struck me was the absence of sound, any sound, then, in the very center of the screen, a tiny dot, a radius, appeared. I watched it slowly expand until it filled the screen with its image – a field of stars and galaxies illuminating the magnificent background of the Universe. The camera started with a slow zoom until it focused on a singular planet. The rate of zoom increased until terrestrial outline was visually distinct. At this point, the planet began to spin like a top, and when it came to rest, it froze on the Northwestern Hemisphere, unfroze and zoomed in to a high, wide angle aerial shot of New York City, froze briefly once again, and then zoomed in with lightning speed, distorting all images until it came to rest on the back of a man's head that literally filled the screen. The camera pulled back slowly revealing the man's jacketed upper torso, his hands raised in front of him and gripping bars... pulled back farther to reveal the man was in a cage.

And a stab of damp cold ran up my spine.

The camera panned the cage three hundred and sixty degrees, revealing a man with a grotesque mask of tragedy covering his face. The screen suddenly went black and tiny white script appeared dead center:

"The events portrayed in this film are true. Nothing has been changed to protect anyone for there are no innocent."

The image of the man in the cage reappeared. Slowly he removed the mask as the credits became superimposed over his face, blocking his features:

DIMENSIONS UNLIMITED,
IN ASSOCIATION WITH
THE UNIVERSE
PRESENTS

The camera zoomed in on the man's forehead just as a hand with a rubber stamp stamped his brow with "THE SPECIMEN."

The actor they had chosen to portray me resembled me so greatly that I let out a clearly audible gasp.

STARRING

Death	Rape
Outrage	Temptation
Life	Lust
Shock	Justice
Murder	Confusion
Fear	Ignorance

WITH SPECIAL GUEST STARS

Deception	Objectivity
Productivity	Realization
Genesis	Growth

Special Effects Courtesy of TELEDOME

WRITTEN, PRODUCED, AND DIRECTED BY
CAUSE AND EFFECT

The scene suddenly shifted and a moment before it came into focus the sound of a raging sea filled the tiny screening room. Again, the high wide angle perspective, this time of sky, sea, sandy beach, and a tiny, almost indiscernible figure at the water's edge. The zoom suddenly slammed into the image so quickly that I literally jumped a few inches from my seat. Again, the backside of the man seated in the sand, his attaché in front of him, strewn paper all around him, and a gun in his right hand held to his temple. The camera switched POV and looked through the man's eyes into the sea.

The scene suddenly shifted to the same man now swimming in the ocean. Fast cut to what at first glance appeared to be a piece of driftwood... coming alive as a bearded, caftaned ancient metamorphosizes from the wood and walks slowly to the man's belongings, gathers up the bullets from the sand, checks the man's wallet and removes a business card, a tight close up reveals Voyages Unlimited... places it in his pocket and reaches for the gun, breaks the chamber and stares in shock at the one full chamber slot. He then looks quickly to the sea. Suddenly, my lookalike's image is superimposed over the Indian, his hand now holding the gun, chamber closed, he raises it to his temple and the shot freezes.

I finally eased the grip on the arm rests and wiped my hands on my trousers. I thought for sure that all now was going to be revealed to me, but now I wasn't sure – they had purposely not shown the Indian removing the bullet from the gun.

The image unfroze and the camera pulled back, way, way back, until the man was the least visually significant object in the frame. It was a very impressive and foreboding shot; the moon just disappearing behind an inky cloud; the whitecaps pummeling the shore, and a tiny, tiny man about to take his life. An incredibly loud hollow mechanical sound filled the room exactly five times, and with each successive CLICK the tiny man became larger; more important to the scene, until the fifth click, all that filled the screen was the right side of his head, the barrel of the gun resting against the temple. The screen instantly went black and the words INTERMISSION (ten seconds) appeared.

I wanted to laugh, but not really. Once again, I was being given the choice. I really did want to get up, take advantage of this option, but that cumbersome accoutrement – my body – had other ideas. Then the image reappeared as yet a tighter close-up – only the trigger finger filled the screen, and finally, my entire body slumped in the chair to the excruciatingly loud hollow mechanical CLICK.

They had very simply forced me to relive that moment, but this time I had supplied a very different corresponding response – my eyes welled as my face broke into a large grin.

The camera closed to the sea herself – to a tiny scow making its slow progress across the Mediterranean; to two men, myself and Rambeau standing on the quarter deck; to a glass of wine, and as I drained the liquid from the glass, the camera closed in tight on the now empty glass' interior and revealed through it the slow motion images of myself passed out, then being carried off the boat and transferred to a sea plane, then being placed on an identical boat, the outline of La Boca de Dios in the background.

And I congratulated myself for having already figured out that one.

The next scene revealed a split screen shot of Alethea's face viewing me for the first time, and on the other side, my seeing her for the first time, and then I received a shock: my painting suddenly appeared for only a brief moment, almost as a subliminal cut over the split screen images, but it was long enough for me to fully realize just how accurately I had captured that initial meeting. The scene also revealed that the actor had been done away with, for it had most definitely been my face taking up the left half of the screen.

The shot gently dissolved into Anarose standing in the tiny cover, drying her hair. She turned and looked directly into the lens, revealing her pride and astonishment. I had almost forgotten how beautiful she was – those violet eyes of hers against that milk-white skin photographed in such a classic manner that one needed to be reminded that she was indeed living matter as opposed to being the masterwork of an artistic genius. I tried hard to quell the feeling that permeated every inch of me, but could not and knew I would never be able to.

The sound of progressively louder and then deafening horse hooves seemed to come from everywhere at once. The carriage shot directly for the camera and for only a fleeting instant revealed the prone "laid in state" goddess. The mist cleared to reveal her standing over me as I lay sleeping on the bench that spanned the Buttercup like some spur in the side of La Boca de Dios. This time, her expression was very alive; pondering, as was mine when the POV switched, and then back to hers and a slightly crazed and saddened look had entered her eyes. The camera pulled back and froze on her against the backdrop of the sky and sea just beyond her. Very fast, almost indistinguishable cuts of images of us reaching out and pulling back from each other, both on the Buttercup and in my room at the Pension. The frame froze with her still standing on the lip of the Buttercup, close to the edge, the sky above and beneath her; a fraction of a moment before she jumped she was standing on the tiny balcony of my bedroom. Her feet on the railing, the camera pulled up and back slightly to reveal her hands thrust straight up and grasping a long iron bar affair that raised her upwards to the balcony immediately above as a mannequin, incredibly Anarose lifelike, was flung from that same terrace.

The next shot revealed myself, staring into the fog below, watching her "body" plummet towards the cliffs, one foot raised to the guardrail while one hand braced me for my plunge. A fast pull back to a man standing in the shadows just the other side of the open French doors pointing a gun like object at my upper back – the sound of rushing air, then my hand slapping at the back of my neck a moment after the tiny tranquilizer dart had found its mark. My body slumped to the terrace floor.

A shot of Alethea and the Judge standing over me, obviously a doctor, checking my vital signs and nodding affirmatively to his employers. Two men in white loading me onto a stretcher. Anarose by the door, fully clothed, and I was on the edge of my seat, attempting to fathom the expression in her eyes, but there was none to be found.

A high angle perspective of the octagonal glass booth, the gas chamber, again my vital signs being checked; again the affirmative nod to Alethea and the Judge. Extremely tight close up of Anarose sniffing the rose, her eyes intentionally avoiding the camera, but were those tears in her eyes that I saw a moment before she looked away? I forced myself once again to keep from pulling the arm rests out of their sockets.

INTERMISSION (30 seconds)

I did not recognize the spectacular topography of the opening scene, and then a title appeared at the bottom of the screen, just as two orderlies carried me off a small private plane, across a grassy field and into a large, double-bubbled structure.

MOUNTAINAIR, NEW MEXICO

The shot revealed Alethea and the Judge greeting a fortyish man warmly as he led them to an elevator. The orderlies and my stretcher-prone body followed them. We were in a large geodesic dome, but only briefly, for we had now entered a second elevator that carried us to a much smaller dome. In the upper dome, I was placed on a raised platform which housed a hospital bed-like contraption. The orderlies strapped me into it. There appeared multi-colored leads, wires, and tentacles all about it. At various stages, low on the walls, were panels with buttons and levers. The scientist dismissed the orderlies, flicked a switch and the huge, what appeared to be lead, shield that circumvented the dome drew back, revealing the clear, navy blue of the sky. For the first time since the film had begun, dialogue ensued. The scientist primarily addressed the Judge.

"Teledome is nothing more or less than being inside a telescope or very high magnification binoculars. It can be used only during darkness. The lead shield covers it automatically with the first rays of the day's sun. We wouldn't want anyone burning to a crisp which is precisely what would happen if you stepped into this room during the day without the protection of the shield. A time lock is on the elevator door so there is no chance of this occurring. Like any good set of binoculars or telescope, Teledome has been prismatically coated, and so, for a clear image, you must remove all interior light sources prior to engaging its operation or the refractions and reflections will distort the images you want the Specimen to experience. The only exception to this is the beam that will shine on him. You can project anything into the beam's interior that can be captured on film. This lever here is the focus. Operate it as he is just coming to consciousness. It will be perfectly natural to have things blurred for a moment when coming out of an unconscious state. A blue light will come on when the Teledome is focused to his particular vision. Do you know what kind of vision he has?"

"Twenty-twenty."

"The setting for twenty-twenty is straight up, like this. As to the human housing device, he will obviously still be unconscious when you place it in him. Be sure his head is adequately elevated, as well as his tongue clamped – that's very, very important, as the shock of what he will see may cause him to gag, thereby swallowing his tongue.

"The vials of drugs to completely numb his sense of bodily sensation are located here, above the headrest, with the red labels. Give him two ccs in each underside of the elbow and knee joints, approximately one hour before Blastoff. [laughter here] It will have the same effect as Novocain over his entire body. Approximately twenty minutes before Showtime, switch on the air cushion. This will elevate his non-feeling body approximately four inches from the surface of the bed. As you well know, even though his body is numbed, his mind will perceive the feeling of motion – that is what this switch is for. For a light sensation of floatation, turn the dial all the way to the right, for a more turbulent effect, to the left, no motion at all, leave in the "off" position. The black lever right next to it rotates the air cushion three hundred and sixty degrees so that you can constantly vary perspective.

"To return to the beam for a moment: When you have it operational, have my assistant hit the lever in Panel Three, which is on the opposite side of the room. The beam is so powerful that it will give the effect of going off into infinity. You have a variety of colors to choose from. Personally, I recommend the Golden Glow… it gets them every time. Now, for sound, already have placed the headphones on him and select from Indian pitch sounds to whirlpool air gusts to the sound of complete silence. You may cassette record any other type of sound and amplify it as loud as you wish. Did you have a specific one in mind?"

"A gunshot."

"Ahhh, then be sure to have my assistant test it as we wouldn't want to cause any permanent damage to the inner ear. He will program the correct tolerance ratio. Button four, I almost forgot, back to the beam once again. You can project images into the beam and zoom them in from any distant visual point you desire, but as it is a technically complex maneuver, give the slide of whatever it is you are projecting to my assistant at least four hours before and he'll take care of the rest. And, finally, keep him in this state no longer than twelve minutes, and only one time in a seven day period. Twelve minutes, because at the thirteenth, the effects of the drug will minutely begin to taper off thus causing tingle; one in seven days because, otherwise, the residual effects you want to produce the next three weeks will be too pronounced. In short, his recollection of the experience will come too frequently as opposed to being triggered in a subtle manner through whatever key phrase you select. When do you plan to begin?"

"Tomorrow night."

Instantly the scene shifted to Pembroke, England, with me lying in the operating theatre, a scalpel making a superficial incision... but not before I had burst into solo applause.

The images blurred and suddenly a new shot came into focus and filled the screen; it was, once again, the back of the actor's head, with the gun resting against the temple. It suddenly moved over to the right half of the screen to make way for the other half of the split screen sequence. It showed me, not the actor, just my face, the same proportions as the back of the actor's head, but this time my hand held a paint brush, the tip of the handle resting against my right temple; my eyes ablaze with energy, the relaxed mouth displaying contentment.

The images went out of focus once again, but this time it wasn't the camera that had blurred, it was my eyes. The image reduced itself to its original dot and the lights in the room came on simultaneously. I suddenly realized I had understandably forgotten all about Claire's absence. I brushed the tears from my eyes and glanced at the vacant seat to my right and smiled, for there lay a black rose.

I suddenly became aware that no one had gotten up to leave; those in front of me rigidly, too rigidly, remained in their seats. As I turned around to look more closely at the audience, my shock gave way to gales of laughter as I realized that Diarma not only possessed a sense of discretion, but one of humor as well. My fellow members of the audience were all dummies – literally. Each and every one of them had an expression painted on their faces depicting the gamut of emotional realization that the subject matter they had just "viewed" had elicited from them. The faces varied from caricatures of outrage and shock to horror and laughter, serenity and joy, to confusion and complacency. I rose, chose the face I most admired to gaze upon and smiled back at it all the way to the door. Suddenly, it came alive in its last row aisle seat and handed me a note. Obviously, by choosing that particular beaming face, I had passed the test and was now being offered some sort of bonus.

As soon as I was in the corridor, I tore open the envelope and read the note:

> *"If you wish any final words, I shall be feeding*
> *our friend where we first found you.*
> *I will wait one hour.*
> *~ A"*

My first thought: Was "A" for Alethea or Anarose? My second concerned the decision I had to make and make fast. Did I really want to see either of them?

I stepped onto the elevator and worried that one around for thirty-six floors.

XXXIX

I was late. I had vacillated over dinner, deciding only at the last minute to go to the rendezvous point. It was already nine o'clock and I had just entered the park. I briefly acknowledged a large dromedary surrounded on either side by an antelope and a pair of reindeer. I stepped up my pace somewhat.

Nine-ten. I came to the top of the shallow flight of steps that led to the plaza that housed the seal pen. No one was in sight. I squinted my eyes in the darkness, peering across and beyond the pen to the monkey cages. Suddenly, the apricot lighting shone down from the overhead lampposts, and instinctively, without really knowing why, I stepped a few feet to my right so that I might be blocked from view by the low hanging branch of a cypress tree.

I checked my watch again.

Nine-fourteen.

Perhaps it had been some sort of final joke that Diarma had conceived. Perhaps she had come and gone not allowing for my tardiness. Perhaps it had all been a test to find out if I really had severed the umbilical. Perhaps at this very moment, from within the comfort of a dark shadow of another tree, they were watching, grading me. I started to feel slightly paranoid when I caught sight and sound of movement on the far side of the seal pen. She was leaning over the railing, her gaze intent on two of the local residents frolicking in the water. She straightened up, clasped her hands behind her, tilted her head back and momentarily eased the tension out of her neck and back. She returned to a relaxed position, her body gently resting against the railing.

From the security of my hiding place, I studied her. Her long shining hair fell freely to her shoulders and as an occasional wisp of it covered an eye, her hand, in practiced mannered gesture, eased it back into place. Tonight she looked a very contemporary goddess. A severely cut double-breasted navy blue suit in high fashion men's style, and under the deep V, wide lapelled coat was a magenta sweater that I knew highlighted her eyes perfectly. The large white collar of a silk blouse spilled casually over the round neck of it. A single strand of pearls graced her neck. Black patent leather boots peeked out from under her cuffed trousers.

I was frozen to the spot where I stood. I simply didn't know what to do. My mind was telling me one thing, my heart instructing another.

It was then that she spotted me. Where is her expression? How am I to read that inanimate face? She did not move but I did. I did not walk towards her or away from her, but rather I side-stepped her for I have just noticed the figure on the bench only a few feet from me. He is hunched over, reading a book by the overhead lamp. Or is it a he? Perhaps a she?

The beginnings of a smile have come over my face as I walk to him/her and none to politely jar the unsuspecting soul from his/her book, his/her thoughts. Without even attempting to disguise your annoyance, you look up into my self-satisfied countenance and just as you are about to challenge my intrusion, I broaden my grin even more, most rudely jab a finger at you and say,

"You decide what I am going to do."

And you slam shut your copy of *Diarma*, as I just stand there hulking over you like some monster of the night.

That's one possibility.

The sun was fading, but its warmth was still strong as I walked across Columbus Circle to the north side of Central Park South. It turned out to be an expensive route, as I was "hit up" three times for a total of seven dollars by the panderers whose territory I had invaded. I checked the time – it was seven-fifty-five. I made a leisurely stroll of it and arrived at the mall fronting the zoo area some fifteen minutes later.

I noted the area was practically deserted as I walked past the cat cages towards the seal pen, behind which stood the rendezvous point and her.

I studied her profile as she tossed the nuts to the small, scampering creature. Cautiously, I approached her but she sensed me anyway as she turned bricfly, smiled, and motioned me to her. I smiled into her eyes for a long moment then shifted my glance to the cage.

"I wonder what became of the other one."

"He probably died. They don't last long in captivity, you know."

And we both laughed.

"Disappointed that it wasn't Anarose that was here to meet you?"

"Yes and no."

"There's no kind way to say it, Christos. Anarose is not for you – she truly is already spoken for. You look wonderful, by the way."

"Thank you. I feel well."

"Come. Let's walk a bit. I imagine you have some questions for me."

"Three to be exact."

"Shoot."

"What if you had been wrong? What if I had not been the Specimen you thought me to be? What then?"

"You realize, of course, that your question is totally academic. What you are really asking me is, are we, Diarma, responsible, or merely lucky? As I told you at the trial, you were researched beyond anything you can imagine prior to being allowed to set one foot on Diarma. On all levels, emotionally, mentally, physically. This was done as much for our protection as for your own. Do you honestly believe we would have risked your very sanity had we not probed and examined your capacities? Were you not always given the choice? Was it not made perfectly clear to you that you could leave any time you desired up to the point you elected to stay for the trial? No, you were never our prisoner in any sense of the word, but rather your own in every sense of the word. And wholly aside from that, what if we had been wrong about you? Just exactly what did you have to lose considering the circumstances under which we found you?"

"You have a point."

"Do you know at what precise point you freed yourself from your own bonds?"

"Of course. When I elected to stay for the trial."

"That's right. Next question."

The wail of a siren suddenly distorted the night air and when it had dissipated, "How many Specimens have come before me?"

"You are the fifth."

"And was Anarose used in the others as well?"

"To one degree or another; in one form or fashion, yes, including the first in which she, albeit unwittingly, was the Specimen. However, no two scenarios are ever alike, as no two individuals are ever alike."

My eyes went askance as I whispered my reply, "I see."

"No, Christos, I don't think you do, for you are still judging her. The Anarose scenario is employed, to one extent or another, because of the universality of experience implicit in male-female relationships. All things spring from same. Life itself. How one comports oneself in a male-female relationship is the single greatest key to the quality of their character. I said Anarose was used – utilized is a far more accurate term – in all the previous Specimen situations, but never as she was utilized with you, for our investigation of you kept returning to one basic flaw – a pronounced tendency to use and discard that while primarily manifesting in your relationships with women, as it does with most all men, permeated most all of your other relationships as well. It is what we refer to on Diarma as The Transition Syndrome. Once having gratified your sensual appetites, you invariably experienced a sense of emptiness.

"The feelings of emptiness were the result of an inability to perceive something of value in that of which you partook. In other words, in the pursuit of sensual gratification, you glossed over the substance of that which you took for granted. Essentially we are talking about selfishness. We call it The Transition Syndrome because in a man like you, such forms of indulgence are truly merely substitutes for deeper connection to a higher reality. It comes to pass that only the act of sex, not its meaning, satisfies. To have and have not. Women, on the other hand, are far more naturally attuned to the meaning of sex as opposed to the act, which is why, generally speaking, it is a far greater experience for them both during and afterwards, and…"

She smiled at me for a moment before continuing.

"You fooled not one of them along the way, for all women, because of this sensitivity, automatically sense the male's feelings of emptiness, the emotional drop-off sometimes referred to inaccurately as post-coital depression. I say inaccurately for it is not a depression but rather a void, nothingness, and, this unmasking, Christos, is the root cause of your most basic conflicts with members of the opposite sex from which so many battles arise. Let me give you a little womanly advice: Learn to perceive them for what they really are or stay the hell away from them for She can either enlighten you or destroy you. For whatever reasons, that is your personal cross, and in the universal sense, that is what She is about. It's getting late. Let's start walking back. What is your last question of me?"

"Who, what, is The Seventh Man?"

"You haven't come to that one yet?"

"Let's say I have an idea, or rather a concept as to its meaning, but…"

"But you're rather reticent to articulate it, is that it?"

"Yes."

"That's understandable, considering its enormous scope and ramifications."

We stopped at the polar bear pen. A sad look entered her eyes as she gazed at the huge animal sitting motionless in the small pool. Addressing it more than I, she said, "Several years ago, when I was still living in New York, I used to come by this pen at least twice a week to visit the polar bear that lived here at the time. He was a marvelous, friendly, playful, and humorous beast. He was also a shameless ham. One sweltering summer afternoon, I came by to find him lying dead right over there beside the pool. A policeman had just put a bullet into his head. I asked what had happened, and the officer told me that a drunk had been taunting the bear with a stick while several people stood around and watched it happen. The drunk repeatedly poked at him through the bars until finally the bear had had enough and took the man's arm all the way up to the elbow into his mouth, refusing to let go. The zookeeper was called, and for some reason neither he nor I could figure out, a tranquilizer gun was ruled out – perhaps they felt it would be too slow-acting. Anyway, several minutes passed, the bear holding on to the man's arm, the man screaming hysterically. Finally, the police arrived, assessed the situation and ordered the killing of the bear. The young officer I was discussing all this with had protested but was overruled by his superiors.

"When they opened the bear's mouth to remove the man's arm, not only had the skin not been broken or scratched, even his shirt sleeve was intact. Any animal behaviorist worth his salt will tell you that bears are the most intelligent land mammal in the Northern Hemisphere. That cumbersome creature had simply held onto that man's arm so as not to be further abused; had displayed no malice whatsoever when a simple movement of the jaws would have taken that man's arm off in a millisecond. When he had finished recounting the event, we turned to each other and at precisely the same moment, said exactly the same thing: 'We killed the wrong beast.' That is a true story.

"Who, what is The Seventh Man? You are The Seventh Man, Christos. Ramapithecus, One; Australopithecus Africanus/Hablis, Two; Australopithecus Robustus, Three; Homo Erectus, Four; Homo Sapiens Neanderthalenis, Five; Homo Sapiens Sapiens, Six... Home Serenius, Seven.

"Simply the next evolutionary rung on the ladder, not a biological one, *per se*, for we have already accomplished all the essential physical adaptations to our environment in order to survive it. Rather, a mental and spiritual evolution. Listen to me carefully, Christos, for in all likelihood, this will be our last meeting for a long, long time. The clearest indications that Homo Sapiens Sapiens are in their death throes is reflected in two major areas of perversion, both of which totally dominate the content of the last half of the twentieth century. First, the absolute and complete disproportion between style and substance that has permeated every basic value, every standard and every art form that is axiomatic to continued growth. I would venture to say that those fifty years, from 1950 to 2000 plus, will go down as the half-century that reflected eighty... no, ninety percent style and ten percent substance. It is the basis for every quote leader's unquote rhetoric, but far more disheartening, it has dominated all our art forms, and art, great art, great communication, is the only thing that can either withstand or transcend the ravages of time and change.

"Art, literature, music and film, today, through the absence of substance has blatantly attempted to elevate style itself to an art form and is primarily geared towards the stimulation of the nerve ends as opposed to the enhancement of the intellect and the nourishment of the soul. When the variations on the theme so vastly overshadow the theme itself, one must assume the theme is all but dead. In short, our self-consciousness has taken us as far as we can go, awareness-wise. Now, it is inverting. That Force up there will not allow that to happen. Did you know that it is now a scientific fact that Homo Sapiens Neanderthalenis co-habitated the earth with Homo Erectus until such a time as Homo Erectus died out by virtue of the survival of the fittest? A case in point of two phases of humanity occupying the same space at the same time. The same phenomenon is occurring today. You look stunned.

"No, not stunned. It's like receiving confirmation of one's very being. It explains so much."

"Of course. It explains all those feelings of alienation you have experienced since you first became aware of yourself. You never did fit into what all this is about. Your conditioning forced you to try but that effort had to produce the one thing that could destroy your very core: Compromise. I am not referring to the kind of compromise that is negotiated by two or more parties towards a more balanced good, although often that is suspect as well, but rather the kind of self-compromise that when one first bows to, results in the clearly audible ring of the 'warning bell'; that when employed a second time, the clang resounds less distinctly, and by your third go around, you don't even hear it at all for it has become a way of life. Compromise. We are ruled by men who no longer hear the bell."

"Then accordingly we can not have much time left."

"We do not have much time left relatively speaking. Mercifully. I told you there were two major areas of perversion. The second one, while being an off-shoot from the first, is devastating enough in its own ramifications to accomplish our demise all by itself. It began because religion, organized religion, that is, could no longer satisfy the needs of the people. This in turn opened the door to the likes of the 'Reverend' Sun Myung Moon, and the fifteen year old Maharishi, to name but two, to prey and capitalize on this unrest exploiting the very essence of spirituality in the process.

"They have tried and succeeded in turning religion into a capitalistic profit-making venture involving millions upon millions of dollars, as Scientology has as well. Unfortunately, the true blame for this corporate church image must be laid to rest on the steps of the Basilica in Rome, for the Roman Catholic Church with its enormous financial assets cannot espouse the Christian Ethic on the one hand, while on the other, allow its parish pastor in one of eastern Long Island's most exclusive resort communities, to charge his dinner at one of that village's most expensive restaurants with his personal gold American Express Card, without being held in both contempt and suspicion.

Yes, we are coming to the end of a reign. We are poised Interregnum – between two reigns. Evolution has always been heretofore viewed in retrospect because never before; not until the dawn of Homo Sapiens, had we attained the equipment, a sophisticated degree of self-consciousness, to perceive it while it was actually occurring. We are, right now today, undergoing a period of Catharsis. First, the Cleansing; the Culling; the total breakdown of the Prevailing Order. You have but to open your eyes, jettison your myopia, and look around you to see it happening in every essential aspect of our existence. Moral, Sociological, Economic, Political, and Religious. It goes without saying that the price of admission to the New Reign, the reign of Homo Serenius, the reign of Cosmic Consciousness, will be very, very high. Many, many will perish. It is the way of evolution..."

For the first time since I had known her, I saw her eyes fill with tears.

"...much higher than it had to be. You see, Christos, we lost almost an entire generation of thought, of inspiration, with the infusion of drugs into the culture and especially the campuses of the world in the Sixties. Great minds could and should be coming to fruition right now, but where are they? They are not to be found for they have become anesthetized by LSD, mescaline, cocaine, hashish, methamphetamines. They offered them a choice of realities: Fight us in the 'real world' and suffer the effects of our not inconsequential power, or, turn on and escape to a reality where the pain and suffering no longer exist, and so, what began as a radical movement of great substance in the Sixties digressed into stylistic rebellion manifesting itself for the most part in long, stringy hair, dirty clothes, drug-oriented and inspired music and a manner of soft spoken empty speech. Please do not think me unduly harsh. My heart goes out to them, for through them I have seen flashes of what might have been had they been less seduced by the likes of Carlos Castaneda and Timothy Leary to name but two and more inspired by the teachings of Mahatma Gandhi and Martin Luther King.

"And so, the culmination of the transition period will be one of enormous upheaval in which many will perish because there exists a deficit of great minds to positively influence a more natural one. This upheaval I speak of will most likely take two separate and distinct forms, one strictly man made through the influences of his causes and effects; the other, a natural unavoidable phenomena. The shifting of the axis – the polar shift due to occur after the year 2000 which will account for vast land mass alterations as well as great loss of life. Scientists now feel certain that the last occurrence of a polar shift instantaneously brought on the Ice Age as great prehistoric beasts were found frozen in place centuries later, perfectly preserved, with undigested food in their stomachs. It is not a gradual process, once the actual shift occurs.

"And so, I repeat, the price of admission to the New Reign will be very, very high. And now you know why Diarma exists: to accelerate the process of evolution, to form the vanguard for the New Reign, for the magnitude of the leap from Homo Sapiens to Homo Serenius pales by comparison all the six steps that precedes him. He must be allowed to prevail, for his knowledge will bring about true understanding."

More to myself than to her, I said, "And what should *I* do, Alethea?"

"Live what you know and nothing, but nothing, can destroy you. I must go now."

I watched her disappear into the milling crowd while trying to assimilate her parting words to me. She had most eloquently provided me with answers, some of which I had already arrived at; others of which were of a revelatory nature. I started to amble out of the zoo area when I spotted the polar bear enclosure, its present inhabitant frolicking in the pool. I placed my hands on the iron bars and stared at the magnificent beast. It chose that moment to exit the pool and on all fours trotted in my direction. Suddenly it rose to its full height, tilted back its head and let out an ear-shattering roar while locking its eyes into mine. In that exquisite moment, I was humbled and awed by its enormity, its majesty, its ferocity, as I am by all of life.

AFTERWORD

Michael Staley

The book you have just read was originally written in 1970, entitled *The Specimen*. It received limited-edition publication in 1980. Between 1970 and 1977, I was represented by the Paul R. Reynolds Literary Agency in New York City, now called the John Hawkins Literary Agency. It was Mr. Hawkins, on the strength of the half-manuscript of my first work – *Dead Ringer* – who brought me into the agency.

One of the very first publishers the completed version of *Dead Ringer* was submitted to, William Morrow, exhibited enough interest in the work to set up a meeting with one of their senior fiction editors, a bundle of energy by the name of Reni Brown. That meeting changed the course of my literary life and is directly responsible for my comment in Chapter XXXVI, wherein Christos confronts me on the beach and I say to him, referring to the editorial process, *"You may technically edit my work because it requires it, but you may not, will not, conceptually edit my mind."*

Now, bearing in mind that, in those days, I was a young man in my early thirties, with hair and buns (that's not hair in a bun by the way – I was never known as Top Knot), and undoubtedly suffering from a degree of arrogance as that of most young men so encumbered, nevertheless my reaction and response to said meeting changed the course of my life.

After the pleasantries and amenities were observed, Ms. Brown, who had a very engaging personality, got down to business, in the course of which she told me that while she thought I was a "great storyteller," the philosophical aspects of the story distracted the reader from the flow of the plotline and had to go. I countered by saying the only reason I was giving them the story was to sneak in what you call the "philosophical aspects," to sugarcoat the pill, so to speak. She then lectured me on the relevance of "genre," as pertains to the marketing and promotion of a novel, and that it had to fit into a specific genre for it to be a viable product. Hmmmm.

I replied, "Essentially, then, I'm a quart of milk or a box of cereal."

I remember her looking at me and shaking her head from side to side before responding with, "Michael, you know we publish Carlos Castaneda, right?"

I said, "No, I didn't know that, but I am familiar with his Don Juan series about the Yaqui Indian.

She replied, "Do you know why we publish Carlos Castaneda?"

I said, "Well, I imagine it's because he's a very colorful writer but, to be honest, a somewhat irresponsible one, as he is popularizing a potentially very dangerous drug – the Jimson weed…"

At this point, she held up her hand and said, "Forget about all that. We publish Carlos Castaneda because we know there are hundreds of thousands of young people out there on drugs who are going to buy his books."

Reality set in with the jar of a thunderclap. I felt as though I had been stabbed in the heart; however, there was an upside for, as I rose from my chair to bid my *adieus*, I knew, from that moment on, I would never neutralize or dilute another written word, ever… Needless to say, my agent was not happy with my performance.

In the early Eighties, *Newsweek* came out with a report on how several youngsters had died from overdosing on the Jimson weed.

And so, over the course of the next forty years-plus, I was forced into a duality of existence – doing one thing to stay alive, primarily in the restaurant business, and something totally other to feel alive: writing. Many times over the course of those years I asked myself, knowing what I know now, would I have made the same decision I made that fateful day at William Morrow? I would like to think so. There was certainly no nobility in that decision. For better or for worse, it was simply spawned by being who I am.

Many would say I was a fool, that I threw away an opportunity that could have changed my life. In their thinking they would be correct that, if I had given a little then, I could have called my own shots down the road. That's what they would have you believe. But it is not what I believe. I believe that that first compromise of yourself can only lead to further negotiations with yourself and, ultimately, something dies within you that cannot be resurrected.

Other than the title change from *The Specimen* to *Diarma*, and certain very minor changes to update the setting to present day, the work remains identical to its original roots. I was going to insert into the final meeting with Alethea some remarks through her as to the relevance of the technological revolution that hadn't really taken seed when I originally penned the work, for it would certainly be germane to the final discussion she has with Christos. I thought of having him bring up the enormous advances in information gathering now accessible *vis-a-vis* the Internet. Said advances are appreciable but, to my mind, while acknowledging the value of such tools, especially as relates to law enforcement and health care to name but two, the major thrust of such endeavors only tends to make us smarter, not wiser. It is my belief that, if we are to evolve, it must be a simultaneous mental and spiritual evolution. The downside is that we appear to be burying ourselves – our individuality – under an avalanche of our own technology. Of course, the abuses run rampant on the Internet, from child pornography and pedophilia to scams of every variety imaginable, all in the name of "free speech." Wholly aside from that, social and communication skills are suffering badly through lack of actual person-to-person physical contact.

Finally, I would like to take this opportunity to express my deep-felt appreciation to Barbara Quin, of Great Spirit Publishing, for her wonderful work in taking my forty-some-year-old manuscript from the manually typed word to the computerized print and e-versions – no simple task, and it is appreciated. But mostly I want to thank her for providing a venue at a very reasonable cost for authors such as myself to get their work into print.

Michael Staley
September 30, 2014
diarma757@gmail.com

Coming in 2015, from Michael Staley:
Loki and Simba

Excerpt

PROLOGUE

SEPTEMBER 29, 1977

His long white mane plastered to his head by the falling rain, the old Indian remained motionless on the boulder that overhung the rushing stream. A rock upon a rock. His time was near – two, three days at most, and he welcomed the moment when his spirit would soar on the wings of wind. In his ninety-seven years of life there had been little he had not suffered, a great deal he had not understood, and more he wished not to.

The hunter was close now. He had observed him for the past day and a half. He was a great one, combining stealth and cunning with seemingly infinite patience. Yet he was not truly a hunter. That is what tugged at him. The man did not hunt for sport, nor did he hunt for food; he certainly did not hunt as one hunts merely to sharpen skills, for he was beyond that. Rather, he hunted only to kill.

Unobserved, he had watched the executioner end the lives of rabbits, squirrels, a beaver, a raccoon, two small doe, and even a tiny bird in flight; each and every time, gathering the small of the quarry and dumping them into a burlap sack like so much garbage. He suddenly rose from behind his makeshift blind and the old Indian studied him in depth: the long torso that appeared deceptively narrow beneath the poncho and jeans that in reality hid long sinewy pop-veined muscles, but it was the thick neck that gave way to sloping shoulders that was the true give-away: a dangerous body that commanded feline reflexes. The killer laid down his rifle, sat in a clearing and gnawed some jerky.

The Indian knew why he rested. The rain had stopped. The sun had shone and was setting and soon the creatures would come to the stream to water and the slaughter would resume. The old Indian thought momentarily of accelerating his own demise by attempting to kill him, but he knew that was too easy. He would anger the Great Spirit if he forced his time and so he made not a move.

Suddenly, a chill went up his back. He could not recall the last time he had experienced the sensation of fear. It took him a moment to identify it, so alien was it. He sensed a presence, malevolence, and was certain his time was now but was utterly confused by the evil tenor of it. His should be a peaceful end. He had lived passionately, voraciously, courageously, then humbly, compassionately, and patiently. Why was the Evil One coming for him? He turned to the sound the same instant the killer did. The prey rose to his feet with incredible agility to meet his attacker and was dead in less than ten seconds. The old Indian watched the attacker celebrate the hunter's death. He buried his teeth into the hunter's jugular. He removed a severed wolf's paw from his pocket and with it gouged the eyes from the head. He took the dead man's right hand into his mouth and chewed off the four fingers and thumb. In a single, slashing movement, he brought the wolf's paw ripping down the center of the man's chest, crushed through the rib cage with his bare hand, and tore out the still throbbing heart. He masticated it slowly until it was consumed. He gathered up the fingers and the thumb and tossed them into the stream. He tore the clothes from the body and then sunk his teeth deeply into the flesh four more times, the fourth bite dismembering the phallus. He spat it out, raised his head to the budding night sky and howled. He removed a steel rod from beneath his great coat and rammed it through the puffy red opening of the groin, ramming it upward until it protruded through the hunter's mouth. It was then, as he looked to the night sky that their eyes met. The old Indian nodded more with his eyes than his head, noted the man had the eyes of a wolf, and immediately returned his gaze to the heavens. His time was close, very close, but he knew that in these, the last hours of his life, he had been privileged to bear witness to a strange and transcendent moment of justice. The roar of distant thunder punctuated his thought.

The man with the golden eyes rose, glanced once more at his staked prize, upended it and impaled it into the muddy earth, all the while wondering to himself, for the fourth time, why the stars in the skies, like the stars in his prey's eyes, all had circles around them. Then he walked into the darkness from which he came.

And the old Indian resumed the remainder of his vigil, motionless, a rock upon a rock.

*****

SEPTEMBER 10, 1977

My name is Dr. Christopher Jerome Maxwell. Between the years 1964 and 1973, I was a senior staff parapsychologist with the Society for Psychical Research (SPR), London, England. During my tenure there, my responsibilities encompassed the research, analysis, and documentation of over two thousand recorded instances of psychic phenomena spanning the spectrum from investigation and verification of precognitive experiences (experiencing the future) to retroactive experiences (experiencing the past); from the graphic monitoring of Out of Body Experiences (OBE), sometimes referred to as Astral Projection, to the bona fide psychic mediums who claimed communicative powers to the spirit world; from teleportation to kinetic movement – moving objects through mental concentration.

Less than one percent of the cases investigated and documented were registered by me, with the SPR being without question, authentic.

In late 1968, utilizing a combination of techniques pioneered by Dr. J. B. Rhine and Louisa Rhine, of Duke University; Robert Munroe of the Georgia Institute of Parapsychology; and S. G. Soal of the SPR, I began clinical experimentation in the practice of a scientific methodology by which to catalyze an OBE at will.

In over three hundred test cases, which I personally oversaw, or in any instance that has ever been recorded, there has never been verification of any verbal utterances, let alone conversation, by the subject with the monitor during an OBE. Data compiled during the experience is primarily accomplished through monitoring vital signs which appreciably fluxuates and, in some instances, a subject has been able to communicate their state of heightened consciousness through a physical gesture such as what appears to the target recipient to be a muscular spasm or jolt. When the subject is questioned upon returning to a normal state of self-consciousness, he will reveal that his astral body did indeed slap or touch that portion of the target-recipient's body that felt affected.

But as to verbal communication, it is generally believed that an OBE is strictly a spiritual experience with all mental faculties highly engaged, and that the worlds the mind perceives, negates, even defies description, for language, after all, is the tally of the self-conscious mind, and consciousness is raised to a much higher level during an OBE. Our set of symbols appears inadequate to depict this state other than in broad generalities such as Light, Color, Motion, and Sound. Upon returning to a normal state of consciousness, however, the subject, depending upon the nature and limitations of the travels can oft times describe, quite graphically, the environs visited, but this is after the fact, never during, and usually is indicative of a lesser state of Cosmic Consciousness.

The justification for this rather long-winded excursion into my field comes now: There was one exception to the above: A quite beautiful young woman who had come to the SPR the first year of my experimentation, deeply troubled by what she referred to as "nightmares but not really." When questioned on this description she simply replied: "I am never asleep when they occur. I seem to be out of my body."

After some twenty tape recorded monitoring sessions, the following communications were documented. Absolutely no hypnotherapy was employed. Never once during these sessions did her verbal communications vary even one word... or syllable, or tone inflection for that matter. There is no question that she was in a state of Astral Projection when the following was recorded – her vital signs dropped very low and at one point ceased to function at all. For the most part, her brain activity registered exceedingly high on the CAT scan. I always began the session by asking her the same question:

"What is happening now, Gena?"

"The vibrations are increasing."

"Where are the vibrations located?"

"In my abdomen, my center, pushing upwards... upwards into my chest... increasing in strength... trying to get out."

"Are you still in your body, Gena?"

"In my head now... my head is so heavy with them... letting go... don't want to."

"Is it causing you pain or discomfort?"

"No... the feeling is euphoric... but I'm scared... I'm so scared... don't want to go... please don't make me go."

"It's all right, Gena. Let go. Let it go."

"Free."

"What's free?"

"My Spirit. My essence... am on ceiling now... looking down at you seated by me on my bed."

"Do you see the Silver Cord, Gena?"*

"No. I am energy, light, and intelligence. I am not form."

"Where are you now, Gena?"

"I am through the roof and into the sky... oh, no, please not there again... please don't send me there again!" (A small, shriek-like sound here.)

"Your own will determines your course, Gena."

"No! Not there again!"

"Where are you now?"

"Water, over water, large expanses of water. Oh, God in heaven! PLEASE, not there again!"

"Can you tell me the direction you are going in?"

"All directions. All directions."

"Do you see anything on the water?"

"A ship, a ship."

"Just one ship?"

"And land. I see land."

"Can you describe the land, Gena?"

"Over water again... now land... now water again."

"Do you still see the ship?"

"Yes. The ship is still there... I see myself on it... land again."

*The Silver Cord is a line of connection from the astral body to the physical one, or shell it has escaped from. This is known as an ecsomatic experience in which the subject perceives a second or astral body. If no astral body is perceived, but rather the subject perceives oneself as pure energy, light and mind, this is what is referred to as an axomatic experience.

"Is it day or night?"

"It is neither and both... the colors... oh, God, the colors are so beautiful!"

"Do you perceive motion?"

"Oh, yes... speed. I'm traveling as much incredible speed... so soothing... NO, I want to come back!"

"Come back where, Gena?"

"To my body... I'm so frightened."

"Just think the thought. The thought of returning will bring you back. Think the thought."

"I can't. It won't let me."

"What won't let you?"

"LOK (sigh), he's waiting for me."

"Who's LOK?"

"No… please, God, not there… please… must go on."

"Go on where, Gena?"

"To the Green and the Yellow… it's getting dark… oh, dear God, not the darkness… please not the darkness."

"Where are you, Gena? Where?"

"No! I'm not Elizabeth… not Elizabeth. I'm Gena!"

"Who's Elizabeth?"

"I see trains… mustn't go there… mustn't go there…"

"What else do you see?"

"A long river… mustn't go there?"

"Go where?"

"To the Green and the Yellow in the old city by the river. Mustn't go there… LOK (sigh), he's waiting for me."

"Who's LOK, Gena? What's LOK?"

"I want to come back… come back… no… can't… almost… there now…"

"Almost where, Gena? Where?"

"In the Green, in the Green."

"What do you mean, Green?"

"And Yellow… and Yellow."

"Is it day or night?"

"Dark. God, it's so dark!"

"But you can see green and yellow?"

"Yes, and I hear water… walking through the Green now… Oh, God. He's there. He's there under the Yellow, waiting for me. NOT ELIZABETH! I'M NOT ELIZABETH!"

"Who's there, Gena? Who's Elizabeth, Gena?"

"LOK (sigh), he's waiting for me under the Yellow."

"Is anybody else around?"

"Yes… a man on a bicycle just rode past me."

"Any other life, Gena?"

"I'm not Gena. I'm Elizabeth… sounds, quacking sounds… water… Oh, no… He's snarling at me… coming towards me now… oh, please, bring me back. NO. Can't go back now."

"Who, what is coming towards you?"

"LOK (sigh) He's coming."

(Her entire pulse has become extremely rapid suddenly, as if her entire system was shot with adrenalin.)

"What does LOK look like, Gena?"

"I'm *not* Gena. I'm Elizabeth. Tall, very tall. Oh, God, those eyes. I can't look into those eyes. Slanted, golden eyes. They're trying to kill me. Killing me. All of me. Forever."

"What do you mean 'all of me... forever'?"

"Not just my body. My spirit. My soul."

"Are you alone? Is there anyone else around?"

(no response)

"What does LOK look like, Gena? Describe him. Is he a man?"

(no response)

"Elizabeth! Is LOK a man?"

"Yes... No... His hair... black and white mane... he's circling me now, snarling... baring his teeth... LOK (sigh), he's stalking me now... springing at me now... biting me all over... gnawing the fingers off my right hand now... running off... burying them... no, no, please, not that... please, not my eyes... he's clawing them out. His teeth are in my throat now... (long pause of seventy-two seconds).

"I'm dead now. (At this point, her vital signs ceased to function for an elapsed time of fifty-two seconds)... turning me on my stomach now... lifting my hair from the back of my neck... carving something... rolling me back over now... on his knees... holding my heart to the sky... He has reached into my chest and taken my heart. Mournful howling/wailing, sad, so sad... He's eaten my heart. Howling and howling. He's ripping off my skin..."

(This entire last section, since the point where she declared herself dead, was delivered in a cool, detached manner as if she were simply an observer.)

And she returned to self-consciousness. Before she could totally reorient herself, I asked her once again who LOK was:

"Who?"

"LOK. L – O – K."

She did not hesitate for even a fraction of a second.

"The Lord of Karma, of course."

Ten minutes later, I asked her again:

"LOK... I have no idea."

An hour later, the same response.

At the time, though somewhat disturbed by the strange, eerie quality of it, I did not become overly concerned by the actual text of the experience. In my field it is a generally known fact that one's deepest suppressed fears can easily surface during an OBE and take on symbolic as opposed to literal significance. They can become extraordinarily magnified even to the point of ludicrousness to the observer/monitor but nonetheless real and horrifying to the subject. I tended to categorize this along these lines – symbolic death experience, or less likely, a symbolic future death experience, the latter being less likely because Gena Peters had exhibited no history of precognition whatsoever, although, it is not unusual that the two experiences – precognition and an OBE – should occur simultaneously.

Ultimately, it, as well as four other tapes all concerning themselves with grotesque manners of violent death to individuals other than herself; all with "LOK" as the perpetrator, proved to be incredibly accurate accounts having left virtually nothing to the imagination. They were simply chronicles of fact, pure, unadulterated, astonishing, horrifying fact.

On the day of her last monitoring session, on September 10, 1969, Gena Peters brought me a gift – a leather-bound hand-written log. On the cover was the gold inscribed, hand-tooled title, CANIS LUPUS – SPRING, 1904 – a true copy of which is enclosed with this statement.

On the very same evening, I read the contents of that log and, to my mind, or any rational mind, it was one of the most unbelievably tragic accounts of man's ignorance ever documented – the degree of ignorance from which lunacy is born.

Copies of the tape recorded sessions with Gena Peters are enclosed.

I make this statement of my own free will in connection with the ongoing homicide investigation into the death of Paul Munroe.

> Dr. Christopher Maxwell
> Society for Psychical Research
> London, England

The above statement was issued voluntarily to the undersigned in connection with the Paul Munroe homicide of February 16, 1977, RE: Open Case #86795-424PC. It was submitted and signed in my presence this date, September 10, 1977.

> Jason Lombard, Capt., SID
> Shield #7871, NYPD

CONTACT GREAT SPIRIT PUBLISHING IF:

... you want to learn more about publishing with Great Spirit Publishing's traditional line of spiritual and inspirational material, or would like to learn about *GSP-Assist* and NABSY, alternatives to an author's "self-publishing" route to publication.

Feel free to visit our website to browse our growing selection of books. All items are available for purchase through PayPal, or online through CreateSpace and Amazon.

Send e-mail inquiries to greatspiritpublishing@yahoo.com.

FIND MORE ONLINE AT:
http://www.greatspiritpublishing.yolasite.com/book-store.php

independent and assistive publishing technologies

Great Spirit Publishing is proud to bring you entertaining and mind-expanding literary works from known and unknown writers. And we can help writers make their publishing dreams come true!

Contact Great Spirit Publishing directly by sending an e-mail to:
greatspiritpublishing@yahoo.com.

Visit us online at
www.greatspiritpublishing.yolasite.com/book-store.php.

Made in the USA
San Bernardino, CA
06 November 2014